C000124795

THE BEYOND

Book 4, The Breeder Files

About the Author

Eliza Green tried her hand at fashion designing, massage, painting, and even ghost hunting, before finding her love of writing. She often wonders if her desire to change the ending of a particular glittery vampire story steered her in that direction (it did). After earning her degree in marketing, Eliza went on to work in everything but marketing, but swears she uses it in everyday life, or so she tells her bank manager.

Born and raised in Dublin, Ireland, she lives there with her sci-fi loving, evil genius best friend. When not working on her next amazing science fiction adventure, you can find her reading, indulging in new food at an amazing restaurant or simply singing along to something with a half decent beat.

For a list of all available books, check out:

www.elizagreenbooks.com/books

BOOK 4 IN THE BREEDER FILES

THE BEYOND

ELIZA GREEN

Copyright © 2020 Eliza Green

The moral right of the author has been asserted in accordance with the Copyright, Designs and Patents Act 1988.
All rights reserved. No part of this publication may be reproduced, stored in a retrieval system, or transmitted, in any form or by any means, without the prior written permission of the author, nor be otherwise circulated in any form of binding or cover other than that in which it is published and without a similar condition being imposed on the subsequent purchaser.
All characters in this publication are fictitious and any resemblance to real persons, living or dead, is purely coincidental.

ISBN: 9798574332870

Copy Editor: Sara Litchfield
Cover: Deranged Doctor Design

Dedicated to dreamers, schemers and lemurs.
(Because rhyming is cool.)

1

Anya

The acrid smell of gun metal settled in Anya's nose.

'Again.'

She cocked the revolver while one of the soldiers a couple of years younger than her swapped the bullet-riddled target out for a new sheet. He scurried back when she popped off a new shot without warning. Three more bullets slammed into her target.

It didn't have a face. She didn't need one. The face of any Copy would do.

A stern woman with black hair and pinched lips came to mind, one of the Copy supervisors from Arcis. The memory of Arcis had been cruelly stripped from her. The Collective, too worried about what she might do if she kept them, had erased the last three months of her life.

But she'd clawed the memories back, thanks to

a machine the Inventor Jacob, her brother Jason and the rebel technician Thomas had designed. Now, everything about that time couldn't be clearer. The tests. The lies. Not to mention the memory-wiping machine the cowardly Collective had used on her.

Sheila, Dom's close friend and now hers as well, stood off to the side, her arms folded and a frown on her face. She'd been there all morning, looking annoyed and close to saying something. Anya knew what this bullet-wasting practice must look like to her. They were about to return to the city and needed all the ammo they could get, but Anya didn't know how else to deal with her grief.

Sheila huffed loudly when Anya aimed at the target again. She ignored her and fired.

'Does Dom know you're using all the bullets?' Sheila said.

Anya paused before her next hit. 'Yeah.'

Shooting targets was distracting her from other things. Julius, who had been the rebels' third in command, and two foot soldiers from the city had taken Alex and Jerome back to Praesidium. Jerome was a newborn and friend she'd met in Arcis. Alex, also a friend, was a Breeder. Anya had rescued him from the Collective's twisted program. She guessed the Collective wanted back all its "property".

None of them had known about the traitors in their camp. That put them all at fault. But the giant boulders to the front of the camp made it impossible to follow them in the trucks. And Dom was refusing

2

to leave until they had transport that could get them there fast and also protect them.

Sheila uncrossed her arms and, with a loud huff, stalked off toward the city hall. Probably to see Dom to tell him how unreasonable Anya was being.

Good luck winning that battle, Sheila.

Anya aimed the gun again.

Four, five, six.

She didn't care if she hit the target. This session wasn't about accuracy. A second revolver, lodged in her waistband, dug into her side.

She removed it and handed the empty one to the nervous boy soldier hovering close by. 'Set a new target.'

'Uh, are you sure?' The boy sounded nervous. 'Max said we shouldn't waste the bullets.'

'Max isn't here.'

One of Praesidium's giant guardian wolves had killed their leader out on the same battlefield where one of the Copies had killed Jason and Warren.

The boy wiped his sweaty brow with his sleeve. 'Sorry, I forgot.'

Her activity had attracted quite the crowd. Male and female soldiers watched her curiously. Before the memory wipe she'd been a nuisance around here, unsure of herself. The soldiers hadn't wanted her around because, above all things, she'd doubted her ability to shoot. After, she had transformed into a killing machine. And that made her useful.

'Reload.'

The boy did and handed the shaking gun back to Anya. She emptied all six chambers, hoping that her activity would dislodge the hard knot in her chest. After a long period of inactivity it felt good to shoot again. Her returned memories had reignited her love of competition. Competition put her back in control.

She wanted to be useful to the rebels' cause. More than that, she wanted to avenge Jason's death.

A lump rose in her throat.

June stepped up beside her, a revolver in her hand. Her gentle smile snapped Anya's grief away.

'Want company?'

Anya relaxed her tense shoulders. 'Sure.'

The boy soldier stood well back, looking like he wanted to flee. Others stood around in an arc. The temporary shooting range rested against the gable of a disused house near the back perimeter fence. The spectators watched with a mix of curiosity and something else Anya couldn't figure out. She spotted three of the female soldiers who'd been rude to her when she'd lost all except one of her memories: the one of Warren attacking her. She and Warren had fought publicly. Without knowing why, the three women had thought it appropriate to take Warren's side.

But that scared and timid girl who had first entered the camp was dead. It sent a thrill through her now to see their looks of confusion while Anya did what she did best. Fight.

She flicked open the chamber and popped in six

new bullets, then snapped it closed. June was one step ahead. She already had the gun at eye level, one hand steadying the other. She brought it down and looked at Anya.

'Best out of five?'

Anya nodded. The person to hit the bull's-eye after five shots would win. She pointed at the boy soldier, then at the targets.

The jittery boy ran up, pinned two targets against the gable and ran back. Both were plain, white sheet of papers with a series of circles drawn on in pencil.

June went first. She needed to let off steam, too. Not only was she carrying a child from Praesidium, but Max's third in command had taken Alex, whom she'd gotten close to. Imogen, Max's second in command, stood off to the side. Her eyes refused to settle as she brushed her short hair back. She chewed on her thumb.

They were all to blame for not seeing the threat in their camp.

Reliving the memory of her brother's crumpled body threatened Anya's resolve. It reminded her who deserved the real blame.

June fired the first shot. Anya wondered if her target had a face. Her memories of Arcis had yet to be returned—Jacob's memory machine had not worked on her and Junior—but it seemed at times like June was remembering on her own.

The boy soldier checked the target when June

5

nodded at him.

'It hit the second last ring,' he said breathlessly.

June lowered her gun and looked at Anya. 'Your turn.'

Anya took aim at her own target, picturing the female from Arcis again. She'd been cold toward her group. Unfeeling. She fired her first bullet in this round.

The soldier marked the hole with an X. 'Anya won that round.'

Winning usually fueled her, but today she couldn't muster up a smile.

'Two in a row,' she said to June, already tiring of her activity.

June aimed at her target before the soldier had cleared the area. He scuttled back in fright just as she fired off two shots.

The soldier checked and marked them. Anya followed with two of her own.

'June was closer,' he said when he went in to check.

'It comes down to these last two shots, I suppose,' said June.

'Make them count.'

June cocked her gun like a pro. She'd had training. All the rebels had.

She raised her arm, steadied it and fired one, two.

The soldier checked. 'Bull's-eye.'

June grinned at Anya. 'Beat that.'

'No problem.'

June might have had training, but Anya had perfected her marksmanship with hours of practice. She lifted her gun twice as fast and, without looking, popped off two shots at the target.

A gasp from the crowd sent a thrill down her spine.

'She didn't even look,' said one.

'I think she hit it,' said another.

Gone was the timid girl who'd arrived at this camp. In her place stood Anya Macklin, strong, brave and willing to fight for what was right.

Even the women who'd written her off before gushed with praise.

Another young woman stood there, Kaylie, who'd been intimate with Dom once. Anya looked over at her. Kaylie gave her a tight nod.

She looked back at the target. She could see her shot was closer to the center of the bull's-eye than June's, but the soldier checked anyway.

'Anya won that round.'

Her fingers fumbled in her pocket for more ammo, but she found none. Dom had said not to use too much. She had counted out enough bullets to soften the hurt but not the supply.

The last two days had been a blur. Everything had happened so fast out on the battlefield. Now, a day after losing her brother, she combed through her memory of events, wondering if she could have done anything different. In the end, Warren had saved

Jason, but another Copy had shot both of them.

The Copies were all the same. Murdering, lying robots.

Except they weren't. Carissa and the ex-guardian wolf that Jacob called Rover had helped them. But Carissa was also hearing one of the Collective in her head. Anya worried that Quintus might say something to make the girl loyal to the city once more.

'You okay?' asked June, touching her protruding belly.

Thanks to the growth repressors in Carissa's biogel, the rapid growth of June's baby had been stemmed, for the moment. It could so easily have been Anya. In Praesidium's medical facility, she and Alex had been pushed together and expected to breed. Sheer willpower had ended that dalliance.

But June hadn't been so lucky. She had been used as an incubator, a vessel to grow the fetuses created between human and Breeder.

Bad for June. A success for the Copies.

'I will be,' said Anya. 'You?'

June rubbed her belly. 'I will be.'

Anya tucked the revolver into her waistband.

Not all the Copies were the same. A medic had helped Alex and Anya to escape. The same medic had prevented Dom from being turned into something that would set a metal detector off at a distance.

'Eh, do you still need me?' said the boy soldier.

Anya blinked away her stillness. 'No. I think

we're done.'

The soldier sighed with relief and scurried off. The others who'd watched their session dispersed, smiling and shaking their heads. Some looked impressed with her skills. Others who had mocked her weaker, amnesiac self just days ago still weren't sure what to make of her.

The old Anya would have apologized for scaring them. The new Anya didn't care enough to hold people's hands. It had been too long since she'd practiced. Over three months, probably closer to four. But she hadn't forgotten the basics.

Set, aim, shoot.

That's all she needed to do. They would be going back to Praesidium soon and she wanted to be ready. Because the city wouldn't know what hit them.

Imogen stayed behind. She approached Anya and June, running a hand over her short hair a second time. Her eyes were red and puffy, like she'd been crying.

'Anya, June?' she said softly. She didn't sound like the confident soldier who had commanded many training sessions.

'Yeah?'

'I... um... just wanted to apologize for what happened with Julius.' She blew out a long breath. 'I had no idea he was under the Collective's control.' She looked at them, then away. 'And now he's taken Jerome and Alex.'

The reminder made Anya's chest ache. She

glared at Imogen. She had worked closest with Julius. How had she missed what he'd been: a newborn under the Collective's command? Jason had died because of her mistake.

Anya gritted her teeth and looked away.

'It's okay, Imogen, we're going to get them back,' June, the diplomat, said.

Anya looked back to see her touch Imogen's arm. Imogen nodded and dropped her gaze. It wasn't her fault, but Quintus wasn't here and Anya needed to blame someone.

'I'm going to check on Dom,' said June, 'see if he's got a plan to get us out of here.' She elbowed Anya. 'You coming?'

The crowd had already dissipated, except for Kaylie and the three women who had been rude to her before. They hung back, looking like they wanted to speak to her.

Kaylie said softly, 'Nice one, Anya.'

Anya gave her a quick smile. 'Thanks.'

'Hey, that was some fancy shooting,' one of the rude women said.

Anya breezed past them with barely a look in their direction.

June caught up and elbowed her again. 'Welcome back. I missed the ballsy you.'

Anya stopped in her tracks. 'You remember?'

June smiled. 'It's coming back to me.'

2

Dom

'I need to speak to you about Anya.' Sheila stood next to Dom in Max's strategy room, hands on her hips. 'She's using up all the bullets.'

Dom leaned over the table, a map of Praesidium resting on it. With Jacob and Vanessa's help, two rescues from the city, they'd been able to draw out a rough plan. It didn't fill in all the gaps of the intricate city, but it was a start. Dom had added his limited knowledge of the medical facility's first floor to it, but he'd been too out of it to remember much beyond his room and the space where they'd operated on him.

Carissa had filled in more from her own explorations. The schematics she'd downloaded on the battlefield right before Quintus had disconnected her were still in her memory banks. But without Jacob's diagnostic machine, currently sitting in his half-destroyed workshop in the city, the maps were unusable.

'Did you hear what I said?' Sheila huffed. 'Anya and June are out there shooting the crap out of paper targets.'

'I know. She asked me if she could practice. I didn't see the harm.'

'Harm?' Sheila threw her hands up. 'She's using up the ammo! Are we even going to have enough left to hit the city? How much did you say she could use?'

Dom loved Sheila, but she could be a pain at times. This was one of those times. He pinned her with a look that he reserved for when they were alone. Which, right now, they were.

'Real bullets don't harm the Copy machines. We have their weapons, the ones they dropped, plus our own. The revolvers will only be used to distract.'

'Okay... will we have enough "distracting" ammo then?' She air-quoted the word.

'Yes, Sheila.'

He sighed. Max's death twenty-four hours ago might have elevated him to the position of commander over the rebels, but he wished everyone would stop complaining to him over every little thing.

'I mean, you're the leader. She needs to listen to you.'

'And I said she could use them.'

He hadn't quite given her that order but he trusted Anya would only use the amount she needed. And yes, he was the leader now. Not that he had a clue what to do. Soldiers had been injured on the battlefield. June had a fast-growing fetus in her belly. Anya using a few bullets wasn't high on his list of concerns.

But Sheila was far from settled. Her lips were pinched and she was tapping her foot.

Dom turned to face her. 'What's this really about?'

It felt like more than a few bullets.

'She won't talk to her.'

'To who?'

Sheila straightened up. 'Imogen! She's sick with worry that everyone is blaming her for Julius going rogue.'

'That's stupid, Sheila. It wasn't her fault. None of us saw what he was. Not even Max.'

Her eyes shifted to the floor, then back to Dom. 'I know, but she feels responsible.'

'Do you want me to talk with her?'

Sheila shook her head, getting angry. 'Tell Anya to stop blaming her for what happened with her brother.'

'She doesn't blame her.'

'Tell her.'

The door opened and Anya and June walked in. He turned from a huffing Sheila and grinned at his girl. Despite the frown Anya wore, having her near calmed him. It also made being commander that little bit easier.

Imogen entered next, followed by Kaylie.

Sheila's face lit up. To Dom's relief, she gave up on her tirade and went straight to the woman she'd gotten close to. Dom nodded at Kaylie. She nodded back, in soldier mode. Even if Anya hadn't returned to him, it never would have worked out between them. But he was glad to have her support now.

His girl sidled up to him, quieter than usual. Anya had been through too much in the last few days. Right now, he'd give her all the bullets she wanted.

She slid her warm hand into his, her eyes on the map.

June came round his other side and nodded at the schematics. 'Hey, how's it going?'

Dom sighed. 'It's not much. What we really need are the areas not covered by this map.'

'What about Carissa's downloaded maps? Will they show more?'

'She doesn't think so. Many of the tunnels we want were never on the maps available to her.'

Anya pointed to a section below ground, a short distance from Jacob's workshop. It showed two tunnels, one leading to the medical facility, which they'd used to escape, and another running parallel to the streets. They'd followed it for a while until a new set of stairs had brought them up and out, close to the Business District. Neither tunnel had been on any map Carissa had seen.

'Could the coordinates be hidden in one of these tunnels?' she asked.

They could be, but he'd been out of it when

they'd used both tunnels. He shrugged at her. 'You'd remember more than me.'

Anya let go of his hand and studied the map more closely. Carissa's recollection of the layout had filled in most of the city's streets and buildings, but not the interiors. A few places had been included, places where Carissa had been more than once. Those included the Great Hall in the Learning Center, where the Collective apparently resided.

Frowning, Anya traced one route with her finger. Dom saw she was on the second floor of the medical facility, where she, June and Sheila had been kept prisoner. And the Breeder called Alex.

'I hope Alex is okay,' she said softly. 'And Jerome.'

June's shoulders rounded. She kept her eyes fixed on the map. 'When do we go, Dom?'

'As soon as we can clear the boulders from the front of the camp. Jacob's out there with Vanessa and Charlie. He's commanding the pair of wolves to move them.'

The boulders were too heavy to move manually.

He sensed everyone was anxious about leaving. Neither Vanessa nor Charlie had offered their thoughts about returning to the city. Go too early and they'd be ambushed. But leave it too late and they could be sitting ducks.

Without Max to guide him, he had no idea how to attack Praesidium when they returned there. But Jacob's reprogrammed orb had shown them images of the city and its force field down. Now was the right time to strike.

The door opened and in walked Vanessa, Jacob and Charlie. Thomas followed closely; the young man in his early twenties was the closest thing to an inventor the rebel camp had. Carissa trailed after Jacob. Her blonde hair was messy and her sweatshirt was dirty, as were her hands. She must have been helping the wolves move the rocks.

'What's the word?' he asked Charlie.

The old man puffed out some air. 'The rocks are large, but Rover and the wolf from the city are making small progress. We need a break before we start in again.'

Dom hated this, sitting around doing nothing. 'We should get moving as soon as the rocks are out of the way.'

Charlie wiped his hands on his overalls. 'Vanessa and I have been talking. We have a lot of injured soldiers. We should make sure they've fully recovered before we go.'

'We don't have time. June needs medical attention. And we need to get Alex and Jerome back.'

'By all means take a small group, but the rest of us should stay here until the injured are strong enough.'

Dom understood Charlie's concerns. He'd watched his son die on the battlefield outside this very camp. If they went to the city with injured soldiers and the Collective attacked again, it would leave them at a serious disadvantage.

But something told him it would be worse if they split up.

'Alex and Jerome have been taken and we don't know what's happening to them. We need to get them back now. '

Charlie nodded. 'Take a smaller team, like I said.'

Dom looked at Jacob. 'Didn't you tell me the orb showed the city's defenses were down?' The Inventor nodded. 'If we wait too long, the force field could have time to recover. By the time this camp is strong enough to fight, the city could be impenetrable again. I don't want to split us up. We travel together or not at all. We need the trucks ready to go as soon as possible.'

Charlie looked away, his jaw tight.

Jacob gripped the old man's shoulder. 'I agree with Dom. It's dangerous to stay here. We have to move out. The city has equipment that can heal the soldiers faster. The longer we stay, the more time the Collective has to regroup. We don't know what information Julius might have passed to Quintus.'

But Charlie still wasn't happy. And neither was Vanessa.

'Can we use the mountain pass to get out of here?' she asked. 'Charlie's concerned we'll be exposed if we leave through the front. So am I.'

Their truck had used the mountain pass above the camp to get in and Dom had considered using it to get out. But he couldn't be sure the Collective didn't already know about that one way in and one way out route. At least in the open they could see their enemy coming.

Jacob echoed his thoughts. 'We can't be sure the Collective hasn't sent Copies, wolves or digging machines to block the road at the base. It's safest to leave through the front.'

'But we'll be vulnerable!' said Charlie. He was breathing hard.

'It won't be like the last time, I promise.' Dom said.

He would make certain of that. Nobody else had to die.

Anya squeezed his hand briefly; the tension in his shoulders lessened a little. She didn't add anything to the discussion, but he knew she would follow his decision. They all would. Even Charlie.

He stepped closer to the man who had become his family. The old man's eyes widened a little at his approach. 'I miss him, too, Charlie.'

'Me too,' said Sheila.

Tears glistened in the corners of Charlie's eyes. Seeing them brought a lump to Dom's throat. 'We have to get our friends back. We also have to find the Beyond. It's what Max was searching for. It's what we need to do now.'

Charlie's lower lip quivered and he looked away. Sheila flung her arms around him.

He made a half-hearted effort to push her away.

'You're making a fuss over nothing. Stop that.'

But despite his scolding, he held on tight.

Dom swallowed back his own tears. Max had been more of a father to him than the asshole who'd beaten him and his mother, and made a pass at a younger Sheila.

June grunted. He turned to see her wince. Anya grabbed her arm to steady her.

She waved her away and bent over a little, hands on hips. 'I'm okay. Junior's being a little testy, that's all.'

Vanessa hooked her arm under hers. 'We should check you out in the medical bay to be sure that's all it is.'

Jacob nodded at Carissa. 'We need more of your growth repressors.'

The Copy, who resembled a thirteen-year-old girl, had abandoned her city and the Collective to help the humans escape. The attack had left her shocked. Apparently Quintus had been talking to her during the battle. Now, she stood taller than a day ago. But her rounded eyes told Dom she was unsure about something.

And that made him nervous.

Carissa nodded at Jacob, then at June.

June flashed the Copy a smile. 'Thanks.'

According to Jacob, Carissa's growth repressors meant she could not age any more. They were also the only thing keeping June's fetus at a manageable size. But it couldn't last.

Another reason they had to return to the city.

Vanessa walked June out. Jacob and Carissa followed them.

Charlie said to Dom, 'I'll support whatever decision you make. I know that girl doesn't have much time.' He nodded at Thomas. 'Back to it, son. It shouldn't be long before the wolves move the boulders out of the way. Until Jacob returns with them, we can shift the smaller stuff.'

'I'll help,' said Kaylie, flicking her eyes to Dom and Anya, then away.

The room cleared until only he, Anya, Sheila and Imogen remained.

Imogen said in a broken voice, 'I'm sorry for not seeing what Julius was.'

Sheila glared at Anya, as if willing her to do something.

Anya's shoulders dropped. She stepped forward and hugged Max's former second in command. Imogen crumpled in her arms. Sheila smiled and breathed out a sigh of relief.

Dom shook his head at Imogen. 'It's not your fault. He had us all fooled.'

3

Carissa

Quintus' instructions to Carissa on the battlefield replayed in her head as she and the Inventor followed June and Vanessa out of the town hall. Quintus had told her to return home, threatening to hurt her friends if she didn't. In the end, she'd chosen to stay with her friends. That's when Max, Jason and Warren, along with several soldiers, had been killed. She worried her that her inaction had been the catalyst.

They walked past the trucks parked to the front of the medical bay building. Beyond the camp's open gates she heard the hum of the anti-magnetic field, back in place while they were not working to shift the boulders.

The Inventor had reassured her that any move to help Quintus wouldn't have made any difference. He still would have given the order to kill. But she'd never know now. She'd betrayed the Collective by ignoring Quintus' demands. Then Julius, the newborn with a neuromorphic chip, had taken Alex and Jerome.

Imogen blamed herself for not seeing what he'd been. But if anyone should have spotted the newborn, it was Carissa.

Maybe her friendship with the Inventor had made her soft.

The old man glanced down at her. She smiled, but his deep frown said he wasn't buying her pretense. She needed more practice to perfect her "game face". The humans could still see through her.

'Are you okay?' he asked.

She nodded, not wanting to talk about what had happened. Not while Quintus' voice continued to play like an echo in her head. She worried he'd found a way to listen in. He had said her NMC was only damaged and that it could self-repair.

Ahead, June and Vanessa burst through the double doors of the medical bay. Keen to forget about Quintus for a while, she ran to catch up. A distraction might be just what she needed to chase him from her mind.

The old man kept pace with her as she marched up to the first free bed, where Vanessa was getting June settled. The bay was close to full of injured soldiers. Seeing them did little to ease her guilt. She turned her back to the soldiers so she wouldn't see them.

A medic came over. June winced and protected

her belly. It had grown since the day before—approximately one inch bigger on all sides. The fetus was growing again.

The Inventor said to the medic, 'We need to give her another growth repressor injection. Could you get the syringe ready?'

The medic nodded and walked away.

Carissa's gaze grazed the soldiers. Some were sitting up. Three additional medics were checking bandaged wounds. Wounds that Copies like her had inflicted.

Her escape from the city, her plan to help the rebels—it had all been for nothing. Max was dead. So were Jason and Warren.

The Inventor shook her arm. 'Carissa?'

She blinked and refocused on him. 'What?'

'I said I need you to roll up your sleeve.'

She blinked again and the medic was back, carrying a large needle that made her shudder. Carissa did as the Inventor asked, sucking in a new breath. But a little pinch was nothing compared to what June must be going through. She couldn't imagine something stretching her insides so fast; it could burst through her skin at any moment.

June winced again. Carissa closed her eyes and held out her arm. A sharp pinch followed and she inhaled sharply. She opened her eyes to see the syringe now contained a clear fluid—her biogel. The Inventor had assured her she could live without some of her growth repressors. Losing some would not affect her own growth.

She trusted the Inventor more than she did herself. He hadn't helped to kill anyone recently.

The medic took more repressors from her. June and Vanessa were watching her. She smiled at them, a pathetic attempt to assure them it was no big deal. The medic removed the needle a second time. Carissa swallowed back tears. It bothered her that she was losing more of herself each time. That she was neither human nor Copy.

'Don't worry, Carissa,' said the Inventor. 'You can make more. It's like our blood. We donate it all the time.'

His comparison made her feel a bit better.

The medic waved a thermo-imaging wand over June's belly. Then, she carefully injected the growth repressors into the cavity around the fetus. The visible movement of the fetus appeared to ease up. June settled back with a sigh.

'Junior wants out,' she said, looking from the Inventor to Vanessa. 'We need to get back to the city.'

Vanessa patted her knee. 'We're almost there. The boulders first, then getting you sorted will be our first priority.'

Carissa hoped their return to the city would not attract trouble. Who knew what awaited their return? She prided herself on having known the Collective once. She'd been able to hide her thoughts from the Ten. But Quintus, the spokesperson for the Collective ten, was acting differently to the way he used to. She could no longer predict his patterns.

And that scared her.

The Inventor pulled her back from the others and spoke in a low voice. 'What's the matter, miss? Are you worried about returning?'

The Inventor understood her—a little too well at times. She wished she had the same skill, but she hadn't learned how to read emotions.

Carissa looked up into his watery blue eyes. Her first thought was to lie to him, but the truth didn't hurt as much.

She nodded.

He responded with a pat on her shoulder. 'You don't have to worry. We'll be okay.'

'How can you be so sure?'

'Because we have a camp full of trained rebels, that's why. Dom will see us there safely.'

'But Julius is probably there, with Jerome and Alex, spilling the rebel secrets to the Collective.'

The Inventor frowned. 'There's nothing we can do about that. But you know what? The Collective may have Julius, but we have the next best thing.'

'What?'

'You.'

She didn't understand. 'Me? I could have stopped this. I could have ended Quintus' obsession with winning the war. All I had to do was go home when he ordered me to.'

He shook her shoulder. 'You're thinking for

yourself, miss. A sentient being with independent thought. You have evolved past what the Collective designed you to be. You became aware of your surroundings all on your own. You are special, and Quintus knows it. That's why he wants you to return.'

It warmed her part-organic heart to hear the Inventor call her special. But when would she feel it?

The old man bent closer to her, and stared at her. 'Do you believe me?'

Carissa wanted to. But predicting Quintus' next move wouldn't be easy, no matter how special he thought her.

'I still hear him,' she blurted out.

The Inventor straightened up fast. 'Quintus?'

She nodded. 'I'm still hearing his voice from the battlefield.'

He released a quiet sigh. 'You're replaying a memory, that's all. It's okay to think about him. He was a big part of your life in the city.'

Carissa twisted her hands to the front. Her nails were dirty from her attempts to shift the boulders from the valley to one side. She wanted to help speed up the wolves' work. The longer the anti-magnetic barrier was down while they worked, the longer the camp would be vulnerable to attack.

She looked up at him. 'Quintus is obsessed. He has been for a while. He made the tests harder for the last group that went through Arcis. He was excited to learn rebels were in the facility.'

She wasn't certain, but Carissa sensed he had

been most interested in Anya.

The Inventor cupped his chin in thought. 'Quintus has always been an anomaly among the Collective ten. I sensed that when he called me to the Great Hall to ask about you.'

'Is it bad to think about someone so full of spite?' That was the only word she could think of to describe Quintus.

'No. Quintus was like a father to you.'

The Inventor was her father. Quintus had been her... teacher. He showed no love toward her. He never praised her when she did something right. His manner was cold, like the machine he lived inside.

Carissa nodded and smiled at him. When the Inventor turned to check on June, she dropped the act.

'I'm looking forward to getting Junior out,' June said.

Vanessa replied, 'We don't know what it is, if it's even human. Don't get your hopes up.'

'I don't care. I need to see what he or she is.'

'Very soon, I promise,' said the Inventor.

June rubbed her now-still belly. 'It can't come soon enough.'

Carissa watched seventeen-year-old June cradle her belly. She was too young to have a child, yet she was looking forward to meeting her what she carried. That confused Carissa.

Quintus had taught the Copies not to care. To care would mean losing innovation, progress. The children born from the Breeder-human combination were not designed to be loved. They were test subjects for Quintus to experiment upon. What life would the children have if they were raised by humans?

The loss of her former life squeezed her heart. It might not compare to this one, which offered more freedom, but she'd become used to comfortable parameters and easy predictability there. Out here, among these chaotic humans, control was dependent upon the actions of others.

But chaos made life exciting. And, it turned out, she quite liked it.

When the medic finished taking June's temperature, the Inventor turned to Carissa.

'Are you okay now?' he asked.

She smiled and nodded, hoping to appease him.

Quintus had hinted at trouble in the city. The Copies under his command weren't to blame for this mess. They were as much victims as the humans were.

Quintus would pay for his mistakes.

'We should get back to the boulders,' she said.

The Inventor lifted both brows. 'I can see you're not okay.'

His ability to read her mind shocked her. 'How do you do that?'

'Do what?'

'Know what I am thinking?'

The old man chuckled. 'Miss, I've been watching you for a long time. I know your tells.'

'Tells?'

'Expressions. You don't hide your emotions anymore. That's all you did in the city, except when you figured out how to erase your memories.'

She looked up at him. 'Is that a good thing?'

June, Vanessa and the Inventor nodded at the same time.

He said, smiling, 'Welcome to human life.'

4

Anya

The food stores had dropped to their lowest levels. With all of Kaylie's team to feed as well as their own, rations were down to the bare minimum. But Anya wasn't worried. During her time as a prisoner in Praesidium, she and Alex had eaten like kings. That meant there must be a food replicator or a garden or something in the city.

The dining hall was busy that evening. Anya sat with Dom at one table while Sheila, June and Imogen sat at another. Kaylie, who'd been helping in the valley, kept to her team. The woman who shared an intimate past with Dom no longer bothered her. Anya had been through too much with Dom to let anything come between them.

She looked over at Sheila's table. Of the six Anya had completed the first floor of Arcis with, only three survived: June, Anya and Jerome. She hoped he and Alex were okay.

Dom dipped his spoon into the meager portion of beans on his plate. Next to it were three apple slices gone brown and a piece of stale bread. His head was still, resting in his hand, but his eyes were not. At least there wouldn't be many supplies to take when they finally left for the city. The dwindling food supplies was another reason they couldn't stay.

She kicked him under the table. 'Hey.'

Dom startled and looked up at her. 'What?'

'Are you okay?'

He faked a smile. Her time in Arcis had trained her to know everyone's tells. But she was most attuned to his.

'No you're not. What's wrong?'

Dom's lips thinned. He looked around, as if he were avoiding her question.

His eyes found hers. 'Did the shooting session help?'

She kicked him again. 'Stop changing the subject.'

Dom pulled his legs back. 'Ow!'

'I didn't hurt you, you baby. If I did, you'd know about it.'

Dom smiled; it was the first genuine one she'd seen from him since Max died.

Max! How could she be so insensitive?

Anya reached out for him and touched the top of his hand. He pulled it back from her, glancing around the room. She paused, her hand in the air, waiting, until he inched his hand forward. Then she swatted it. Lightly. He laughed.

Her own smile lasted mere seconds. 'How are you coping without Max?'

Dom's shoulders dropped and she worried she'd sent him into a deeper, darker pit.

'I'm fine,' he said.

She wanted to ask more but Vanessa, Charlie, Thomas, Jacob and Carissa entered the food hall and drew Dom's attention away. All eyes were on them, covered in rock dust, looking like they'd come from some deep excavation project.

Dom sat up straight. They approached their table. Other soldiers looked hopeful. As did June, who had also perked up at their arrival.

Vanessa sat down beside Anya. She scooted up to make room for her. Charlie sat next to Dom. Jacob and Carissa remained standing.

'It's done,' Vanessa said. 'The wolves shifted the last of the problematic boulders out of the way.'

Anya could smell the effort that had gone into the removal. She and Dom had offered their help, but Jacob had said the wolves would work better with a trusted few.

'All of them?' Dom asked.

Charlie nodded. 'Like we planned.' His lips were pinched. 'I guess we can go now.'

All eyes were on Dom for his next answer.

Anya's heart tugged for him. The weight of responsibility had been thrust upon him so fast.

'It's not the right time.'

His reply surprised Anya, matching Charlie's earlier disputed one. What had changed his mind?

'Of course not now,' said Jacob, resting his fingers on the table, 'but in the morning. We need to get June urgent medical help.'

Dom blinked, as though he'd forgotten. 'Of course. In the morning. We'll head out after breakfast.'

Vanessa got up. She headed to the food counter, and Jacob and Carissa did the same. But Charlie stayed seated.

'You need to tell them what's happening,' he said to Dom, nodding at the room. 'It's what Max would have done.'

Dom's shoulders stiffened. 'Of course. I'm sorry.'

He stood up and announced to an eager group, 'The wolves have moved all the boulders, clearing a path for the trucks to leave. We will head to the city in the morning. Everyone should pack up tonight.'

A restrained buzz ran around the room. But that energy didn't hit their table. Something was off about Dom and Anya wanted to know what.

Dom asked Charlie, 'Did you turn the anti-magnetic field back on?'

'Yes.'

'And the spotters?'

'They'll stay up on the pass until we're ready to go. You should order them down at dawn.'

Charlie stood up and clapped Dom on the back once. He followed the others to the counter for food.

The second he left, Dom shoved his plate of food away and stood up. 'I'm going to pack.'

He left the room, leaving Anya alone.

She checked her watch. It was only seven thirty. What was there really to pack?

Sheila frowned at her and mouthed, *What's wrong with him?*

Anya replied, *Max*, even though she wasn't sure.

Sheila nodded. Whatever issues she'd had with her at the shooting range had disappeared. Anya had no energy for grudges.

She followed Dom out into the hallway. There was no sign of him, but there were only two places he might be. She checked the strategy room first, but he wasn't there. Next, she went upstairs to the room he'd been using as his bedroom. One of the officer's rooms.

She cracked the door open to see Dom lying on the bed, his arm draped over his eyes. She opened the door wider and stepped inside.

He didn't move. 'I don't want company right now.'

His voice was low and soft. She didn't believe him.

Anya closed the door and sat down on the bed. 'That's too bad because you're getting it.'

Dom lifted his arm and peeked at her. Then he

draped it back over his eyes. At least he hadn't told her to go a second time.

She squeezed his leg. 'What's going on with you?'

'Nothing.'

'You missing Max?'

'Of course—we all are.'

Anya peeled his arm away from his eyes. He protested with a sigh.

'I sensed from the conversation downstairs that you're not excited to be leaving the camp,' she said.

Dom looked at her. 'I'm not.'

'But you were all for it earlier in the strategy room.'

'I can change my mind.'

Anya scooted closer. 'Not when June needs help and food is running low. Plus, Alex and Jerome are prisoners in the city.'

Dom sat up, sighing louder. 'All valid reasons I know, but I'm worried.'

'About what?'

He refused to look at her. 'About losing more people. What Charlie said earlier bothered me. We don't know what's waiting for us when we leave here.'

The danger had occurred to her, too, but Anya couldn't see another way. 'We have to go. Julius could be spilling rebel secrets as we speak, instructing the Collective about our habits. If we stay here, we give the Collective time to regroup. We damaged its arsenal during the battle. According to the footage from Jacob's orb, the city's defenses are down. We need to go now. If we stay, we die.'

Dom rubbed his eyes with the heel of his hand. 'That's what I'm worried about.'

'That we'll die?'

He looked at her. 'That we'll make it inside the city, unimpeded, and they'll take us prisoners again.' He looked down at his lap. 'Max would know what to do. I'm not a good replacement for him.'

She grabbed his hands and shook them. 'Of course you are. You're amazing. You've come up with a plan to get us back there. Max would be proud of you.'

Dom looked at her. His eyes were heavy with tears. She wanted so much to kiss away his fears.

Instead, she swallowed. 'Jason would be proud of you, too.'

He stilled when she mentioned her brother. She hadn't spoken about him yet. All she could think about was getting revenge for his death. After, she would grieve properly.

Anya rubbed circles on the back his hand. 'What's the plan for when we return?'

'It's a wait-and-see situation. Jacob's orb recording is a day old. Anything could have happened since then. The city could have reinstated their barriers, leaving us with no way in.'

'We got out with Carissa's help. Can she get us back in?'

Dom shrugged. 'She was part of the system then. Her frequency matched that of the barrier, allowing her to open it. I'm certain they've changed it.'

So was Anya. But she needed to believe their return would not be difficult. Something had to go their way.

Dom looked close to retreating inside himself again. She hated seeing him like this.

'Do you want me to help you pack now?'

Dom's lips quirked into a smile. 'I packed the last time.'

He nodded at a green rucksack in one corner of his room.

'Okay, that's two of us. So, what's left to do?'

He shrugged at her, but the doubt in his eyes lingered. She needed to kick him out of his funk. She had to become someone he could lean on, the way she'd leaned on him. Wasn't that what partners did for each other? Helped each other out?

She brushed her lips against his. He gasped with surprise; it was the most delicious sound in the world. It pushed her to explore more of his mouth. Her fingers played with the buttons of his green, rebel jacket. She popped the first one. A suddenly impatient Dom popped the rest. He shucked out of it and dropped it to the floor.

His T-shirt came off next, black and plain, but it offset Dom's olive skin and deep-brown eyes perfectly.

Anya slid her hands over his stomach. Dom's breath hitched when she touched ragged skin. He pulled her to him using the same arm the medics in Praesidium had placed their tech inside. She felt the power in his touch, but also Dom's control of it.

He pulled off her T-shirt next. She sat before him in just her bra and combat trousers. His eyes trailed over her and the look set her skin on fire.

Dom deepened their kiss, pulling back to lick her earlobe briefly. She groaned; both sensations sent a thrill through her. Dom switched to a kneeling position and pulled off his trousers, then worked on hers. She lay on her back, giggling at his failed attempts to get them past her heavy, black boots.

Anya sat up, and while she untied the laces Dom kissed her neck.

'Hurry up, please,' he murmured against her skin.

'I'm working as fast as I can.'

She got the boots off. Dom wasted no time in pulling off her combats. Wearing just her underwear, she lay back down on the bed. Dom rested his cheek against her stomach. She played with the soft curls in his hair.

'I love you so much, Anya Macklin.'

Her heart nearly exploded in her chest. 'I love you, too, Dom Pavesi.'

5

Anya

Ten trucks rolled out past the relocated boulders, through the front of the valley, its anti-magnetic protection disabled. Anya sat in the first truck. Dom was driving. In the back were half a dozen soldiers, plus packs of food, ammunition and guns. The other nine trucks were similarly packed.

The truck jerked over some smaller rocks that hadn't been cleared, forcing Anya to grab the door handle to steady herself. Dom gripped the steering wheel hard, his knuckles turning white. His stern gaze was fixed on the opening to the valley.

Anya was worried, too. Nobody knew what might be waiting for them. Jacob had sent his reprogrammed orb out to check the landscape an hour ago. The orb had returned with footage that showed it to be empty. But an hour was plenty of time for Praesidium to make a move. Anya looked up to see the orb zipping ahead of their truck, but without a monitor to see what it recorded, it was useless.

She sucked in a quiet breath to steady her nerves, hoping Dom wouldn't hear it. She wanted to be strong for him, but the idea of returning to the city put her on edge. It wasn't that long ago that she'd been the Collective's prisoner.

But they had to go back.

Dom slowed when the truck neared the entrance to the valley. He leaned forward, trying to get a better look.

'Should we check on foot?' asked Anya. It would only take a minute.

'No.' He leaned back. 'If there's trouble, we can move faster in these things.'

He inched the nose of the truck out. Anya craned her neck, not seeing any large diggers or Copies waiting for them. She released a breath.

'Maybe they had other things to do,' she said, settling in the seat.

Dom frowned. 'Maybe.'

He flashed his rear lights, signaling to the others behind him. Then, he rolled the truck out.

The orb zipped overhead as the last of the trucks exited the valley, heading out a short way before returning. It kept close to the truck that Jacob was in. The two wolves galloped alongside him. Her and Dom's truck rumbled over the dirt landscape. Evidence of the recent fight lay strewn across the battlefield. A few Copy corpses remained, alongside two digging machines the rebels had dismantled.

Anya frowned at the scene. 'Why didn't they reclaim their dead?'

It was a stretch to call the machines dead, but to the Collective these once-living beings were their creations. It must want them back. It had gone to a lot of effort to take Jerome and Alex, both children of the city.

'I don't know. We don't know anything.' He shuddered as his narrowed gaze assessed the scene. 'Let's just be glad they aren't waiting for us.'

Their truck sped past the broken machines that had turned parts of the landscape into a mini junkyard. The other trucks followed. Rover appeared at Anya's window, keeping pace with them. His eyes were set ahead and his tongue lolled to the side, as though he were enjoying the run. Next to him was a second, smaller wolf that Anya presumed was female. During the battle, Jacob had cut her connection to the Collective. When she'd come back online, she'd listened to a new voice. She and Rover were inseparable.

Anya felt better knowing the beasts were on their side.

Dom was concentrating on the route ahead. She did the same, hoping the wolves would alert them to any approaching danger. The city wasn't far, maybe fifty kilometers away. By truck, and with the weight they carried, they'd be there in an hour.

Ω

It didn't take long for the city to come into view. Nothing but flat land lay between them and it. Ahead, an arc of buildings marked its perimeter, making it look like an oasis in its desert-like surroundings.

Dom stopped the truck. Being exposed like this made Anya shiver. The other trucks staggered their stops behind theirs. One truck drove up next to them. Charlie rolled the window down. Vanessa was sitting beside him.

'What now?' he said to Dom.

'I don't know. Any idea if the barrier is still down?'

'Jacob might know. But I think he'll suggest we try it for ourselves.'

Charlie got out of his truck. Dom did the same and they walked to the window of another one. Anya watched the pair in the mirror as they spoke to Jacob. Jacob shook his head. Carissa next to him perked up, eyes wide. Her gaze flicked between Charlie and Dom, then to the city.

Their limited choices caused Anya's pulse to hammer in her throat. The girl had gotten them out once. If the barrier was back up, there was a chance she could get them back in without them having to ram it. But, as they'd discussed, it was more likely the Collective had already changed the frequency codes and the girl was no longer aligned with it.

Dom and Charlie returned to their trucks. Dom

slid into the driver's seat next to her while Charlie stayed by Dom's window.

'Jacob says there's no way of knowing from out here if the barrier is still active. He says it gives off a weird shine when it is, but today'—Dom pointed up at the overcast sky— 'it's not that easy to see it.'

The city looked ordinary to her, not shiny at all.

'Then we drive at it. If the barrier's up, it will stop us,' she said.

Charlie raised one brow. 'It's not the worst idea.'

Dom appeared to think about it. He looked at Anya. 'You think it will work?'

She grimaced. 'I have no idea.'

Dom gripped the wheel and looked ahead of him. 'That's good enough for me.'

Charlie climbed back into his truck.

Dom said to him and Vanessa, 'I'll try it first. If I make it through, the rest of you follow me.'

He turned to the grill separating the cabin from the back of the truck and ordered the soldiers out. Turning to Anya, he nodded at the door for her to do the same.

'No way. I'm going with you.'

Dom shook his head. 'It's too dangerous.'

'Yes, it is, and that's why we're both doing it.'

Besides, it was her idea.

'Come on, Anya...'

She folded her arms. 'Make me.'

He gave her a withering stare, but Anya stayed

43

put.

'I guess we're at an impasse.' She stared ahead of her. 'Let's go. June needs us to get in there.'

Dom shook his head and rolled up the window. 'Okay, but hold on to something. The lack of seatbelts in this thing will be a problem if we meet resistance.'

Her hands started to sweat, thanks to the kick of adrenaline pumping through her body. She wiped them on her combats and gripped the door handle. Dom stuck the truck into first and floored it, quickly shifting up through the gears. The truck swapped the dirt road for a paved one that marked the main entrance into Praesidium. The Business District was to the left and accommodation to the right, separated by a deep strip of grass that created a buffer between the city and the real world.

Dom increased the speed as he aimed for the entrance. It would either have a barrier or it wouldn't.

Anya's breaths shortened to fine points. If this didn't work, little would protect them from the kickback. Dom couldn't have looked more nervous if he tried. He kept his wide-eyed gaze ahead. Anya rattled out a breath as the entrance grew closer.

The wheels of the truck hit a bump designed to slow vehicles down. The truck skidded to the left, and their speed slowed. Dom righted the truck and launched it at the open entrance. A screech built up in Anya's throat. She squeezed her eyes shut, waiting for the impact.

But it never came. She opened her eyes to see Dom still driving. Along the central road. Inside Praesidium. They had made it. A laugh bubbled out of her. Dom screeched to a halt next to a tag machine just past the Business District. Anya checked behind her to see the other trucks filing in. The barrier was down. She looked ahead of her, her chest still tight with stress.

The place was too quiet. Where was the welcome party?

'This doesn't feel right,' she said, huffing out her stress.

Dom loosened his stiff posture, but only a little. 'No it doesn't.'

A knock on the window startled them both. It was Jacob.

They climbed out of the truck. Three dozen armed soldiers filled the spaces between the vehicles.

Anya and Dom gathered with Charlie, Vanessa, Jacob and Carissa.

'Where's the resistance?' asked Dom.

Jacob shook his head. 'I thought there'd be an army waiting for us.'

Anya had dreaded this moment, but to get revenge on the Collective, this was where she needed to be. If her parents' deaths had pushed her out of reality, Jason's death had pushed her back into it.

In truth, that had already happened with the return of her memories from Arcis. Knowing the Collective had forced her through nine floors of hell, all while she had to watch her friends die, was reason enough to make it pay.

But standing in this city, she felt as empty as the city looked.

Dom handed her a weapon. One of the revolvers, for defensive purposes only. He carried a more lethal weapon: the Disruptor. But it only worked by stealing the power from the machines. Without any power present, the gun was currently empty.

Sheila, June, Imogen, Kaylie and Thomas got out of their respective trucks. Kaylie instructed her team to set up a defensive arc.

Anya walked along the central road, putting a little distance between them and the trucks. A high wall stood to one side of them; the entrance to a large, three-tiered accommodation block lay to the other. It felt strange to be back in the city while free.

To her left, inset into the wall, was the door they'd used to escape from the underground tunnels. In the distance, a large, white building sat taller than the rest.

'It's the Learning Center,' said Carissa.

Anya frowned. 'What's in there?'

'There's a download/upload room. But it's also where the Collective live, or rather where its program does.'

Anya examined the building at the heart of Praesidium. With no sun and no barrier, the plain, white exterior looked duller than she remembered. In fact, the entire place looked flat.

'Do you think they're still in there?'

Carissa shrugged. 'I can't sense them.'

Jacob came to stand next to her. He cupped his hand over his eyes and looked into the distance. 'That doesn't mean anything, miss. You've disconnected yourself from the Collective.'

'But I can still hear Quintus.'

That was news to Anya.

Jacob looked down at her, apparently not shocked by the news. 'Was it your memory or was it him?'

Carissa blushed. 'I don't know. It sounded new.'

'What did he say? Tell me.'

Carissa shifted on the spot, as if uncomfortable. 'He wants me to come home. But he said that same thing to me on the battlefield, so I can't be sure it wasn't a replay.'

Jacob patted her on the back. 'It's okay.' He frowned at the Learning Center. 'We'll be okay.'

At one time, Anya would have blamed the Copies for everything. But the more time she spent with Carissa, the more she saw that the girl had only been following orders. Humans were to blame for this mess. They'd blindly followed the Collective inside Essention. Anya had permitted it to enroll her in Arcis and she'd lost her memories because of it. If humans followed less and took action more, perhaps this world would be a different one today.

She lifted her gun, glad to have chosen a side that cared enough to fight.

But still, the empty city chilled her. Their group walked toward the Learning Center. Anya glanced at the accommodation block to their right and the apartments that appeared to be vacant. Dom appeared at her side suddenly. She jumped in fright.

She was doing that a lot lately.

'You okay?' he asked. 'You look a little on edge.'

'Yeah. Just don't like being back here. You?'

His gaze swept the accommodation. 'Yeah.'

Sharp movement from inside the block startled her. She stopped just as Rover growled low and deep. A dozen Copies streamed out of the building, all armed, all running at them.

'This is an ambush!' yelled Dom. 'Fall back!'

But their trucks were a half a kilometer away.

Between them and the vehicles were four wolves that had not traveled with them.

6

Dom

Dom jerked back at the sight of the Copies. He didn't remember much about this city. From the time he'd arrived to his departure, everything had been hazy. But one Copy had stuck in his mind. One of his guards, who'd not only treated him poorly, but also pretended his mother, Mariella, was still alive.

Yeah, he remembered him all right. And now that Copy was running at him. Not just one, but twelve of him. Each version of his prison guard wore the same sneer on his face.

'Everyone, fan out!' he ordered.

If they couldn't get to the trucks, they'd have to fight.

The Copies fired at them.

Kaylie shouted to her team and they fired back, long enough for Rover to get into position and provide them with cover. The bullets bounced off his exterior. Jacob and Carissa cowered behind him. Rover's mate did the same as him, facing off against Copies she'd once listened to. Charlie and Vanessa hid behind her. Dom didn't have the firepower to help them. He hoped he wouldn't need it.

Dom's nemesis came running at him. He couldn't tell which one was the Copy he'd battled with. Did it matter? In his eyes, they were all the same.

His gaze flicked to a cowering Carissa, eyes set wide, and Rover and his mate defending her. Okay, maybe not all the machines were the same. He checked for Anya. She and June had merged with the line of soldiers, their revolvers poised and ready. Sheila and Imogen, too. Thomas crouched low with the Atomizer, which was capable of punching a hole in Praesidium's tech. Rebel soldiers hit the Copies with blasts from their Electro Guns. The electricity bounced off some kind of personal shield the Copies wore. But not all of them appeared to have one. Two went down.

Kaylie and her team were driving forward.

Thomas kept low as he shuffled closer to Dom. Dom raised the Disruptor, drawing the spent energy out of the air to charge it.

'Use the Atomizer to punch a hole in their shields,' he said to Thomas.

Sheila and Imogen slipped back behind the soldiers, who had fanned out. They were attempting to sneak up on the Copies, who were huddled in groups of three. One from each group appeared to hold what looked like a shield, while another fired around it. Anya popped off a shot at one of the Copies. It bounced off the front of the shield before hitting the Copy's outstretched arm. Dom's former guard jerked his arm back.

The purpose of the bullets wasn't to kill; it was to distract. Thomas aimed the Atomizer at one shield and fired. A hole appeared in the shimmering, transparent barrier. Before the Copies could refocus, Dom fired the partial energy from the Disruptor at the shield; it hit the guard. He reversed the action on the gun and sucked the Copy's energy plus that of the shield back inside the weapon.

Now, he had real power. The trio of guards regrouped and huddled behind the remaining shields. Dom wondered which one was his actual guard. Many Copies lived in this city. What was the purpose of replicating just one?

To create an infinite army, perhaps?

Kaylie and her team fired their Electro Guns at the enemy. It gave Sheila and Imogen time to pick up the discarded weapons belonging to the Copies. Kaylie and her team tossed their spent weapons on the ground and kept firing with active ones.

Dom took cover behind a tall, white tag station. Thomas stayed with him.

'Hit their shields again and I'll blast them with the Disruptor.'

Thomas nodded. His fingers were white from

clutching the Atomizer too tight.

Electro Gun shots from the Copies hit a couple of soldiers who hadn't moved fast enough. They went down. The enemy moved in, but Anya and June popped off shots at their heads to keep them back. Behind him, Dom heard an exchange of growls and a 'Carissa, get back!' from Jacob. He turned to see the wolves that had blocked their retreat to the trucks were moving in. Rover and his mate snapped and snarled at the unwelcome visitors. The wolves launched themselves at each other in a weird display of dominance.

He faced forwards. One of the Copy guards had broken off from the pack and was almost at him. A light shimmer from his personal shield distorted his face.

Rattled, Dom raised the Disruptor and set it to fire, but a blast of electricity near his fingers forced him to drop the gun. Thomas scrabbled back from the danger.

'I thought it was you,' the Copy said with a sneer.

His prison guard. It had to be.

The other Copies moved in on the others' location. He heard a scream. Female. His eyes searched the crowd, but the guard blocked his view. Thomas raised the Atomizer.

The Copy flicked his gaze to him. 'I wouldn't do that. I've got a gun on him.'

Thomas lowered the Atomizer.

Dom clutched his arm, the one that the blast had hit. The one without the tech in it. 'I didn't expect you to still be here. Where is everyone?'

'Gone.'

'Really?'

'Would *I* lie to you?' he drawled.

Dom lunged for the spare gun in his waistband, but his ex-guard blasted the ground. The electricity bounced around and hit his metal arm, making a weird, twanging noise.

'Ah, yes, I forgot about that,' the Copy said. 'I hoped the infection might have killed you, but I suspected it hadn't.'

Seeing his prison guard again stirred up his worst memories, but all Dom felt for him right then was pity. At least Dom had his freedom.

He smiled.

That only angered his former guard. 'What are you smiling at, Original?'

'I'm just wondering why the Collective chose *you* to copy, chose *you* to put your life on the line to stop us.'

The Copy sneered in response. 'I volunteered.'

That made Dom laugh. 'Really? The Collective likes to protect its best assets. If you were one, you wouldn't be here. Did you use that crude machine to make copies of yourself?'

The guard's sneer lifted the edges of his mouth. He glanced back. 'Looks like your team is on the back foot.'

Dom saw the fight was almost over, but it wasn't his team that was losing. Rover and his mate were managing to keep the connected wolves back.

A sharp sting caught his leg, sending him to his knees. His former guard lorded over him, looking ready to finish the job he'd tried to do while Dom was prisoner.

'I volunteered for this because I wanted to be the one to kill you.'

He pressed his finger down on the release trigger. Dom reached up and grabbed the end of the gun. With a strength he had yet to test, he ripped the gun from the Copy's iron grip and tossed it away. The guard stared at him, wide-eyed. Dom got to his feet and tore the shield away. He grabbed the Copy's neck and pushed him back against the tag machine.

His mother appeared to him. She was standing beside him, telling him everything would be okay. She told him to squeeze harder. So he did.

The Copy's mouth fell open. He looked as though he was struggling for air.

These things aren't real.

Dom's fingers dug into the Copy's soft flesh. That was the only part that truly disturbed him: how real these things felt. It reminded him of Anya's Copy and her almost-successful attempts to seduce him.

Dom blinked and shook his head. Mariella stayed with him, whispering, 'Keep going, my child. You're almost there.'

He didn't believe his mother wanted him to kill

another. Even at the end, his father had not destroyed her goodness, but he had definitely destroyed Dom's.

The Copy became his father, Carlo. He continued to squeeze.

A warm hand on his arm broke him free of his obsession. He blinked.

'Let him go, Dom.' It was Charlie. Jacob and Vanessa were with him. 'He's not worth it.'

Dom glanced at the Copies to see they'd been dealt with, except for this one.

He refocused on his former guard. 'I have to. I need to.'

Carlo refused to die. He lived on in his angry son.

'No, you don't,' said Charlie. 'Don't let your time here turn you into one of them.'

Dom blinked again. 'You want to let him go?'

The guard's eyes were closing, but a flicker of hope was lodged in them.

'No, we'll lock him up. We might need him.'

Dom released his hand, remembering why they were here. The Copy coughed and rubbed his throat. Like he was a real person.

Dom stepped back from him. He buried his anger caused by memories of his dead father, and remembered who he was. A leader.

A leader didn't waste time on the smaller things. Or the smaller people.

He glared at the guard. 'Where are the prisoners?'

His nemesis smiled. 'What prisoners?'

'The ones who were brought here. Jerome and Alex.'

The Copy shrugged.

Dom waved his hand at him and turned away. 'You'd better get him out of my sight, Charlie, before I kill him.'

Rebel soldiers restrained the remaining Copies. Dom saw bodies on the ground. His heart seized with fear until he saw Anya was okay. He breathed out. June was with her. They were staring down at the fallen.

His gaze flicked to June, who was holding her belly. 'And we should get June to the medical facility now.'

Charlie touched Dom's shoulder. 'We will. But not everyone made it, son.'

7

Anya

Just twelve Copies and four Guardians against three dozen rebel soldiers and two wolves? That was a fight the Copies could never have won.

Rover and his mate pushed the wolves back, but before Thomas and Dom could use the Atomizer and the Disruptor, they ran off. Rebel soldiers picked themselves up from the dirt. Six were dead.

Charlie said something to Dom. His eyes searched the scene frantically. Anya met his gaze, then looked down at Kaylie's body. June stood next to her, equally shocked.

Dom strode over to their location. He stopped cold when he saw the bodies of those who'd fought to keep everyone safe.

'I'm sorry, Dom,' said Anya. 'I know she was your friend.'

Dom hunkered down next to the half dozen

soldiers who'd been unlucky. Including Kaylie.

He stared at her for a long moment. Then he stroked her face gently. 'I'm glad to have known you, soldier.'

His expression hardened as he stood up.

A lump rose in Anya's throat. There was too much death. She picked up the spare Electro Guns the dead soldiers had dropped, checking the power indicator on the side of each. She'd used one of these in a timed maze on the fifth floor of Arcis. They'd been told to shoot holographic discs. She'd shot something else that day: Warren. Anya sensed that his parents abandoning him had turned him cold, but he'd redeemed himself a little in the end. He'd tried to save her brother. She pretended there had been nothing in it for him, no redemption—that it was just a selfless act.

Dom rubbed June's arm. 'We need to get you to the medical facility, now. I'll ask the soldiers to collect our dead. The wolves will protect them while they do. We'll bury them once you're stable.'

The Copies were down, but Jacob manually disabled eleven of them by pressing a button at the back of their neck and accessing an open panel there.

Good to know.

A few of the soldiers kept the remaining Copy guard under control. They only needed one to enter any building in Praesidium—the one Dom was currently flashing eye daggers at. Anya could only guess the story there.

A section of their team pressed on to the medical facility. Vanessa walked ahead with June, Jacob and Carissa.

'Is it safe to bring one of the Copies with us?' she asked Jacob. 'What if he's connected, like the others?'

Jacob shook his head. 'We need him active, in case we need to access off-limit areas.'

He looked back at Dom, who was following behind the soldiers in control of the Copy guard.

'This one stays with us,' Dom snapped.

'Lucky me,' the Copy quipped.

Dom swatted him across the top of his head and shoved him on.

Anya wasn't sure how Dom had been able to tell the twelve Copies apart, but this one had rattled him enough that he'd just tried to kill him.

The lack of resistance bothered Anya. Twelve Copies and a few Guardians? Was that really all there was between them and the medical facility? Everyone moved more cautiously than before. If another attack happened, they would be ready.

Dom dropped back to walk beside her, constantly scanning the area.

'Are you okay?' she asked.

He blew out a breath. 'Yeah. Just a little shaken.'

'Was he one of your prison guards?'

'The worst.'

Dom hadn't spoken about his experience in the

medical facility and she didn't want to pry. But she'd seen his condition and experienced the place for herself. Some things didn't need elaboration.

The group entered Zone C, midway between the exit and the large, white structure at the heart of the city. Carissa glanced nervously at the Learning Center. She was holding one arm and looking more nervous than Anya felt to be back here.

They approached a familiar, gray building with a grass verge to the front. Seeing the medical facility from the outside made her shiver. But the fact no one was stopping them worried her more.

She assessed the deserted streets and the rooftops she could see. Jacob's rogue orb zipped overhead. What she wouldn't give to see what it did right now.

'Where is everyone?'

Dom's brow creased. 'I don't know. Maybe they don't have the manpower to fight us.'

'Maybe.'

She looked back to where the train track sat idle above the street. This entire place was like a ghost town.

'I hope there's still power here.'

'Me too,' replied Dom.

The double doors showed damage, probably from the time of their escape. They'd made it to the lobby only to find the door was locked and Copies were trying to break it down. Her Copy medic had helped them to escape the clutches of two guards who had caught up with them. One of them had killed Yasmin. Anya wondered if her medic was still alive.

'Do we need special access to this place?' Dom asked Carissa.

Carissa nodded and approached the door. She tried the handle but it wouldn't budge.

With wide eyes, she looked back at the group. 'I don't know how to open it, other than with my chip.'

Each of them had removed their tracking devices soon after they escaped the city.

Dom stepped forward and shoved the prison guard ahead. 'You do it.'

The Copy grunted from the rough treatment, but pressed the chip in his wrist to the plate on the left. It flashed green.

That confirmed this city still had power.

'At least you're good for something.' Dom turned to the others. 'Get ready.'

Anya lifted her Electro Gun to eye level and aimed it at the door. Her revolver was tucked in her waistband. Others fanned out around the lead group, creating a semi-circle, guns pointing out.

Dom poked the Copy in the side. 'Open it.'

He did and Anya braced for an attack, an ambush. Anything.

None came.

'It's empty,' the guard said.

'Lucky for you,' Dom growled at him. He shoved him inside.

Anya's knees nearly buckled when she stepped

inside the place that had held her and so many others prisoner. She caught Sheila's shiver and saw June's lips thin with tension. This place was evil. But hopefully something good could come out of it.

Her memories of this place had remained intact, not stolen by the Collective's machine. It had been less than a week since she'd been here. So much had happened in that time.

Carissa led the way to the lift. The door refused to open for her.

Dom shoved the guard toward it. 'Open the lift.'

While the guard did, he eyed Carissa. '173-C?'

Carissa's blonde hair fanned out as she turned sharply. 'What did you call me?'

'That's your name, isn't it?'

'M-my name is Carissa.'

'That's not what the Collective calls you.'

His sneer unsettled Anya, but her attention was drawn back to June, who appeared to be in discomfort.

Vanessa was holding on to her elbow. 'Can we get moving, please? This girl needs attention.'

Dom shoved the Copy into the lift. His three rebel soldier guards entered it after him. Vanessa entered with June next. Then Charlie. Carissa and Jacob followed until it was full.

'The rest of us will follow,' said Anya. There was more than one way to access the levels below. 'Where are you taking her?'

All eyes were on Carissa for the answer. She looked around nervously. 'The Nurturing Center, third floor down.'

'Where the babies were being kept?'

She nodded.

The lift doors closed.

Anya said to Sheila, 'We'll use the stairs.'

'Okay, let's go.'

Anya and Dom followed Sheila, Imogen and Thomas as they took three sets of stairs down to the third level. At the bottom, they exited into a white corridor. Anya squinted beneath the harsh, overhead lights. She'd forgotten how bright this place could get. Her medic had brought her down here once, when she was trying to convince her that having a baby by force was a good thing.

Anya followed the sound of soft voices up ahead. They met up with the others in an open area, set before the door leading to the Nurturing Center viewing corridor.

Carissa walked up to a different, plain wall that had a slight shimmer to it. She glanced down at her wrist.

'It needs a Copy's chip to open it.'

The soldiers shoved the guard forward. With a grunt, he waved his wrist in front of the wall. A part of it transformed into a door, showing a new corridor that appeared to give them access to the area behind the rooms and the viewing corridor. Vanessa helped June inside, followed closely by Carissa and Jacob.

Dom ordered the remainder to watch his ex-guard before following them. Anya entered the new corridor, keeping back. This was Carissa and Jacob's show now. She had no idea what this equipment did or how it worked.

She entered a room—one of three—that she'd only seen from one side: through the viewing corridor. Her chest tightened suddenly. Her incarceration, her forced connection with Alex... it was still raw. She needed to find Alex and Jerome, to free them both—if they were here at all.

Their rescue would have to wait. Right now, June needed help.

Anya stood back while Vanessa helped June sit on a gurney in the middle of the room. A machine containing seven vials made of clear glass stood off to the side. Each vial contained an amber liquid.

Jacob stroked the front of the machine.

'Do you know how to use this?' he asked Carissa.

She walked up to it and frowned. Anya wondered if Carissa was accessing the files she'd grabbed before disconnecting from the city.

'This machine accelerates growth.' She shook her head at Jacob. 'We can't use this on the fetus while it's still in June. They use this machine to grow the babies once they're out the host's womb.'

The truth made Anya shiver. It could so easily have been her. She had seen the other two rooms from the side of the viewing corridor. They'd held

64

children of varying ages. Had they been products of that growth machine?

A hand on her back startled her. 'Are you okay?'

Dom was looking down at her. His brown eyes settled her nerves and she nodded. 'Just remembering.'

He flicked his eyes up to Carissa. 'So, where do we take her?'

'The Harvesting room on the first floor has surgical equipment,' she said.

June's eyes widened. 'Harvesting? Surgical?'

Dom nodded. 'I can vouch for that.'

'Anything that can take the baby out?' asked Vanessa.

Dom's lips thinned. 'More than there should be.'

Vanessa helped June to stand. 'I'm sorry, we need to move you again.'

June nodded, but Anya saw she was in huge discomfort. And also that her belly was growing in size again.

As they left the room, Jacob said to Dom, 'We're going to need you to come with us. You've been there before.'

Dom jerked a nod and followed. But when Anya didn't move, he stopped. 'Are you coming?'

'I want to see if I can find Alex and Jerome.'

Dom smiled. 'Of course. Be careful.'

He bent down and grazed her lips with the

softest kiss.

'I will,' she whispered.

8

Carissa

Where was Quintus? Or the rest of the Collective? Carissa had felt a slight tingle in her head, where her neuromorphic chip was, when she'd passed the first of the tag stations. Quintus had told her she couldn't break her ties to the Collective, that she belonged to the Ten always.

She followed Vanessa and June to the lift. Now wasn't the right time to check if the ten voices were still active inside the Great Hall.

But soon. Because she had to know.

Jacob encouraged her on with a gentle nudge and she picked up her speed. Ahead, the soldiers steered along the Copy guard, known to Carissa as 148-C. His clones were gone. That they existed at all meant the replication machine technology must still be working. And that the city might have sizable power reserves.

Carissa almost touched the NMC connection disc that used to allow her to hear the Collective. It made her nervous to attempt connection now. If the Collective was still online, it could use the connection to kill her.

The Inventor's hand on her back startled her. She jerked her finger away and looked up at him.

'Is something the matter, miss?'

His eyes were pale and warm. She hated that he could see right through her moods.

'No, nothing.'

She resumed her walk, keeping her pace even, keen to keep her distance from 148-C, who kept glancing back at her. Her memory banks held a report on this Copy. He'd been reported to Quintus for bullying Dom while he'd been prisoner.

'It must be strange to be back in the city, miss,' the Inventor said. She snapped her attention to him. He was looking around. 'I must admit it feels strange to be back myself, even though we haven't been gone that long.'

Carissa had become so used to seeing the Inventor in the city she sometimes forgot that he'd been a prisoner here. In her own way, Carissa had been one too. She was a child of the city, destined to live out her days here. Cared for by the Collective. Shaped and molded by Quintus.

But never loved by him.

Carissa hugged herself as she walked, injecting pace into her step and passing the others. She wanted to make it to the lift before 148-C did.

'Slow down, miss.' The Inventor huffed out a breath. 'I can't move as fast as you.'

She reached the lift and slipped in beside Dom, Vanessa and a wincing June. The Inventor arrived a moment later. He flashed her an irritated look and climbed on board. She pressed the button before 148-C's arrival with the soldiers.

A restrained 148-C arrived with this escorts. Carissa kept pressing the button.

'We should go, Jacob,' she said.

The Inventor frowned at her, then looked at 148-C. He waved at the soldiers holding him. 'Take the stairs. We'll meet you up there.'

148-C smirked at Carissa, as if he knew his presence bothered her. A deep chill ran through her biogel and made her hands tingle. She hated not being connected, not knowing what was going on.

The second the doors closed, Carissa's fear lifted.

The Inventor's eyes were on the door.

'Thank you,' she whispered, too softly for him to hear.

The doors opened and they exited into the first floor. Carissa had not visited this floor before. Her interest had lain in the second floor, where June had been. She'd only seen the first floor as part of the maps. But Dom should remember it well.

Their dark-haired leader shuddered. He pointed ahead. 'This way.'

The route brought them to a long corridor with a solid wall and door on one side, and several corridors opposite it. The soldiers, who had taken the stairs, arrived with 148-C.

Dom led the way, looking more confident going in than he'd been coming out of this place. His shoulders sagged a little, but he kept his head and chin up.

'In here,' he said softly, pointing at the door on the left.

148-C smirked.

Dom opened the door fast, pointing his gun inside. 'Clear.'

He stepped inside, but not before hesitating.

Vanessa helped June inside the room.

'Stay out here and protect us,' said the Inventor to the spare soldiers. He cast a cool look over 148-C, then nodded at the two armed soldiers flanking him. 'Bring him in.'

The soldiers pushed him inside. Carissa, last into the room, closed the door.

The room was bright and white—a prominent feature of the city. A nod to the cleanliness the Collective strived for daily. There was a gurney in the middle of the room. Above it, several closed panels were set in the ceiling. The walls, smooth and white, had hidden nooks. All the walls in the city did. The Collective despised disorder. Everything had to be in its place. If it wasn't needed, it must be out of sight.

Carissa clasped her hands to the front while

Vanessa and Dom got June settled.

June looked around the room, worried. 'What happens in here?'

'Many interesting things,' replied 148-C.

Dom grabbed 148-C's arm, making him yelp. 'Shut your mouth, unless I ask you to speak. Got it?'

The guard nodded slowly, not looking too put out by Dom's threats. Dom let go. 148-C rubbed his arm where Dom had used his enhanced strength on him.

'Ah!' June cried out.

Carissa rushed over to her. 'Are you okay?'

'I will be. Junior's getting a little antsy.'

Carissa pulled up her sleeve and looked up at the Inventor.

He pushed her arm down. 'We're past your growth repressors now, miss. It's time to take Junior out.' He squinted at the walls, the ceiling. 'How does this place work?'

Dom pointed. 'Up there. The medical equipment.'

Vanessa held on to June's hand. 'How do we get it started?'

'He knows how.' Dom grabbed 148-C's arm roughly.

'I've forgotten,' he said coolly. 'It's been so long since you were here.'

Dom twisted 148-C's arm behind his back. The Copy yelped. 'I seem to remember you being squeamish about blood.' 148-C's eyes widened. 'Help us now, and I'll spare you the gory parts.'

The Copy nodded tightly. Dom let go, but the soldiers flanking the prisoner kept their weapons pointed at him. He walked over to a panel and pressed it. It revealed a control pad.

Dom stood at his shoulder. 'How does it work?'

'You type in the procedure you want done. Then the arms do the rest. You remember them, don't you?'

Dom slapped him on his ear. 148-C hissed.

'What command to we need to deliver the child?'

148-C glanced at Carissa. 'She's more likely to know than me.'

All eyes were on Carissa, including June's.

She shook her head. 'I never worked here.'

The Inventor stooped, drawing her focus to him. 'Miss, you have the commands. You know what they are. Think.'

She shook her head again. 'But I'm not connected.' She pointed to 148-C. 'He is.'

'We can't risk him issuing a false command. Think, miss. June trusts you.'

Carissa bit her lip. She tried to remember, but the pressure turned her thoughts blank.

The Inventor shook her arm gently. 'Do your best, miss.'

She nodded.

There were too many eyes on her; she closed her eyes to concentrate better. She thought back to her visits on the second floor. She'd spoken to the head medic about the procedures. 28-C had called June "Patient Zero" and said that she was awaiting fetus transfer. But that was before June had received the implant.

She opened her eyes. 'Try this command: fetus removal.'

Dom typed in the procedure. Panels opened in the ceiling. He jerked his head up. A sudden shudder matched the fear in his eyes.

The first metal arm extended down, almost hesitantly. It had a set of pincers. June's eyes widened. Carissa rushed over to her and held her other hand.

'It's okay,' she said, even though she'd never witnessed operations in this room. She'd only read reports about the work that went on in the Harvesting program. She turned to Dom. 'Talk to her.'

He left the control panel and came to June's side. 'It's okay. It usually starts with a morphine injection.' He pointed to an arm carrying a needle. 'See?'

The second arm raced toward June. She recoiled from it.

'Dom?' June whispered.

The needle jabbed her vein roughly and stayed there. She cried out.

Dom smiled. 'It's okay. You won't feel the next part.'

Carissa wondered about his time here. But a

third and fourth arm extending down dragged her thoughts back to the next part. One had a set of retractors. The other had a laser and was cutting through the fabric on June's clothes. The pincers held the clothes apart while the laser continued to cut. It made a neat incision in June's belly. The retractors pinned the skin back, exposing the womb.

So much blood. Carissa had never seen that much before. The smell of iron filled the air and made her feel dizzy.

148-C said, 'You promised I could leave!'

Dom nodded to the rebel soldiers and they took him outside.

Carissa covered her eyes, peeking now through slits in her fingers. The set of pincers lifted the baby out. Vanessa had her jacket off and was holding it out for the arm to place it in. The arm hesitated, then dropped the baby into it.

A fifth arm sealed the tear in the womb and the retractors retreated up and into the ceiling. The pincers held the skin closed while the arm with the skin-repair tool mended the horizontal slice in June's skin. Carissa removed her hand from her eyes and examined June's belly. Except for a slight bulge from the trauma, her skin was healing nicely. June sighed with relief, but her eyes were on Vanessa, cradling her bundle.

'Give her to me,' she said.

Vanessa looked up at her, surprised. 'How did you know the sex?'

'I had a feeling.'

Vanessa smiled at the baby Carissa couldn't see and handed her to June. And that's when she saw her. A human baby. No flaws. No horns. No strange additions. Just flesh and bones.

Then it began to cry. The noise pierced her eardrums. She covered her ears.

'Jacob!' she cried out. 'Stop the noise immediately.'

The Inventor just laughed. 'That's what babies do, miss. It's their way.'

'I don't like it. Stop it.'

The Inventor continued to chuckle, which only irritated her more.

'I can hear it a mile away.'

It was something the Inventor used to say. She hoped she got the context right.

The Inventor froze. He looked at Dom and Vanessa, then at June.

What had she said wrong?

'They'll hear her before we reach safety,' said the Inventor.

And then she understood. The baby was making too much noise.

Vanessa grabbed Carissa's shoulder, startling her. 'The growth machine. Do you know how to operate it?'

That, she'd seen in action. Newborns being grown into toddlers in a matter of hours. She nodded. If it stopped the crying, she was all for it.

June cradled her bundle.

Vanessa touched her shoulder. 'Are you sure about this?'

June nodded, her lower lip quivering. 'None of this is her fault. She needs all the protection we can give her.'

9

Anya

Being back inside the medical facility sent a deep shiver through Anya. For obvious reasons. The place lacked the usual bustle that she'd experienced while prisoner. But none of that mattered. Not when Alex and Jerome were still missing.

She was halfway up the first set of stairs when she heard someone behind her. Anya stopped and stared down at Thomas, who had paused on the step.

'I can do this on my own.'

'I know, but I need to feel useful,' he said. 'I'm trying not to think about what happened.'

Thomas was a tall, skinny twenty-year-old with brown hair similar to Jason's. His pale skin told her he preferred being inside to out. Just like Jason did.

Had.

A lump lodged in her throat.

'Were you and Jason friends?'

Thomas stared at the floor. 'I didn't know him for long.' He looked up. 'But I'd like to think so.'

The loss pinched at her fragile heart. She gripped the wall with the tips of her fingers, to steady herself.

'Jason didn't have many friends, but I can see why he picked you,' she said. Thomas smiled at that. 'Come on, I suppose I could use a second set of eyes.'

Thomas resumed his climb and she sensed, as she climbed higher, that he also needed a distraction. She stopped short of the door to the second floor. Thomas paused two steps below her.

She turned to him. 'Were you and Max close?'

He sighed and nodded. 'If it hadn't been for him and Charlie, I wouldn't be here.'

'It seems we both have the same person to thank for that.'

While Max had not rescued her from this medical facility, he had attempted to rescue her from the ninth floor of Arcis after he, Jason and other soldiers had successfully stormed the facility.

Anya studied Thomas' face. 'I don't remember you from Arcis.'

'I was never in Arcis.'

'We were on the ninth floor. The rebels... they came for us. Jason was with them...' She could barely say his name without bursting into tears.

Thomas smiled sadly. He leaned a shoulder against the wall. 'Preston went instead of me.' His smile dropped away. 'He was killed by the Copies.'

'I'm sorry.' She couldn't think of anything else to say.

Thomas shrugged as if it wasn't a big deal.

'The weapons—your designs—they got them past Arcis' force field?'

Thomas nodded, looking away. 'That was the only thing that worked well that day.'

'They saved us out on that battlefield. They gave us the upper hand.'

Thomas smiled sadly. 'They didn't save everyone.'

'Come on, let's keep moving. We don't know who's around.'

She clutched the Electro Gun hard to her chest, as if the feel of the cold metal might stop the hurt there.

She slipped through the door to the second floor. Sweeping her gun around, she checked for signs of Copy life. There were none.

Thomas stopped next to her, keeping his own Electro Gun raised.

'Where is everyone?' she asked him. 'This place was active when I was last here. It's like everyone dropped tools and left.'

'Maybe they were ordered to leave. With the city's defenses down, it would only be a matter of time before we showed up.'

Maybe. She hoped Jerome and Alex hadn't been cleared out, too.

'We should check this floor anyway. It's where

Alex was. It's possible they returned him to this floor.'

Her trainers squeaked as she sneaked down the main corridor. Thomas stayed behind her, covering the rear. She arrived at a corridor with several doors down it that ended in a dead end. This was where she and Alex had been trapped for a week. Sucking in a breath that was designed to steady her nerves but had the opposite effect, she stopped outside her old room.

She tried the handle. It didn't budge.

Anya knocked on the door. 'Hello? Alex, are you in there?'

She heard a noise on the other side. 'Anya?'

It was him. Her heart pounded faster. 'Alex! We're going to get you out of here.'

She turned to Thomas, not sure how. 'The access cards open these doors. We'll need that Copy guard to open it.'

'Maybe not.'

Thomas handed his gun to her. She pointed both their weapons at the entrance to the corridor. He pulled out a small tin from inside his coat pocket and opened it.

Anya saw an array of tools, narrow in design. 'What are you going to do with those?'

He smiled. 'Why, pick the lock, of course.'

Anya nestled both guns in the crooks of her arms. She hoped she wouldn't have to use them. The revolver in her waistband was her backup in case the electricity ran out. Not a great backup plan though.

Thomas got to work on the locking mechanism. 'They may use electronics to lock the doors, but every piece of electronics I've ever seen always has a manual override.'

His explanation took Anya back to Brookfield. Jason used to sit at the kitchen table with Praesidium's equipment spread out before him. He'd ream off an explanation of how the inventions worked. She wished now she'd paid more attention.

Thomas cursed, then said, 'Aha, here it is.'

Something clicked and he got the door open. Waiting inside was a worried Alex. No Jerome. She stepped inside the room, eyeing the big bed she'd slept in. Suppressing a shiver, she gave Alex a hug.

His hug back was brief, rushed. 'How's June?'

'She's fine. They're taking the baby out.'

His eyes widened. 'What?'

'June's fine. Listen, where's Jerome?'

'I don't know. We got separated when we arrived here.'

Anya exited the room, glad to leave the familiarity behind. 'This floor's empty. Where are all the Copies?'

'I don't know that either. They blindfolded me when I got here.'

'Blindfolded?'

Alex shrugged. His eyes shifted to the way back. 'I need to see June.'

'Jerome first.'

His wild gaze softened. 'Of course. We should

81

check this floor.'

Anya handed one of the Electro Guns back to Thomas.

Alex eyed the exchange. 'Any for me?'

She paused, then pulled the revolver out of her waistband. 'You remember this?'

She'd taught Alex and others how to shoot in the rebel camp.

He hesitated, then took it. 'Aim and shoot, right?'

She checked each of the rooms in the same corridor by knocking on the doors. Nobody answered their call.

They spread out and checked three more corridors in one go.

Searching the corridor farthest away from their starting point, Alex called her over. 'In here!'

He pointed to a door.

Thomas worked his lock-picking magic faster than before. Alex eyed his methods. Anya was equally impressed.

The door swung open. A relieved Jerome stood there, hands on hips. 'What took you so long?'

'Thomas insisted on doing things the old fashioned way.'

Jerome's lips curled up into a shaky smile. Anya hugged her old friend. Warren's old friend. They'd all lost someone they cared about.

She pulled back. 'Come on, we've got to go.'

'Where?' asked Jerome.

'To see June,' said Alex. 'Where is she now?'

'They were headed for the first floor to deliver the baby. There's surgical equipment there.'

Alex marched on ahead to the stairwell. Without pausing, he crashed through the doors and up one flight of stairs. Anya followed him, frowning. She knew he must really want to see her, but they still needed to be cautious.

They arrived on the first floor and followed the smell of iron. They stopped outside a room.

No, not iron. Blood.

Her own blood ran cold at what awaited them inside.

Alex sucked in a breath and jerked the door open. He peered inside. Anya checked past him. It looked like a bloodbath in there. Alex stood clear of the mess, staring at it.

She pulled him back from the door, hoping June was okay. 'She's not here. Come on. I know where she will be.'

'Where?' asked Alex.

'We should try the third.'

The machine Carissa had said accelerated growth was there.

Alex stormed back to the stairwell, taking the stairs down two at a time to the third. Anya followed, curious about this angrier Alex. She guessed being back here again must be one time too many.

She hurried to catch up with him. Thomas and Jerome were on her heels.

'What's the emergency?' Jerome muttered.

Alex burst through the door for the third floor and followed the corridor back to the Nurturing Center. Outside stood the soldiers and the Copy guard. The guard's eyes widened when he saw Alex. Then Jerome.

Jerome strode up to the Copy and grabbed a fistful of his uniform. 'Thought you could keep us here, did you?'

The guard said nothing, did nothing, except narrow his gaze at him.

Alex pushed past the soldiers blocking the way inside the hidden corridor. Anya went after him, Jerome on her heels.

'What's up with him?' he said.

'He's worried about June.'

Alex burst into the first room, calling June's name.

A breath rushed out of Anya when she entered the room and saw June was okay. Jacob, Carissa, Charlie, Vanessa, Dom and Sheila had surrounded her. She was sitting on the floor in front of something —or someone. She couldn't see what.

'June!' said Alex.

She turned and her face lit up. 'Oh my God, you're okay.'

She scrambled to her feet and crashed into Alex, hugging him tight.

Alex stroked her hair, but his eyes searched for something. 'Where is it?'

A smiling June pulled back from him. 'She's okay.'

'She?' said Anya.

June nodded at her. 'We had to use the growth machine.'

Anya stepped closer to the machine, its vials of orange liquid now half empty. Inside the machine and behind a Perspex window was a child sitting on the floor, looking about twelve months old. She had black hair and her eyes were a vivid blue. She looked nothing like June.

'Meet my daughter,' June said.

Alex fell to his knees in front of the child, as though in awe. He touched the Perspex glass between him and the child. The quiet child, reminding Anya of the children she and Dom had seen on the eighth floor in Arcis, regarded him curiously.

He waved at her. She waved back. 'She looks so real...'

June giggled. 'She is. Flesh and blood.'

Alex turned and grinned. 'Flesh and blood.'

10

Dom

'Where did you find them?' Dom asked Anya. He'd pulled her away from the others, who were fussing over the child.

She kept her eyes on Alex. 'In our room.'

Dom's heart twanged with jealousy. He still didn't know what exactly had gone on between the pair. It hadn't been that long since everyone had escaped the city. Alex and Anya clearly had unfinished business if she was referring to it as "their room."

Anya blinked and looked up at him. 'Our old room, I mean. It wasn't really ours. I never felt good there.'

He appreciated her attempts to ease his mind. Was he worried? No. His Anya was back. Was he jealous? Always. While Dom had been fighting for his life, Anya and Alex had been getting to know

86

each other. It bothered him that they might have seen each other naked.

Dom shook his head to rid himself of the pessimistic thoughts. He always looked for the worst in any situation.

Anya was staring at him, her deep-blue eyes round.

'If it helps,' she said softly, 'I thought he was arrogant at the start.'

'And now?'

She looked back at Alex; he was smiling and cooing at the child. 'Now he's just... Alex.'

When she turned back around, a deep frown marked her forehead.

'What's wrong?'

Anya blinked and smiled. 'Nothing. I just didn't know Alex liked babies so much.'

'Maybe it's June he likes. The baby is just a bonus.'

She shrugged. 'Yeah, maybe that's it.'

Dom wished he knew what she was thinking. But too much had happened since the return of Anya's memories for him to push her. Jason had died. Max, too. Even Warren, the weird boy who'd caused trouble in Arcis, would be missed by some. A muted version now stood where his vivacious and plucky Anya used to. He hoped to find her again, and pull her out of her grief.

Dom settled for gripping her hand and squeezing it once. She looked up at him, her eyes filled with a new energy. Then that energy vanished and she looked away.

Someone cleared their throat. Charlie. He, Jacob and Vanessa were looking at Dom.

'Son, what now?' said Charlie. 'June is out of danger and the child is fine. We need to move to the next step in our plan.'

His former guard was not in the room and could not hear him. But Dom lowered his voice anyway.

'Now we search the city, see if we can find the coordinates to the Beyond.'

'What about food?'

He hadn't thought about it.

'I don't know where to look.'

'Carissa?' Jacob asked the girl.

She looked up at him, wide-eyed. 'There is a storeroom close to the shops in the Business District. I don't know what's in it.'

Charlie nodded. 'That should be our first place to check.'

Yes, their supplies were low, but Dom's plan had always been to get out of here as soon as possible. Meeting opposition had diminished his hope of that happening. Maybe they should stock up the trucks. They believed the rebel Janet, whom Anya's parents had helped, to have hidden the diary containing coordinates for the Beyond somewhere in the city before she was captured by the Collective. But everything they had to go on was hearsay. They could be here for a while.

Anya squeezed his hand sharply. It knocked him out of his thoughts and he blinked.

'No, we brought food with us. We will stock up later. Our priority now is to find the coordinates.'

'Okay,' said Charlie with a nod. 'We try and locate all the hidden tunnels. To do that, we're going to need schematics.'

Jacob said, 'Carissa can help. She has cached copies of all the files. We'll be able to access them using the diagnostic machine in my workshop—assuming it's still there, of course.'

The reprogrammed orb had shown blast damage near Jacob's workshop.

'But Carissa's files may not list the tunnels we need,' said Anya. 'If the tunnels are hidden, that means from the city, too.'

'We have our own set of maps,' said Vanessa, patting the bag she carried that contained their efforts so far. 'If we compare both sets, we can concentrate on the areas the Collective doesn't know about.'

It was their best chance. But the lack of Copies in a city that had been teeming with life just days ago still bothered Dom. 'We need to check the city, see who's still here.'

Vanessa nodded. 'The Copy guard should be able to get us into locked places.'

Keeping him around only reminded Dom of the bad things that had happened here. But Dom was the leader now. And leaders didn't have feelings—only the last word.

'Agreed.' His eyes went to the new child. She was looking up at the group through the glass with wide, blue eyes. 'What about her?'

Vanessa glanced back at the toddler. 'The infant is still too young. A year at most. We'll need a couple more hours to mature her.'

'How old will she get?'

Vanessa nodded at the half-spent vials of liquid. 'Old enough not to slow us down.'

Dom gave a discreet shudder. How must June be feeling to see her child grow before her eyes? He would ask Sheila and Imogen to keep an eye on her.

To the room, he said, 'Everyone who doesn't need to be here, move out. We're going to search this city for Copies. I want to make sure there are no threats waiting for us. We should start with this facility.'

Alex remained on his knees next to the growth accelerator machine. His hands were pressed against the glass. A smiling June gazed down at him.

Dom tapped her on the shoulder and she looked up at him. 'Hey, how are you feeling?'

She nodded and touched her belly. 'A little sore, but mending. The tech in this place is unbelievable. I can't believe how fast I healed after she came out.'

Yeah, it was something else, all right. The same tech had torn him apart. He hid his discomfort behind a smile.

'We have injured soldiers. Maybe you can use

90

the machine to heal them,' she said.

The thought had crossed his mind, but they didn't have the time. 'Rest is all we can offer them right now. We need to know how to command the technology. I won't put them in that room without controls in place.'

'You did with me.'

'That was an emergency. We had to.'

June nodded. 'You need me to help with the search?'

'No. You and Alex should stay here, look after the child.'

'I'll stay with her,' said Vanessa.

'I'll leave a few soldiers with you. Hopefully the search won't take long.'

He ushered everyone else out of the room and back to the main area beyond the shimmering wall.

Waving at the entrance, he asked his ex-guard, 'How long will it stay open?'

He shrugged as if he didn't want to answer. 'As long as it likes.'

Dom glanced at the Copy's wrist. 'Does your chip open it?'

'You know it does.'

'Well, how about I cut off your hand and give it to my men?'

The Copy's eyes widened a little. 'They c-can open it from the inside.'

'Good. You three stay here,' he said to the rebel soldiers. He pushed the prisoner toward the stairs.

'You're coming with us.'

Jacob announced that he and Carissa would head to the workshop. 'We should get her files so we have something to compare the data to.'

Dom nodded and three soldiers plus Thomas went with them. Thomas took the bag containing the maps with him.

That left Sheila, Imogen, Charlie, Anya, Jerome and the remaining half dozen soldiers to search the medical facility. The rest—Kaylie's team—were collecting their dead. He'd told her team they would help after they'd done a sweep of the city, but Kaylie's team didn't want to wait. Right now, the wolves were protecting them. Soon, the remainder of Kaylie's team would take half the trucks and bury their fallen close to home. He didn't know if they would return; they didn't answer to him.

For now, checking for Copies had to be everyone else's priority. They did a sweep of the floors together, starting in the lobby. At least his captive guard was useful for opening the doors that weren't accessible to just anyone.

Dom swept his Disruptor inside each room, including the guards' station. There was hardly any technology on that floor, and no way to check if the force field around the city was still down.

They moved to the first floor—the scene of his torture. Without June's emergency to distract him, his feelings about this place hit him properly. He breathed through his nose to calm down. Anya walked on ahead with Jerome. They checked corridors and any rooms that could only be accessed with the Copy guard's chip, while the others did their own sweep.

Charlie stayed with him.

'You okay, son?' he asked.

'Yeah, why?'

He concentrated on the next corner he couldn't see around, gun at the ready.

'You seem on edge, even though this place looks very much abandoned to me. Why are we wasting time searching it?'

'I'd rather be overcautious than not. Max taught me that.' Charlie visibly flinched when he mentioned Max's name. 'Sorry.'

'It's okay. Max was a good leader. He'd be proud of you. We all are.'

Everything on this floor came back clear. The team moved to the second floor, where Anya had been. It was her turn to tense up.

They worked methodically, ignoring any rooms the Copy's chip couldn't open. Anya said the rooms couldn't be opened from the inside anyway.

Sheila led the way to more rooms.

'Down here,' she said, stopping outside one. 'This was my room.'

She opened the door after the soldier unlocked it. A boy of around nineteen was sitting on the edge of the bed. He looked up, shocked to see Sheila.

His face sported a yellowing bruise. Sheila

pointed at it. 'I gave him that, when he got fresh with me.' She lunged at the boy and grabbed his arm. 'Looks like you're coming with us after all.'

The boy protested, but Sheila was too strong for him.

Their checks rounded up more boys than girls. More Breeders he assumed. Like Alex.

Twelve victims. No Copies.

They returned to the third floor an hour later to find Vanessa waiting for them outside the special entrance. 'The child is almost ready.'

He remembered the strange children he and Anya had seen while in Arcis. They hadn't cried or interacted. They'd just sat there and colored, or played alone.

'When we're ready to move her, we'll meet up with Jacob at the workshop,' he said.

Vanessa pointed to a door that was in the same area. 'Through here leads to the viewing corridor. Beyond it is a tunnel that will take us to the workshop.' Dom vaguely remembered this space from the time of their escape.

She looked at the new additions from the second floor. 'Is this everyone you found?'

Dom nodded. 'But I expected to find at least one Copy in this place.'

11

Carissa

Walking along the empty streets filled Carissa with fear. She darted her gaze around, watching for any signs of movement. She'd never seen the city so quiet before—not even at night.

Noise comforted her. Silence made her nervous.

The Inventor was walking too slowly—again. But he'd insisted all three of them travel above ground so he could check on the wolves. Carissa saw the pair in the distance near the trucks. Both of them were sitting down. She took their passive state to be a good thing. But still, the walk unnerved her. Thomas walked as slow as the Inventor. She tried to hurry the pair up by running on ahead. But each time she ended up backtracking.

'I won't get there any faster, miss. I don't move as fast as I used to.'

The Inventor had never moved fast. But a knot

of worry injected nervous energy into her step.

Her mind flitted between racing ahead or staying with the Inventor and risking them being ambushed. Thomas carried the Atomizer and an Electro Gun. Three soldiers shadowed them. Their presence put her mind at ease a little.

As they neared heart of the city a shiver caught her by surprise. The bright, white exterior of the Learning Center looked idle. That place had been her sanctuary once.

No more.

She kept her back to the building. If she couldn't see it, in her mind it didn't exist.

Carissa eyed the long structure opposite it instead. Broken bricks from its outer wall littered the courtyard in between. They'd seen the damage during the orb's brief journey home. A digger had ripped through the retractable roof. The steel girders and part of the wall lay in pieces, but the door leading to the stairwell was still intact.

She rushed to the door and opened it a crack.

One of the soldiers barked at her, 'Wait for me!'

Carissa froze her hand on the handle. The soldier pushed her back and nudged the door open with his gun.

'Clear,' he said.

She trotted down the stairs, her anxiety lessening as she returned to the one place the Copies didn't like to venture.

The workshop looked the same as she remembered it: a counter against one wall with a sink. Spare bellies, legs and tails that used to hang from rafters close to the retractable roof now lay on the floor. A ragged hole in the roof opened out to the sky. The two diggers that were being repaired were missing. This was where she and the Inventor used to hang out. The Inventor had built Rover here.

The old man entered the space, hands on hips. 'Except for the mess, it looks okay.' He stepped over broken rafters and spare parts and headed to the counter, where the diagnostic machine had been left. 'All the equipment is still here. Looks like they only wanted the diggers.'

'That's good, right?' Carissa asked.

Change wasn't always a positive thing, as she had learned.

He grunted his answer and flicked a switch on the side of the machine. It hummed into life. The Inventor released a breath.

Sweeping debris off a chair, he pulled it out into a clear space and patted it. 'Here, please, miss.'

Carissa walked over to it and sat down. She was familiar with this routine having been through it several times before. A smiling Thomas joined them, clearly fascinated by the workshop set up. The soldiers waited by the entrance. Rover's nose and that of his mate was visible through the sky opening.

She concentrated on the machine with the small, black screen that would reveal the data in her memory banks. 'I may not have the maps anymore.'

She'd downloaded what she could while out on the battlefield and connected to Quintus. But she had no way to check if the downloads had been successful.

'The machine will verify that, but I'm confident you have them.' He turned the machine around so he could see the screen better. He lowered a metal arm with two wings over her head. 'All documents are stored in your biogel, like an imprint.'

'But what if the Collective has changed things?'

'Then you might not have the latest version, that's all. But we have our own maps.'

Thomas stepped forward and opened the bag Vanessa had brought to the city. He pulled out the rolls of maps and placed them on the counter.

The Inventor positioned the wings over her head. He connected the flexible ends with magnetic tips to Carissa's two discs.

She felt a buzz inside her head, followed by a ticking sound. The connection tickled her skin; she scratched it.

The Inventor eased her hand away. 'Careful, miss. I don't want you to get a shock.'

She placed her hands on her lap and concentrated on the screen while she felt the connection search through her memory banks.

The Inventor frowned at the screen showing her brain's information. Over one shoulder, Thomas lingered. She saw a list of folders populate the screen, listing all her knowledge. But it didn't include everything. Some things she'd learned on her own, without Quintus' guidance or the Collective's. Things that would only show up if she was in the Great Hall and Quintus was dragging them out of her.

The Inventor perched one fist on his hip and leaned closer to the screen.

He pointed to a folder. 'That one, miss.'

She recognized the folder that contained the maps of the city, but it was grayed out. Carissa tried her old code by thinking it, but nothing happened.

'I can't get into it. My permissions aren't working,' she huffed.

This was a mistake. The rebels should never have trusted her to do this.

Thomas looked over Jacob's shoulder. 'We can try a dictionary attack.'

'A what?'

'We try permutations of numbers in the hopes we hit upon one that works.' Thomas looked at her. 'What code were you trying to use?'

She rattled it off. It wasn't anything special. Just her Copy number—173-C—and a few other identifiers.

'Wait, no.' Thomas stroked his chin, looking worried. 'If the Collective has blocked her from the system, anything she tries with her Copy code could time out. I'm not sure a dictionary attack will work on the active folder.'

'So what do we do?' said the Inventor.

'We should try to access the backup of the folder. Her permissions might not have been altered there.'

Carissa watched Thomas enter a few commands on screen. On occasion, he asked Carissa to open certain files. Some required no pass code—like the files that recorded the times of the Copies' daily downloads. Other things, like the frequency code for the force field around the city, were locked. Why, when the barrier was currently inactive?

Thomas typed in a few new commands. Bright-green text appeared on screen.

'All computer systems are the same,' he explained while typing. 'If I can find the backup storage, we might be able to grab the last saved copy.'

Jacob frowned over his shoulder. Carissa zoned out while he worked.

Her eyes grazed the room that she'd spent so many hours in, watching the Inventor work. Having seen him in the rebel camp enjoying the freedom he claimed to have lost, she couldn't picture him working here again. She now saw this place for the prison it was.

'I have it!' Thomas said. She snapped her attention back to him. 'Call out your command to me again.'

Carissa did and he typed it in.

'It's not locked,' he said sounding relieved.

A new document opened on screen. It was a black map with a white outline showing the schematics of the city. She leaned in closer, breaking her connection to the machine. She gasped and checked the screen. But the image remained. It was a general outline of the city above ground that showed its concentric design.

'You need to go deeper than the surface,' said Carissa, standing up. 'You need the maps with the tunnels.'

Thomas opened a second one. It showed the medical facility layout and the library.

Carissa studied the library. This version included the secret room that Canya—Anya's Copy—had been staying in. The one the Copies hadn't known about until Carissa told them about it. That meant the Collective had updated the map recently.

She examined the medical facility. The secret tunnel between the workshop and the Nurturing Center had also been added.

'These are recent,' she said.

The Inventor nodded. 'That's something, at least. We can use them to find areas that haven't been cataloged by the Collective.'

Thomas produced a piece of paper and a pencil from the bag. He superimposed the paper over the screen and began sketching.

She watched him work. 'What are you doing?'

'Drawing the layout. We can't take the machine with us.'

The Inventor hurried over to the counter. He opened a drawer and removed several new pieces of paper. One with an image on it floated to the floor. Carissa bent down to pick it up.

She stared at an image of herself. The drawing was done in pencil and was a good likeness.

'What's this?'

The Inventor glanced at the page, then at her. 'I used the spare time to draw.'

'Me?'

'Things—people I care about.'

She held the picture to her chest and checked inside the open drawer for more. There was another picture—of Rover. She plucked it out and held it up.

'You like him,' she said matter-of-factly.

The Inventor nodded. 'He saved us.'

'He's not like the other wolves.'

'No, he's not. He's like you. All the images I drew are of those who did not fit this place.'

She crumpled the page with her image to her chest. 'Can I keep it?'

The Inventor smiled. 'Of course. I meant to give it to you. It's not perfect, but I thought you might like it.'

Carissa studied the drawing. The lines were sharp and overlapped in places. Her nose was disproportionate to her eyes, which were set a little far apart. Her smile was a little misshapen. The children could draw better.

It was perfect.

'I've got the medical facility layout and the library,' said Thomas. 'What's next?'

Carissa forgot about her drawing for a second. 'The Learning Center. Accommodation for the Copies. Check for all the buildings the Copies have—had—access to.'

She returned to her seat and set the picture down on her lap. Thomas had found a map of the Learning Center.

The Great Hall took up most of the ground floor. There appeared to be a room next to the screens that the Collective often appeared on. She didn't remember seeing it any time she'd been there.

Thomas sketched the layout and opened the accommodation that she'd lived in after she'd been connected. Copies and humans had lived separately. Newborns in human care were the exception. He then moved on to the school where Carissa had attended lessons.

When he finished, the Inventor switched off the machine.

She gripped the drawing. 'Is that it?'

Thomas nodded. 'That was all that were available in the folder. It should give us something to go on.'

'I agree,' said the Inventor.

She looked at him. 'What now?'

'We should return to the others, miss.'

Jacob and Thomas rolled the machine back to the counter. Before Carissa left, she snatched up the wonky vision of Rover that Jacob had sketched to take along with her own picture.

12

Anya

Anya looked up to see Jacob, Thomas and Carissa walking past the viewing window. They had used the escape tunnel to return to the Nurturing Center.

Anya rushed out to meet them, keen to escape the tight space that included a strange child and a cooing June, Vanessa and Alex. Seeing how June's baby had transformed from a newborn to a three-year-old in a matter of hours unnerved her. Everything reminded her too much of her time in Arcis.

Dom and Charlie went with her. Just beyond the hidden entrance, Dom's former guard leaned lazily against the wall, surrounded by rebel soldiers. He perked up the second Anya appeared. She rushed past him just as the door to the viewing corridor opened. Jacob stepped through, followed by Thomas and Carissa. Thomas had the backpack containing the maps, plus a few extra sheets of paper in his hand.

104

Carissa was clutching two folded-up pieces of paper. When Anya eyed them, the girl's eyes widened and she shoved both into the waistband of her trousers.

On a different day Anya might have asked her about it, but her interest lay in what Thomas held. Two things delayed them finding the Beyond: the child in the next room and discovering the coordinates.

At least she had some control over one of those things.

'What did you find?' asked Dom.

Jacob's eyes flicked to the Copy prisoner. He was standing up straighter and appeared to be interested in their progress.

'You want to have this discussion here?' the old man asked.

Dom glanced back at his guard. 'I'm not sure I care anymore. They know we're here.'

The eight Breeders and four girls they'd rescued from the rooms were sitting in the second area visible from the viewing corridor. They had appeared nervous on the walk back. Four soldiers were keeping an eye on them.

Jacob shrugged lightly, then nodded at Thomas.

Thomas pulled one piece of paper out of the bunch he held and slapped it up against the wall. It was a rough sketch.

Of where?

'The library,' Thomas said as if answering her silent question. 'We only have the layout details the

Copies know about. It appears from Carissa's downloads that they added the extra tunnel we just used plus a hidden room beneath the library.'

Vanessa stood at the entrance to the hidden corridor. How long she'd been there, Anya didn't know.

Vanessa moved over to Thomas, frowning at the page. 'The room below ground was off grid for a while. But they definitely knew about it before we escaped the city.'

'Could there be any additional rooms hidden in the library?' asked Dom.

Vanessa shook her head. 'If there were, I would have found them. I spent hours in that place daily.'

'And we're certain this Janet person didn't hide the diary in plain sight?' asked Charlie.

Anya didn't think so. To do so would risk discovery. A diary would need to be hidden well. If the Collective had been aware of its existence, she was sure it would have mentioned it during its interrogation practices on the seventh floor in Arcis.

Anya looked at Thomas. 'What else did you get?'

He set two new pages next to each other on the wall. He nodded at the left page. 'The medical facility, which includes the tunnel we just used. Beneath that, Jacob's workshop and'—he nodded to the page on the right—'the Learning Center. I have more, but only one set of hands.'

He jerked his head toward the papers nestled in

the crook of his arm.

Anya took the other sheets from him. She pinned the Copy accommodation block and the school to the wall.

'We should rule out any areas the humans didn't have access to,' she said.

'Carissa?' asked Vanessa. 'What places were off limits?'

The girl didn't think about it for long. 'The Learning Center, the Copy accommodation, the school.'

'So we check the areas where the humans had freedom?' said Anya.

Vanessa blew out a breath. 'That's still a lot of area to cover.'

'Then, we split up.' The sooner they started, the sooner they would find Janet's diary. 'Some of us should search the regular accommodation, some the library. Anywhere else?'

Her knowledge of this city was limited.

'What about the Business District?' asked Carissa, her eyes rounded. 'We didn't venture there often.'

Jacob looked at Dom. 'It's a possibility.'

'And we could check the storage room there for food,' added Charlie.

Dom nodded. To Thomas, he said, 'Do you have schematics of the Business District?'

Thomas rifled through the last few pages and shook his head. 'It wasn't available as a download.'

Vanessa said, 'The Business District has a limited number of shops and everything is above ground. It wouldn't take much to check if any of the shops has secret tunnels.'

Dom nodded, his gaze flicking to his Copy guard. 'We check it out. And he comes with us in case we can't get in anywhere.'

Ω

Anya stood outside the medical facility with Dom, Vanessa, Jacob, Charlie and Carissa. Sheila, Jerome and Imogen joined them. Last out were a dozen armed soldiers who were escorting the Copy prisoner. The remaining rebel soldiers stayed behind to protect June, her baby and the teenage rescues.

Anya shivered at having Dom's former guard near. If he wasn't glaring at Dom, he was smirking at him. He gave her the creeps, but she could only imagine what Dom must be feeling, what emotions his presence evoked. If Dom was bothered by it, he wasn't showing it. His shoulders were back, his face void of emotion. His eyes were actively scanning the area—the way he used to do in Arcis.

'I think we should stick together and search one area thoroughly before moving on,' said Charlie.

'Agreed,' Dom said. 'I don't want to dilute our firepower.'

They were in Zone C: the midway point between Zone A and the Learning Center, and Zone E and the Business District. Anya had only seen the city layout once from the higher vantage point of the train tracks, where the hovering train currently lay idle.

She gripped her gun tighter, not liking how quiet this place was. Would she have felt better if the place was swarming with Copies? *Maybe.*

They set off on foot and entered Zone D. Vanessa waved them past a large accommodation block that was three stories high. 'This is where we used to live, but the apartments were studio in design and basic. I can't think of anywhere safe Janet might have hidden the diary. I think we should try the Business District first. We had more freedoms there.'

Anya walked behind Vanessa, who took the lead with Charlie. Dom followed close behind the pair. They were basing their search on a discussion Anya had overheard her parents having. She worried her intel might be wrong, that they were wasting their time searching this city for a set of coordinates that might not even be here or, worse, might be worthless.

Sheila walked beside her. Similar to Dom, her gaze combed every inch of this place. Like Anya, Sheila hadn't seen much of the city either.

'It's bigger than I thought,' she said. Her gaze settled on the accommodation block.

'I don't like being here,' said Anya.

'Why? Because it's empty?'

'Yeah. But also because this place feels wrong.'

Sheila snorted. 'That's because it was—is—a city for Copies. We were just the entertainment. Like in Arcis.'

Anya swept her gun around, checking for spotters or orbs that might be following them. There was no sign of Jacob's reprogrammed orb. She wondered if it had abandoned their group.

'Except Arcis wasn't pretending to be something else,' said Anya. 'It was a training facility. It never sold itself as anything more than that.'

Sheila glanced at her. 'And what do you think this place is supposed to be?'

She shrugged and looked around. 'I don't like how it mimics a human city. I mean, the Copies, they're not real, but they live as though they are.'

Jerome glanced back at her. She bit her lip at her insensitivity. 'Sorry, I didn't mean you, Jerome.'

The dark-skinned, young man dropped back to walk beside her. 'You did, and it's okay.'

'No, it's not. I meant the Copies without humanity. Those who follow the Collective's orders aren't real.'

Carissa glanced back at her next, and she shut her mouth.

Jerome said, 'I'm still not used to the idea that I came from here. And what about your Breeder? Wasn't he born here?'

Yeah, Alex had been created in this city.

She blushed. 'Forget I said anything. I don't know what I'm talking about.'

Jerome chuckled. 'Believe it or not, I get it. The Copies in Arcis, they freaked me out when I saw them on the ninth floor, frozen. I had no idea I was a newborn—one step removed from them.'

Anya nudged him with her elbow. 'You're more than that, Jerome. You were created here, but you lived among humans. That makes you more human than the Copies.'

Ahead, Carissa's shoulders stiffened. She elbowed Jacob and whispered something to him.

Jacob looked back. 'Carissa wants to know if she is included in your real-not-real summation.'

Detecting anger in the old man's voice, Anya blushed harder. 'No, I mean, I'm not sure. Carissa has helped us. That makes her different, that's all.'

Sheila snorted with laughter.

Anya ignored her. She blew out a relieved breath when Carissa's tense shoulders softened slightly. Maybe she should think before she opened her mouth. None of them were perfect. They'd all had strange starts in life.

Dom glanced back and grinned at her. Yeah, she knew she was being an idiot. She just wanted to get out of here. Find the Beyond... and then what? She had no idea what awaited them. But it had to be better than this.

They passed by a white pillar taller than them. A tag station. Carissa glanced at it, then at her wrist.

'Do you think the coordinates are really here?' Jerome asked.

'It's the last place to look, according to my parents.' She sighed. 'But honestly, I don't know.'

Sheila said to Jerome, 'What happened when the Copies brought you back here? What happened to Julius?'

Jerome watched the ground as he walked. 'No idea. They separated us for a few hours and interrogated us. Just one Copy asking questions. Nothing major. They brought us back together briefly before they dumped us in separate rooms, no food or water.' He looked at Anya. 'Then you showed up.'

'Did they hurt you?'

Jerome shook his head. 'Nah, just questions, like I said. But everything was rushed, like the fight in the flatlands beyond the camp rattled them. The barrier was down when we arrived here. They must have fled the city soon after, expecting retaliation from the rebels.'

'I'm sorry we didn't come sooner.'

Jerome smiled. 'I'm just glad you came at all.'

Sheila patted him on the arm. 'We don't leave our team behind.'

They approached a courtyard before the start of the Business District that Anya remembered from their attempt to escape. A standoff had happened between them and the Copy guards. Now, the area was empty. That bothered Anya more than seeing a line of armed Copies ready to return them to their rooms. She kept looking up, expecting to see a line of spotters. Her neck hurt from twisting it so much.

Their group entered the plaza area with half a dozen shops on either side. Everything was closed up.

She wondered what had happened to the people.

'We should search the city after for survivors,' she said.

Dom turned to her. 'Good idea. Although, it's likely they escaped when the barrier came down.'

The first shop they came across was a clothing store. A garish, yellow dress hung in the window. She noticed Dom startle at the sight of it.

'What's wrong?' Anya asked.

Dom blinked. 'Nothing. It's just, I've seen it before.'

'Where?'

His lips pinched and she didn't need him to elaborate. Anya's Copy had worn a similar outfit when she'd tried to seduce him. She hadn't seen the attempts or the dress, but the newborn Canya had kindly replayed most of the details for her.

'Oh,' was all she said.

Dom pushed against the door. It was unlocked. A bell overhead rattled.

He turned back to the others. 'Split into groups of three and check the shops in this row. Carissa, show Charlie where the food storage unit is. Use the prisoner to access any locked spaces. We'll meet in ten and sweep another area.'

Dom, Vanessa and Anya entered the small shop.

Vanessa looked around the space. 'Your newborn came here to buy her dress.'

'So I heard.'

'She wanted to emulate you, but also become someone else. It was an odd experience to watch her go through puberty in the space of a week.'

Anya lowered her gun with a shiver. 'Maybe we should check this place and get out.'

Knowing her newborn had been here made her want to leave.

Vanessa started her checks behind the counter, pulling out boxes and emptying them on the floor. There weren't many to search, just three. From what Anya saw, they only contained a few pieces of paper.

'They were well organized,' said Anya.

'Not so much organized as there wasn't much paperwork. The goods came from looted towns and were dropped off at the shops. The patrons paid with credits on their tags. Paperwork existed to give humans a sense of normality.'

'Did you ever shop here?' Anya asked.

Vanessa nodded. 'The towns had some good stuff.'

She finished up her search behind the counter. Anya walked over to the rails of clothing set against one wall and pulled them out. She knocked on the panels, listening out for the sound of hollow walls. Nothing. Dom slipped into an area at the back of the shop. She followed him into what looked like a changing room. It had a full-length mirror. She stood in front of it and winced at the sight before her.

The hair that Charlie had lovingly cut into feathered layers a few days ago was pulled back off

114

her face. Strands hung messily around her face, which was streaked with dirt. She scrubbed at the skin using her knuckle.

'Do you think Canya tried on her dress in here?'

Dom surprised her with a kiss on her cheek. 'I don't care. She could have worn the sexiest, red dress ever designed and I wouldn't have noticed her.'

With a sigh, Anya gave up on cleaning her face. She was only spreading the dirt around. 'I could do with a shower and a clean pair of clothes right now.'

She glanced at her combats and black T-shirt. She looked like the soldier she had always been and less like the frightened girl who'd turned up at camp.

Dom grinned at her in the mirror. 'I love you in this look. It's so... badass.'

Anya's lips quirked from the compliment. 'Yeah, I suppose I am.'

But her smile faded when she remembered why they were there.

'When we get out of here,' said Dom, 'I'm taking you on a real date.'

Her heart pounded faster. 'With flowers and chocolates?'

'Yeah, and a big glass of wine.'

'I've never tasted wine before.'

She had, once, with Alex. During their forced seduction of each other. But that time didn't count as special.

Dom smiled. 'Neither have I.'

He knocked on the panels in the changing room.

The walls sounded solid enough.

Vanessa poked her head in. 'Anything?'

Dom shook his head. They returned to the plaza where the other groups of three had gathered.

'Anything?' he asked.

Charlie said, 'The food storage unit is empty.'

Others reported back that their search had turned up no false walls or nooks.

'Okay, we continue our search of the other shops.'

'And if we don't find anything?' asked Charlie.

'Then we search this entire city from top to bottom.'

13

Dom

Dom checked the last shop in the plaza with Anya. They found no hidden doors, no loose floorboards and no secret rooms in any of them.

They lingered in the shop filled with knick knacks—soaps, hairbrushes and mirrors—from their towns.

'There's nothing here,' he said sighing.

'We haven't checked the rest of the city.'

He laughed. 'The rest of the city is huge.'

This was becoming an impossible task. Maybe Charlie and Vanessa's idea to return to the camp was a good one. It made his skin crawl to be here.

'If we all split up, we can get it done faster,' Anya said.

That's what worried him—splitting up. He'd led Max's old team into this city without giving much thought to what they'd do when they got there. So far they'd wandered around, armed with a few maps Thomas had sketched from Carissa's memory banks.

He dragged a hand down his face. 'I'm a failure.'

Anya grabbed his arm. The move startled him and he stared at her.

'No, you're not. Never say that.'

She let go, her gaze darting away to places they'd both checked.

Despite her confidence in him, Dom couldn't let the feeling go. 'Max wouldn't have charged in here without a plan. Vanessa and Charlie told me we should take a small group for June, and wait until the injured were strong enough to travel.'

'If you'd done that, we wouldn't have survived the ambush by the replicated Copies. And June might have died. Plus, Copies might have blocked off the camp, leaving us with dwindling supplies of food.'

There was no evidence of food here either, but they'd had no choice but to return to Praesidium. Finding the Beyond was just not as easy as he'd hoped it would be.

Anya was staring at him, as though willing him to believe in himself. He wished he had her confidence.

'It was a stupid plan, Anya. June is safe. Maybe we should head back to the camp.'

'No, it wasn't. We have to find the Beyond. There *is* no other plan.'

He worried Jason's death was making her

reckless. 'We could go back to the camp and use the comms to round up more rebels in different towns.'

'And how long is that going to take?' She shook her head. 'We're here now. We keep looking.'

Dom released a hard breath. 'Okay, where to next?'

She frowned at the ground. 'We work logically until we arrive at the center of this city.'

The Learning Center. Where the Collective supposedly lived. What were the chances the coordinates would be found there? If they were there, how had the Collective not found them?

Anya walked out of the shop toward the waiting team. Dom followed her out, gauging everyone's mood. After two hours, they were all flagging. That didn't surprise him.

He nodded to Charlie, who shook his head. 'The shops are all clear.'

'Clear on our end,' said Vanessa. 'It's possible we're chasing our tails here. Maybe we should leave the city and regroup.'

He didn't want to give up yet. 'If Anya says the coordinates are here, then we keep looking.'

Vanessa stepped forward, her expression stern. She pulled Dom aside. 'I think we should discuss this in the library.'

'Why?'

'To work out our next move.'

'Our next move is we keep looking.'

Vanessa eyed him. 'Dom, we can't just hit

every place. Let's stop in the library for a minute. Charlie needs to catch his breath.'

His gaze went to the oldest member of his team. Charlie was standing tall but he could see from his face that two hours on his feet was taking its toll. He couldn't believe he'd been so insensitive. He looked at Jacob next, who also looked fit to drop.

He blinked. 'Sure, I don't know what I was thinking.'

'That you wanted this to work. Come on.' She urged him forward with a gentle push. 'Let's take a break and talk about this.'

They returned to Zone C and the library. Dom approached the building made of glass and honey-colored wood. It was a contrast to the other mostly white-and-gray structures the "white city" had become famous for. This one almost looked like a human had designed it.

Vanessa stepped up to the door. It was locked.

She turned to the soldiers. 'Bring the Copy here.'

The soldiers shuffled his former Copy guard to the door and pressed his wrist to the control panel next to it. The door clicked open and Vanessa entered the premises. None of the rebels had their chips anymore. While Dom was happy about that, it put too much reliance on this figure from his painful and torturous past.

Charlie entered next and Dom followed him inside the library. Vanessa walked over to a table farther back from the dusty collection of books on tall shelves, set against the glass walls. She sat down. Charlie did the same with a puff. Dom joined them at the table while Anya and the others wandered around the space. The soldiers regarded the impressive array of books with wide eyes and smiles. Some ran their fingers over the spines. Dom assumed they must have come from the cleared-out towns. One picked up a book and began to read.

Jacob walked around with Carissa, who was pointing out books and telling him, 'I read that one.'

He wished he could join them. But as leader, he straightened up in his chair instead of relaxing.

Vanessa had her hands clasped on the table, a serious look on her face. Charlie was looking down at the table. He'd sensed something was off with them for the last hour.

'What?'

Vanessa narrowed her eyes a little. 'Charlie and I were talking.'

'About what?'

'About the likelihood of finding the coordinates to the Beyond in this city.'

He didn't understand. They'd all agreed to this plan. 'You want to give up?'

'No, we're not saying that,' said Charlie. 'But it's too dangerous to stay here. We don't know if the Copies will return. The fact that this place is cleared out worries me.'

Sheila joined them and sat down.

Dom had no plan B. But he had a feeling the pair might. 'What's your plan if not to search here?'

'Return to the camp, radio for help, bring the scattered rebels together.' Vanessa lifted her hands and dropped them. 'We've got fifteen soldiers, give or take. We lost half of Kaylie's team and the other half is burying them someplace away from the city. We don't know if they'll return. The numbers we have aren't enough. It will take us too long to search everywhere.'

Dom leaned forward. 'That's why we're concentrating on the places where the humans had access, not the Copies. If Janet left the diary anywhere, it has to be in one of those locations. Some place easy for others to find it.'

Charlie placed a hand on his arm. 'Then what, son? We all leave for this "Beyond" place? We don't even know what it is, or if it's another place of control.'

Dom didn't believe what he was hearing. He sat back. 'You really think returning to the camp is going to fix things? We'll end up trapping ourselves there.'

Sheila piped up. 'It's better than getting trapped here, Dom. June is better. Her child will be old enough to walk soon. I agree with Charlie and Vanessa. This place isn't safe. We should leave.'

Dom ran a hand through his hair. He searched the room for Anya. She was standing close by, a book in her hand. Her eyes were on their discussion. On him.

He looked away from her, needing to find the strength to do this alone. 'Max wanted this. Max wanted to find the Beyond.'

Charlie shook his head. 'He wanted freedom and he got killed for his dream. We don't even know if the place exists. Vanessa and I are not prepared to lead the youngsters into a battle, or some unknown place where anything could happen.'

'But you think I am?' That's what this was about—his ability to lead. Or lack of. 'You don't trust me to do this.'

Sheila leaned forward, her voice a whisper. 'We're not saying that, Dom, but this situation needs experience.'

Not her too?

Vanessa added, 'Both Charlie and I have more of it than you. Pass the responsibility to us. Let us keep everyone safe.'

Dom stared at Sheila. He'd expected her to at least have his back. She was staring at the table.

What he wouldn't give for this to be over.

He shook his head. 'I have as much rebel experience as you, more, even. I spent time here.'

Vanessa leaned back. 'So did I. In this very library.'

He scoffed. 'Our experiences were not the same.'

'Perhaps not, but the problem persists that this city is not safe.'

That bothered him, too, to be inside a city with

no conflict. The thought drove him to his feet.

'Where are you going?' asked Sheila.

He ignored her and walked over to his ex-guard, lounging against one of the stacks while his warders perused the shelves next to him. The Copy straightened up when Dom approached him.

'What's the deal with this city?'

'Excuse me?'

'You heard. Where are all the other Copies?'

The prisoner shrugged and smiled. 'Left as soon as the barrier failed.'

'So, why were *you* left behind?'

He shrugged again. 'They trusted me to stop you.'

A fight with six dozen Copies, not one, would have been more successful for them. The fight had been too easy.

'Are they coming back? The Copies?' asked Dom.

'I don't think so.'

'And the Collective? Is it still here?'

He would have asked Carissa, but she was no longer connected to the city.

'It left.'

Dom was getting tired of the one-dimensional answers. 'Where did it go? How did it leave?'

The prisoner shrugged. 'One of the Copies downloaded their ten consciousnesses into a machine. They took that machine with them.'

'What is the Beyond?'

The Copy averted his gaze.

Dom grabbed the front of his uniform. 'What is it?'

The guard looked back at him. Dom wasn't sure how to read all emotions in these things, but he thought he saw jealousy.

'I don't know. It's a place the Collective is curious about. It's a place I've never been.'

He pushed Dom off him. The soldiers restrained the prisoner.

Dom turned and walked away. It didn't matter where. Without more detail, he was flying blind. Maybe Vanessa and Charlie were right. Maybe they should return to the camp and wait for more help.

He stopped and his gaze found Anya. She was clutching the book tightly. Her eyes were wider than usual. From where he stood, her grief was palpable.

Vanessa came up to him and touched his arm. 'Let's leave this city, Dom. We can hit this place again soon, but for now we should plan from the camp.'

The Copy guard flashed him a look. *Surprise? Worry? Relief?*

He shucked her off. 'With respect to you and Charlie, I'm in charge. That's how you wanted it, that's how it will be.'

Charlie shrugged as if he'd run out of ways to convince him. 'Okay, what's your decision?'

He glanced at Anya, who looked too stiff to be comfortable. 'We keep looking.' He saw her shoulders relax. 'The city is on the back foot. I intend to take advantage of that.'

14

Anya

Finding the Beyond would give her answers. That's what Anya believed. Right now, Jason and her parents' deaths had been for nothing. Senseless. The answer to why they had to die rested there.

She sighed with relief when Dom went against Vanessa and Charlie's advice. But when she caught Dom's former guard looking at her, eyes narrowed, she straightened up and gripped her weapon tighter.

'What are you looking at?' she asked him.

The Copy smirked at her. One of the soldiers slapped him across the face. The Copy laughed. Hard.

Anya strode up to him and pressed the barrel of her Electro Gun into his chest. She felt him flinch. 'What's your problem?'

'Filthy, dirty Originals. That's all you are.'

It was Anya's turn to laugh. 'And yet, you were modeled after us. A little ironic, don't you think?'

The smile on the prisoner's face disappeared. 'I'm nothing like you.' He looked away. 'The others are, the cowards who abandoned this city.' He looked back and sneered. 'I chose to stay, because I care about my home and I don't want to see you take it over. You should know you're all wasting your time here.'

Anya shoved the gun into his gut.

Behind her, Dom said, 'Take it easy.'

'Wasting, why?'

The Copy lifted his chin. 'The Beyond doesn't exist. If it did, we would have found it by now. But you, pathetic Originals, you can't organize yourselves in an open-field fight.'

Anya poked the prisoner in the ribs with the tip of her gun. 'Say that again.'

He grunted. 'I heard what happened out there. We're all connected, you see. The Collective, it tells us everything.'

Anya doubted that. Carissa had been talking to Quintus. He'd contacted her before their escape from the city, while in the camp, during the battle.

'Not everything.'

Anya pulled her gun back and marched out the door. Outside, the light hurt her eyes, but it wasn't as strong as she remembered it being when she'd visited the library as a child. The lack of barrier around the city must have removed the light distortion. She looked back at the walls of books lining the library. When they found the Beyond, she would get a bookshelf of her own and fill it with as many books as she could. Maybe, when things settled down, they could return and clear this place out.

The others joined her outside. Dom stood beside her and rubbed her back. It soothed the edges of her temper as she eyed the accommodation block a short distance away they had yet to check.

'Are you okay?'

She didn't answer him, pointing. 'We should try the block next.'

'Look, he's an asshole. He likes to stir the shit. Don't listen to him.'

She looked up at him. 'Listen to who?'

She marched on ahead to the block, bristling with irritation. What if the Copy guard was right and the Beyond didn't exist? If the Collective was clever enough to create Copies, surely it would have found it already?

Anya arrived at the accommodation block first. The concrete structure was set out on three levels with no plants or life of any kind. The doors to each unit she could see faced out. The block carried on farther back, creating side corridors with possible doors there.

She hesitated, not familiar with this place and not sure where to begin.

Jacob arrived at her side. 'I'll take the lead from here.' He walked on. 'This place I know.'

They organized themselves into groups of five to search the rooms on each block, leaving the soldiers to watch the prisoner. Some of the apartments were unlocked, others locked. They used the Copy to open the locked rooms. Anya searched one room, a studio-type apartment with a bed in one corner, a living room space in the other and a kitchenette. A bathroom was separate to the living space. It wasn't much bigger than her and Alex's room in the medical facility.

She walked around the space, checking under the bed, behind it, beneath unmade duvets and under creased pillows. She checked the seams of the mattress for signs of tears. Then she walked the room slowly, listening out for loose floorboards. The kitchenette consisted of a small counter and a kettle. The cupboards were bare.

This room was depressing. Even her and Alex's room had had more character than this. Who had lived here—or, rather, been forced to live here?

She left the apartment and searched the unit next door. That one had a bed stripped of linen. It looked like it hadn't been lived in recently.

She exited that apartment—if she could call it that—and met Dom outside. 'Where are all the people who lived here?'

Dom shrugged. 'They may have fled to the towns. The barrier has been down for a while.'

She supposed that made sense. 'Anything?'

He shook his head. 'The rooms are empty. Any idea which room Janet may have used?'

'I don't. We'll have to search them all.'

The next hour blurred into gray linens and bare cupboards. The rooms all started to look the same, but the checks happened faster. Loose floorboards, ripped mattresses. Hollow panels.

She was exiting the last room in her block when Dom came out holding what looked like a book. He frowned at it, then his eyes flicked up to Anya's.

Her heart pounded in her ears. 'Where did you find that?'

'Beneath the floor in one of the rooms.'

He opened the book. Anya stood by his shoulder, clenching her fists. Dom flicked through it. It appeared to be less like a diary and more like a stock book with ledger entries.

'Is it hers?' she asked breathless.

'I don't know.'

Dom flicked through more pages, containing lists of numbers. 'Are these the coordinates?'

Anya leaned in closer. 'They could represent longitude and latitude.'

Dom flicked on. 'There's too many, and no clue as to which ones might be the correct coordinates...' He stopped on the last page, which had a hand-drawn map on it. 'This looks more recent.'

Anya narrowed her eyes. There were no discerning markers. It was just a quick sketch, as though the route had been penciled in a hurry. 'How can you tell?'

'See, the pencil lines are hastily drawn. Someone took their time with the numbers.' Dom looked around. 'You said you saw your parents gave this to Janet. Why is this book here and not outside the city, like before?'

Anya took a guess. 'Because when Janet was taken to the city she had the book on her?'

'Would the sketch have been in this before or after she arrived? Surely the Copies would have searched her belongings.'

It didn't make sense to Anya either. 'She must have sketched it while she was here.'

She studied it. A sweep of a horizontal line, then a vertical one, a short zig without the zag, then straight. It would be impossible to know where this was without more context.

Dom rubbed his chin. 'If she sketched it after she arrived, it was either from memory or a map of somewhere inside the city.' He became more alert. 'We should check Thomas' sketches of the buildings. One of them might match up to this.'

Anya's heart pounded too fast. 'You think the way to the Beyond is *in* the city?'

He shook the book in the air. 'I don't know, but something compelled her to sketch this *after* she arrived.'

A new thought occurred to Anya. 'What if Janet wanted to be taken to the city?'

His eyes widened. 'Because this was the last place the rebels had yet to search. Those who still looked only presumed they knew where it was. If she found it, she was letting the next rebel know.'

'We could have the coordinates, Dom. I'll tell the others.'

Dom stopped her with his hand. 'Don't tell Vanessa, Sheila or Charlie yet.'

'Why?'

'Even with this, they might still push for everyone to leave. I'm worried that if we do we might not get back in.' He let go and waved the book in front of him. 'This might be it, our ticket out of here.'

'What about the rest of Kaylie's team?' Kaylie's open eyes and pale face flashed in her memory. She touched Dom's arm. 'They're burying their dead. Should we wait for them to return?'

Dom shrugged. 'I don't know them well enough. They were following Kaylie's orders. Without her, they might be on their way back to their camp.' He tapped the cover. 'This was our reason for coming back here. It still is.'

'I'll get Thomas.'

For the first time, she had hope.

15

Carissa

Anya came rushing out of block C, looking for Thomas. The Inventor asked her why.

She whispered, 'We found something,' and showed him a book.

The Inventor smiled.

'It looks promising,' he said as he leafed through it.

His smile made Carissa's heart sink.

'We should compare the drawing with the sketches Thomas did.'

Carissa wished she had the same enthusiasm.

The Beyond was a place the humans wanted to find. What would happen to her when they did? Would the Inventor leave with his friends and abandon Carissa to this city that no longer felt like home?

'But what are these numbers?' he asked. 'They

look like ledger entries.'

Carissa pulled the book down so she could see it. She'd recognize that schedule anywhere. 'They're not ledger entries. That's a list of the Copies' movements.' She pointed at one set of numbers that repeated on each page. 'And here's where the system carried out a health check, from 1-1.15am.'

Anya stared at her. 'Which means the people could potentially go anywhere.'

'But they didn't. They always stayed in their accommodation.'

The Inventor, followed by Anya, rushed out of the accommodation block, calling out for Thomas. The brown-haired boy emerged from block D clutching the backpack with the maps in it. The others gathered around them while Dom stood at the back. Carissa muscled her way into the center.

'We need to see your drawings again,' the Inventor said.

Thomas opened the backpack and pulled out the folded pages. He unfolded several and placed them down on the ground. Carissa checked her waistband for the two sketches—one of her and one of Rover— that the Inventor had drawn. It might be the last thing she had of him soon.

The soldiers crowded around Thomas.

Dom barked at everyone, 'Stand back. Give him some room.'

Carissa wasn't skilled at reading the humans' expressions, but she'd come to recognize tension.

Dom's shoulders were lifted slightly toward his ears, his fists clenched by his side. His nostrils flared as he looked on. Success mattered to him. But being in this city clearly worried him. It worried Carissa too. Where had Quintus gone? Why had he stopped all communication with her?

Quintus knew how to get in touch. He'd said her neuromorphic chip was self-repairing, but he had not contacted her since the battle. She'd expected the usual twinge or pull from her chip to indicate she was on the network again. But so far her head remained quiet.

A breeze caught the edge of one piece of paper and whipped it up. Anya, Sheila, Imogen and Jerome lent the tips of their boots to keep the edges down. Without the barrier, the city was open to the elements. Carissa preferred the fresh air now. Before, the air had been stifling here. She hadn't realized how much until she'd left the city. It had been normal. Until it wasn't.

Anya knelt down next to Thomas and held the book out on an open page. The Inventor assessed the drawings from over Thomas' shoulder. Charlie and Vanessa looked at each other, as though they were shocked by the find.

Carissa's gaze went to the Inventor. Not once did he look at Carissa. Not once had he asked her what she thought about the Beyond.

'What about this map?' asked Anya, keeping the edge of the first page flat with one knee.

She handed the book to Thomas, who rotated the drawing in the book. He frowned at the pages, then set the book down over each one.

He looked up with a sigh. 'It's not any of these.'

Before him was a sketch of the places Carissa still had maps of in her head: the library, the Business District, the accommodation blocks they'd just searched. The medical facility had also been converted to pencil and paper. That one showed the tunnel connecting the Nurturing Center on the lowest level to the Inventor's workshop.

The Inventor turned and sought her out. Carissa was filled with new hope. Maybe he would ask her what she thought about the Beyond. Maybe he would tell her not to worry.

'Miss,' he said, resting his hands on his knees. He nodded at the drawings. 'I need you to look at the sketch in the book and see if it looks familiar.'

Carissa's hope plummeted. With a weak nod, she said, 'Okay.'

Thomas stood and showed the open page to her. The sketch was something a child might have done. Penciled in haste, it seemed. No care or attention given to the strokes.

She looked up at the Inventor. 'It's not very good.'

The old man waved his hand. 'Not important, miss. Please concentrate on the image. You've seen the maps for other areas in this city. One of them might compare to the drawing.'

She ignored her hurt and concentrated on the sketch. Maybe she wouldn't find the place it matched. Maybe she could pretend, long enough for them to give up and return to the camp. June was okay. Her baby would soon be old enough to know what was going on.

But an image flashed in her mind as she studied the poorly drawn sketch. She gasped.

The Inventor grabbed her arm. 'What is it?'

She kept her eyes on it. She'd been there before. Not by choice, but by summons.

Carissa swallowed. 'It's part of the Learning Center.'

Anya stood up fast. Dom was by her side in a flash, hand on her back, as if to stop her from leaving.

The Inventor glanced at the others. 'It's where the Collective lives. I've been there once.'

He looked down at Carissa, his eyes widening. 'Where in the Learning Center, miss?'

She squirmed beneath his gaze. When she didn't answer, he grabbed her arm and shook it.

'Is it the Great Hall? That's just a large room. This drawing clearly has corridors.'

She shrank back from him, never having seen him so intense before, and pointed at a broken line on the drawing. 'That's the entrance. It breaks off into various corridors where we—the Copies—upload.'

She hadn't uploaded or downloaded for days. Did that make her less of a Copy now?

The Inventor released her arm. 'I'm sorry, miss, I need more. The entrance, then where?'

She studied the sketch, which she superimposed over a map in her memory banks. 'The entrance, then the corridors for the download rooms.' She closed her eyes. 'The corridor on the left brings you to the Great Hall, but this one—' she gestured ahead '—takes you to another area, behind the Great Hall.'

She opened her eyes.

Everyone was staring at her. She concentrated on the only face that mattered: the Inventor's.

He was frowning at her. 'Will we be able to access it?'

She shrugged. 'I've never seen the space behind the Great Hall.'

'Could it be beneath the Learning Center?' said Thomas.

The Inventor rubbed his chin. 'It's possible. Maybe we can access it through one of the unexplored tunnels.'

Dom stepped forward while Thomas collected up his sketches from the ground. 'We should search for it above ground first, to get a feel for any access points.' The rebel leader looked at Carissa. 'How likely are we to run into trouble there?'

Carissa closed her eyes, searching for any connection that might hint that the city was still online. She opened them. 'I don't know.'

Dom nodded at the others. 'Okay, we should return to the medical facility. Get June and the others, and get the hell out of here.'

The rebels walked on, forgetting about Carissa's crucial help. Not one person thanked her.

The Inventor stayed with her. He patted her on the shoulder. 'You did good, miss.'

She looked up at him. 'I did?'

He smiled and nodded.

Then why did she feel like she'd sentenced herself to a lifetime of being alone?

The Inventor frowned at her. 'What's wrong, miss?'

'I can't feel anyone here.'

'That's good, isn't it? It means the Collective is gone.'

She looked up at him. 'The Collective lives inside a program, Jacob. Where would it go?'

She marched on ahead, needing to be alone. 148-C watched her curiously. The Copy had punished Dom and pretended his mother was still alive. This guard's obsession with Dom had been in the report sent to the Collective. She wondered if 148-C had been left behind on purpose.

His cold Copy eyes watched her closely, making her skin crawl. She marched ahead faster, then stopped and rubbed her arms. Looking back, she saw 148-C had a small smile on his face.

Tired of this Copy's games, Carissa strode up to him. He visibly flinched.

'Where is the Collective?'

148-C stared at her like she was insane. *I might*

well be.

'Gone. I don't know where.'

'How did they leave this place? Who helped them?'

The guard shrugged. 'I don't know.'

Anger bloomed in her chest. She beat his arms with her fists.

It only made the Copy angry. 'I said I don't know!'

Her breaths came short and fast.

The Inventor rushed over to her. 'Miss, what's wrong?'

'Something isn't right, Jacob.' She looked away from him. 'This place... I don't know.'

He placed a hand on her shoulder. 'Why don't you run on ahead and check on June? We'll catch up.'

She nodded and looked at Zone C. The medical facility wasn't far, maybe five minutes' walk. It would be good to stretch her legs and clear her head.

Hugging her body tight, she walked away, feeling her stress halve the farther from the group she got.

Halfway into her fast walk, a voice stunned her into stillness. Her biogel ran cold.

'173-C, I've been looking for you.'

'Quintus,' she breathed, glancing behind her. The others were a distance back. 'W-where are you?'

'I'm close. I'm safe. Don't worry.'

'A... are you in the city?'

'173-C, I need your help.'

Her stomach lurched. Carissa swallowed hard against the feeling. 'What help?'

'Have they found the Beyond yet?'

She didn't see any point in lying.

'No, Quintus,' she whispered, even though she was alone.

'How close are they to discovering it?'

'I don't know.'

It was the truth.

'Listen to me, 173-C. I need you to keep close to them. When they find it, let me know.'

Despite the healing properties of her neuromorphic chip, she couldn't sense any other minds here. 'How? I'm not connected to anything.'

'You're connected, just not to the others. Do this for me. It's very important.'

She turned on the spot. 'Where are you? Are you watching me?'

'I got away, 173-C. So did the others. When we couldn't resurrect the barrier around the city, we retreated to a safe place.'

'So you're not watching me?'

'No, 173-C. I can only speak to you in your head.'

Her pulse slowed upon hearing that.

'You killed their leader, Max, in the open.'

'That wasn't me, Carissa. Septimus ordered the strike. I tried to stop him.'

It sounded like something that voice of disagreement would order. Quintus was the only one she really knew. 'I'll keep close to them, Quintus.'

'Good. They trust you.'

'How do I contact you?'

'Reach out to me using your NMC and I'll hear the connection.'

'Can you hear my thoughts, Quintus?'

'No, 173-C. Only your voice when you facilitate the connection.'

That settled her worry. It also explained why she'd been able to switch between speaking to the Inventor and Quintus on the battlefield without Quintus knowing.

She thought of something else. 'Are there more Copies in the city, Quintus?'

'Just the ones you encountered. We might be gone, but we still need to know the location of the Beyond.'

'Why?'

'So we may have our answers, 173-C. It's been our purpose all along. It's what we've all been working toward for months.'

For so long, Carissa had given her unwavering loyalty and trust to the unseen Collective. Yes, Quintus had tried to kill her friends, but he'd always protected her. Regardless, if the Collective wasn't really gone and her NMC was still active, it could still terminate her, like in the old days.

She nodded.

'Say it, 173-C. I need to hear you promise you'll help.'

'I promise, Quintus.'

Quintus sounded relieved. 'I knew I could trust you, 173-C.'

The voice in her head vanished. Carissa ran back to the others. On the way, she dug out the sketch of her and a pencil she'd stolen from Thomas' bag when he wasn't looking. She scribbled something down on the back of her portrait. Concentrating hard on her picture, she didn't see someone in front of her.

A pair of legs stopped her cold, causing a breath to rush out of her.

'Steady there, miss. What are you doing back?'

She put a finger to her lips. All eyes were on her, including 148-C's. She showed the page to the Inventor.

His lips moved as he read it. He gasped and passed it to Dom.

She replayed her own scrawl in her head. The last line stuck with her.

This is a trap.

16

Anya

Anya watched in confusion as Dom grabbed the piece of paper from Jacob.

He frowned at it, then looked at Carissa. 'Are you sure?'

The girl nodded. Anya's skin chilled. What was she sure of?

Without explaining, Dom pushed the others on.

'Back to the medical facility now,' he hissed in a low voice.

He grabbed Anya's hand tightly and pulled her along.

She stumbled and almost dropped her gun. 'What's happening?'

Dom looked ahead of him. His jaw twitched—a sign he was stressed.

She stumbled alongside him, feeling like a naughty child being led to her room. Dom rarely got

145

angry, but when he did it was for good reason. That's why she didn't stop him or demand answers. She allowed him to pull her along.

The gray exterior of the medical facility came into view. Dom pointed silently, covertly, for everyone to go back inside. Anya looked around her. Maybe there were Copies watching them. Or, worse, orbs. She clutched her gun tight, a difficult task with Dom gripping one of her hands. She tried to release it, to give her more control. But Dom gripped her with his super strong arm.

With a gentle sigh, she jogged along.

Vanessa and Thomas ran on ahead. Sheila and Imogen followed them, their guns raised too high to settle Anya's nerves. She finally eased her hand out of Dom's. He glanced at their parting hands, but nodded when she pointed to her gun. Jacob and Charlie shuffled along. Carissa and Jerome stayed with both of them. Rover popped his head up from behind a cluster of bushes. Then he came running and his mate followed. Carissa, who'd been terrified of these beasts once, regarded the sniffing pair with mild curiosity.

The Electro Gun slipped in Anya's sweaty hands. Vanessa and Thomas made it to the double doors and disappeared inside. Charlie and Jerome followed. Ahead, the soldiers pushed the Copy prisoner toward the double doors. Sheila and Imogen waited by the doors for the others. When the Copy resisted, Sheila poked him in the back with her gun.

The tension around Anya made her hands sweat more. Still, she could only guess what was happening.

Jacob and Carissa idled by the door. Rover whined and nuzzled Jacob's hand.

Carissa looked up at the father figure beside her. 'Can we bring them inside, Jacob?'

Jacob patted the wolf's nose. His mate came in for the same attention. Both beasts whined with excitable energy.

'No, miss. They're too big.'

'But we got Rover into the bunker after we escaped the city.'

Anya remembered it. They'd found solace in the basement of a nearby town while the city searched for them.

'Will they protect us out here?' said Anya.

'I don't know,' said Jacob. 'Rover will, but this one?' He patted the other wolf's head. 'She might still be programmed to listen to the Collective. If it recalls her, she may turn on us.'

Everyone's haste made sense now. Anya glanced around her nervously. 'The Collective, it's here?'

Dom looked around him, too, as though worried about who might be listening. 'Quintus contacted Carissa just now.' He glanced at the double doors. 'We need to get off the streets.'

Jacob whispered in his wolf's ear. Rover whined and nuzzled his hand.

'Come on, miss. Rover and his mate will patrol

for us outside.'

They hurried inside the medical facility. Anya's spine stiffened at the thought of the Collective watching them. It was Arcis all over again. She'd spent three months in that place, being watched by a set of invisible beings. On the other side of the doors, her fear lessened. Dom and Jacob picked up a discarded chain from the floor and wrapped it around the handles of the door. Anya remembered that chain. During their escape, she and the others had found the door locked and guards ready to kill them. If it hadn't been for her Copy medic, they might not be alive. Yasmin had not been so lucky that day.

Anya wondered if her Copy medic was still alive.

The men finished up with the door. Anya never thought she'd be happy to be stuck inside this facility.

The group gathered in the foyer, as if waiting for Dom's arrival.

Vanessa stepped forward, a frown on her face. 'What now?'

Dom nodded at the lift. 'Get to the Nurturing Center. We'll come up with a plan of action there.'

Some of the group piled into the lift. The remainder entered the stairwell until it was just Dom and Anya left. They slipped inside.

On the third step, Anya pulled him to a stop. 'What did Carissa's note say?'

Dom looked down at her. His warm, brown eyes melted her insides a little. 'She said this was a trap.'

'A trap?' The thought chilled her. Her heart pounded too fast. She gripped her gun tighter. 'What do we do?'

Dom held the Disruptor in one hand. He cupped her face with his other one. Sorrow and fear were lodged in his eyes. 'I don't know.'

They were a team now. Teams backed each other up.

Despite her worry, she smiled. 'We'll figure it out together.'

A sliver of tension lifted from his crinkled eyes. They resumed their descent to the first level. At the bottom, Dom closed the door behind him.

He paused in the space where he'd been tortured for close to a week. It sickened her to think the Copies—the Collective—had put him through that. Her experience—of flirtation, injections and good food—had been mild compared to his.

She caught his shiver. To keep him from reliving it, she pulled him into the next stairwell going down. Ahead of them, an echo filled the stairwell then vanished. The others had reached the next level already.

Dom paused midway. He slumped against the wall.

'What's wrong?'

Dom shook his head. She pressed her palm to his chest, feeling the rapid beat of his heart.

'I don't know what I'm doing,' he said closing

his eyes.

'Of course you do. We're going to the Nurturing Center. We'll discuss a plan of action there.'

Dom released a long breath.

She shifted her hand to his face. 'Hey, look at me.'

He did; his eyes were bright, pained. She saw the doubt in them, coupled with shock at this new turn of events. Max was dead and Dom had been thrust into a role by Vanessa and Charlie. But Dom had always been a leader. Their time in Arcis had proven just how much.

'This will be okay,' she said. 'You and I survived this place once. We can do it again.'

Dom looked down the stairwell to where the others had gone. 'Vanessa, Charlie, Sheila... they might be right. Maybe we should leave the city.'

'Without having looked for the Beyond?'

She couldn't believe what he was saying.

'They told me this place had a weird vibe to it. I should have listened.'

And yet the pair had forced Dom into a leadership role.

Her anger flared. 'If they wanted to dictate things, maybe they shouldn't have told you to become leader.' Her voice echoed loudly in the stairwell. She lowered it to a whisper. 'We need to find the Beyond, Dom. Until we do, none of this stops. The city, the towns, the camp we just came from... the Collective found us there. It will always find us.'

Dom looked up at the ceiling. 'But what if we don't have enough people power to escape?' He lowered his gaze to her. 'What if we're signing our death certificates by staying here? What if the right move is to leave and return with more soldiers? We've got a couple dozen people and a small fraction of those are soldiers.'

'There's Kaylie's team. They might come back.'

Dom sighed. 'Kaylie's team are gone. Even with them, that's not enough to fight a second, larger wave.'

She rested her head on his chest. The tension in Dom's body lessened a little.

'We also have an orb and the two wolves,' she added.

'The orb is useless right now, and according to Jacob one of the wolves might turn on us.'

His voice rumbled in her ear, pressed against his chest.

She pulled back from him. 'We also have a Copy with a hotline to Quintus, a newborn, a Breeder and a man with a bionic arm.'

She glanced down at his limb.

Dom held it up, flexed his fingers and gave a little grin. 'I keep forgetting about this.'

'Not to mention a former medical guard who can get us into places.'

Dom's smile faded. 'I don't like that he's here.'

'I can take him out if you'd like?'

She lifted her Electro Gun.

One side of Dom's mouth lifted again. 'No, but thanks. Apparently, he can get us into places.'

Anya glanced at the closed doors at either end of the stairwell. 'If this is a trap, I don't see us getting out of the city without a fight.'

'I wish Max were here.'

Anya wrapped her arms around him. He tightened his grip on her.

'Me too. And Jason. Hell, even Warren in some sick and twisted way.' She pulled back. 'But it's just us. Even if we left the city and rounded up extra people to help, there's no guarantee we'd succeed. The Collective could get the barrier working again. This is a rare opportunity to find the Beyond. We have to take it.'

'But if it's a trap...'

'Then we fight our way out. Returning to the camp before we've tried is suicide. Above all else, we'd run out of food.'

With a nod, Dom resumed his walk down the stairs. 'Where do you think the Copies have all gone?'

'Maybe they're all in the Learning Center.'

She'd meant it as a joke, but the look of fear on Dom's face forced her to lighten the mood. 'The Collective doesn't know where the Beyond is. Quintus seems to operate separately to the main group. It could be a smokescreen and only he remains.'

'I hope so.'

They exited the stairwell to the second floor and entered the final one leading to the third. Exiting at the bottom, they both took a breath before rejoining the others. The on-edge group had gathered in the space before the hidden corridor and the door to the viewing corridor.

Anya assessed the mood of the group. Thomas was folding his pages with the maps on and stuffing them into his backpack. Next to him was a quiet Jacob. Carissa was frowning at a sketch on a page in her hand. The Copy prisoner was slouched against the wall, looking bored.

Vanessa and Charlie were chatting separately in one corner away from everyone. She'd need to keep her eye on that pair.

Sheila and Imogen were standing with the other soldiers. None of them were talking. Some of them, still injured from the fight in the battlefield, slouched or sat against the wall.

Dom's arrival softened Sheila's hardened look.

She came over to him. 'Well? What's your plan?'

Anya glared at her. 'It's not up to him alone. We all make that decision.'

Sheila's eyelids fluttered in surprise. 'I didn't mean...' She swallowed. 'What's *our* plan?'

Anya folded her arms. 'Oh, so you're on board now, are you?'

Sheila flicked her gaze between them. 'I'm sorry, Dom. I thought leaving might help. I didn't think we'd find anything. Not so soon anyway.'

'It's fine, Sheila,' said Dom. 'But we all need to stick together.'

He looked over at Charlie and Vanessa.

Anya needed a moment to process what had happened up top, and she could see Dom did, too. She was about to suggest they check on June when someone tugged on the end of her top. She jerked back, and her gaze landed on a six-year-old girl. The girl had flawless skin and a rosebud mouth.

'What the hell...? Who are you?'

The crowd parted and a grinning June came through. 'Don't be afraid, Anya.'

The soldiers stared at the girl. They obviously hadn't seen her coming, either.

June placed a protective hand on the girl's back. 'This is Frahlia.'

Carissa appeared at the child's side. She was staring at her.

She looked up at June. 'My niece?'

June chuckled. 'In a way, I suppose so.'

Carissa smiled down at the girl.

Stunned into silence, all Anya could do was to stare at the child. She had blonde hair, but a shade lighter than June's. Her eyes were a strange shade of blue, different to June's pale blue ones. She'd never seen eyes that vivid before.

No, wait, she had. Once, on the eighth floor of

Arcis, when she and Dom had discovered a group of children who were being kept separate to the babies. She reminded herself that this was not June's biological child. She was a product of a Breeder and an unwilling victim. Perhaps the rapid growth machine had given her the unusual eye color.

Anya shivered. Had things played out differently, this child could have been hers.

The girl stared up at her. She looked innocent enough, but the situation gave Anya the creeps.

Aware that June was waiting for a response, she looked at her and said, 'Frahlia?'

June beamed. 'A hybrid of Frank and Tahlia.'

Anya smiled. She couldn't think of a better way to remember them.

'Can she talk?'

June frowned. 'I don't know...'

She hadn't noticed Alex standing behind June. His eyes were on the child. His blond hair was probably a closer match to the child's hair than June's.

'She can. The machine grows not only the body but the brain, too. It matures her intellect enough to match her age.'

Just like Alex had been grown and matured too fast.

A thought hit her. Could this child be from one of his forced interactions? She knew so little about what had happened before her arrival.

Alex had a wide grin on his face, looking like a

proud father. Anya had been too busy fighting the breeding program; it had never occurred to her that Alex might actually want a child.

'She's perfect, isn't she?' he said, placing his hand on the top of her head.

The child flinched and hid behind June's leg.

Alex's smile dropped away.

'She just needs time to adjust,' said June.

Alex nodded, looking too stiff to be comfortable.

17

Anya

Anya squashed her back into the wall, keen to distance herself from the readymade family before her. June was a mother. The man Anya had been forced into a room to breed with was a father. Things were changing too fast.

Frahlia watched her with curiosity. Her odd, blue gaze made Anya look away. She crossed her arms and concentrated on the others. This child—and others like her—was the reason Anya and the others had spent three months in Arcis and why she, June and Sheila had been held prisoner in this place. She was also the potential reason why Dom had been tortured.

'So what now?' said Jacob, his voice snapping her back to reality.

'Charlie and I still think we should leave the city,' said Vanessa. The pair had been chatting together in one corner. 'More so since Carissa confirmed this is a trap.'

A worried Anya looked at Dom. They had to keep going. Who knew when they might get another chance?

To her relief, he shook his head.

'Nobody's leaving. We came here to find the Beyond and took a massive risk by doing so. We're not leaving until we locate it.'

Vanessa lifted her hands. 'It's a mistake to stay, Dom. You know that, right? We'll be outnumbered.' She glanced at Carissa. 'The Collective is still here.'

Except Anya didn't believe it was. 'Carissa heard Quintus, nobody else. Same as when she heard him on the battlefield. Same as when he contacted her in the camp.'

Vanessa blinked. 'What are you saying?'

'That Quintus appears to be acting alone. He might have become separated from his group. It's possible the Collective escaped the city and Quintus is trying to fool Carissa into thinking he still has its backing.'

Carissa, who'd been quiet since she'd received the message, breathed out. A small smile played on her lips as she looked down at the ground.

Anya rested her hand on Dom's back in a show of support. 'Dom's right. We need to keep going. Whatever we do—stay or leave—we're bound to meet resistance. At least here we have a shot at getting out.'

Vanessa still looked unconvinced.

Charlie shrugged. 'Okay, we stay. What do we do?'

Dom said, 'The sketch in Janet's book matches up to the schematics for the Learning Center. We don't know if the lines correlate to corridors above ground or tunnels below, but I say we start below.'

'You suggesting we use the tunnels to access the Learning Center? Is that even possible?'

'I don't know, but we should try. The Collective appears to know less about what happens beneath the surface.' Dom nodded at the child. 'Frahlia is old enough to travel. June is healed, yes?' He flicked his gaze to her and June nodded. 'All that's left to do is count how many active weapons we have left.'

The injured soldiers perked up and showed Dom their weapons. Apart from the revolvers and the homemade Atomizer and Disruptor Gun, they had a few Electro Guns that still had a charge. The first bunch of guns had been taken from the fallen Copies during the battle in the area outside the camp. The second lot of weapons had been taken from the fallen doppelgangers of the guard, who was listening to everything they were saying.

'What about the Breeders and girls we found?' asked Sheila.

'They come with us,' said Dom.

Jacob pointed at the prisoner. 'What about this one?'

159

Dom's lips thinned. 'He comes with us.'

Charlie clapped his hands at everyone. 'You heard Dom. Let's pack up and get ready to move.'

Ten minutes later, the group gathered at the door leading to the glass viewing corridor. With them were the eight Breeders and four girls they'd rescued from the second floor.

After Quintus had made contact, Anya had expected a group of Copies to ambush them below. The fact that nobody came only strengthened her belief that Quintus was acting alone.

They could leave through the main entrance, but it could be safer to use the stairs nearest Jacob's workshop. His space was opposite the building they needed to access.

Dom led the way, Disruptor charged and ready. Fully charged, it could steal a machine's power after a successful Atomizer blast. Thomas carried the Atomizer. The gun could blow a hole in the side of any machine. He hitched the backpack containing all the maps higher on his back.

Anya followed him, carrying both a revolver and an Electro Gun. Her nerves jangled at the thought of ending this nightmare, of finding the place that other rebels had died to find. And that her parents had fought to protect. How many had discovered its location and actually made it there? One, ten—none?

The group moved silently along the viewing corridor. She glanced into each of the spaces. Her Copy medic had showed her this space when she'd been a prisoner. She'd tried and failed to convince Anya of her purpose here.

Nobody spoke as they swapped the corridor for a bright, white space that replayed their footsteps back in a weird echo. Ahead of them was a set of double doors. Dom pushed through and they entered a new corridor, more roughly hewn and darker in appearance, but not so dark that they couldn't see their way. This was the route they'd used to escape once before. They'd met resistance then. Now, everything was too damn quiet. Anya lifted her gun higher.

She checked the charge in her Electro Gun. The guns fired thirteen blasts of electricity. She had seven shots left.

Jacob caught up with Dom out ahead. Naturally, Carissa fell into step behind the Inventor. Anya wondered if the Copy would come with them to the Beyond.

Jacob pointed. 'It's a straight run to the workshop from here.'

Anya followed the leaders and Carissa. She heard heavy breathing behind her. The walk was not a taxing one; it must be fear that quickened some people's breaths.

They stepped through a dismantled, brick opening and entered a new corridor. Bricks lay scattered on the ground. Jacob kept up easily with Dom. Or Dom had slowed down for the Inventor. Anya couldn't tell.

Jacob pointed to a stairwell leading up. 'This will take us to the courtyard outside the Learning Center.' He released a long breath. 'There's no other way inside that I know of.'

Dom stopped at the base of the stairs, nestled against a flat wall of tunneled stone. With one hand on the rail he made no move to climb. He looked back at Anya. She saw the fear lodged in his eyes. And the look that meant he was questioning his decision.

Anya lifted her gun higher and nodded.

With a soft breath, Dom looked up and started his climb. Other gun-toting soldiers fanned out behind him, pushing Anya farther back from Dom. The distance rattled her. She needed to be near him. She needed to protect him.

Dom turned to Jacob. 'What about Rover?'

'Don't worry. When I call him, he'll come running.'

Nobody breathed in the stairwell. Anya dared not look back at the others. If she saw any trace of fear her legs might not work.

Dom crept up to the top of the stairwell. Four soldiers followed him. She was fifth in the pecking order. The remaining soldiers with guns brought up the rear of the pack, protecting those without weapons.

Dom opened the door a crack and looked out. Anya held her breath. She wished it were her going first. Seeing Dom take all the risk made her pulse pound too hard.

He said, 'All clear.'

She sighed with relief, but sucked in a new breath when Dom disappeared through the open door. She lunged after him, needing to be his eyes and ears in case this was the trap Carissa had said it was.

She emerged into the bright courtyard. Opposite the stairwell was a large, white building made almost entirely of white panels, intermixed with glass ones. She shielded her eyes against its brightness, still reflective enough to bother her. Dom moved forward.

She hissed at him to wait, but he didn't listen.

Sheila appeared at her side and tugged on her sleeve.

'He doesn't get to have all the fun,' she said. 'Come on.'

They raced ahead, not waiting for the others. Dom had stopped at the door to the Learning Center. He was rattling it, but it wouldn't budge.

'Wait!' one of the soldiers shouted.

Commotion behind her turned her around. The eight Breeders and four young women were running in the direction of the city limits.

Dom said, 'Let them go. I'm not making them stay.' He tried the door using his strong arm and grunted. 'It's locked.'

His strength wasn't enough to open it.

Dom looked back and clicked his fingers. 'Bring the prisoner here.'

One of the soldiers pushed the Copy guard ahead. He stumbled forward, almost hitting the door.

'Open it,' Dom barked at him.

'I don't have access to every building.'

'I don't care. Try it.'

With a sigh, the guard offered his wrist. Dom yanked it closer to the panel next to the glass doors. The panel flashed red.

That's when Anya saw a flash of movement inside the building. A head bobbed up from behind a counter.

Dom was too busy pressing the Copy's wrist to the door a second time to notice. Something clicked and the door released suddenly.

'Dom, wait!'

The words had left her throat, but it was too late. Dom had flung the doors open and was marching inside. New Copies appeared like apparitions from behind counters.

She heard Dom say, 'Oh shit...'

Someone fired at him. Anya saw red. She charged into the lobby with her gun pointed at any Copy in uniform she saw.

Chaos erupted behind her. She heard the others scramble to take cover.

A whistle followed, then Jacob called out, 'Rover, come here!'

Anya focused on the scene ahead of her. She scanned the faces of the Copies quickly, looking for one she recognized, one she might be able to reason with. She saw only one repeated four times.

The Collective must be using copies of Copies

as shields.

One attacker struck a young boy soldier on the head. The boy went down with a thud. Dom grappled with the gun of a second Copy. Anya fired her Electro Gun at a different one, not wanting to hit Dom. He held the attacker off with his strong arm. Electricity bounced around the space and set her teeth on edge.

She hit one of the Copies. It went down. She hit another. A shot came from somewhere else and whizzed past her head. She ducked. It hit a fifth Copy who had been hiding down a corridor.

'Sorry,' said Sheila. 'Had to act fast.'

Anya straightened up. All five attackers had been incapacitated.

Outside, one of the wolves growled. She looked out to see the others fighting against a second wave of Copies. She rushed outside and added her efforts to take the new threat down. But when she fired, nothing happened. She checked her Electro Gun; it was out of charge.

Anya tossed it away and patted her waistband for her revolver. She couldn't feel it. It must have fallen out. Cursing, she ran back inside the Learning Center, plucked up a discarded weapon, checked the charge and made to leave. The sight of someone down one corridor stopped her cold. Dom's Copy guard had her revolver and was pointing it at the head of one of the soldiers.

Nobody else had noticed him threatening the boy.

'Step away from him,' she said, holding her gun to the side.

'Let me go and you can have him,' said the prisoner.

His eyes shifted, like he was nervous.

'There's nothing out there for you. Where will you go?'

The Copy's eyes shifted again. 'To find the Collective.'

'I thought the group was here.'

He shook his head. 'The Ten wouldn't risk staying with the barrier down. They just wanted you to think that. I know how they think.'

She didn't understand. 'Why attack us then, if they're not here?'

'It was the Collective's idea. If you thought we were protecting something of value, you would not give up. The Collective wants you to find what it cannot.'

'Again, that doesn't explain the show of force. If you needed us here, why try to stop us a second time?'

'Call it a survival instinct. Originals are disease ridden. We are simply keeping that disease from our doors.'

'Even though the Collective wants us here?'

The Copy sneered. 'The Ten aren't susceptible to your filthy biological germs like we are.'

The guard backed up into a corridor. He shoved the soldier toward Anya. She put her hands up to stop the boy's momentum. By the time she looked up again, the Copy had disappeared inside a room at the end of the corridor.

She raced after him and jerked the handle down. What she saw sent a chill down her spine. On one wall was an array of screens. In the middle of the room were close to one hundred Copies, all standing, all deactivated.

She searched the room for the Copy guard. A door at the far end opened and closed. She cursed and closed the door with a tight shiver.

Back in the lobby, the fight was under control. Nobody had been injured.

An out-of-breath Dom strode over to her, eyes wild. 'Where did you go?'

'The prisoner, he got my revolver. He got away.'

'Shit, where?'

'Through that door.' She pointed. When Dom went to follow, she stopped him with a hand. He stared down at her. 'He's gone. I checked.'

Jacob entered the foyer. 'What's going on?'

'The prisoner escaped,' said Dom.

Carissa appeared next, hugging her middle, her wide eyes combing the space. This place must have meant more to her than it had to the humans who lived in this city.

Anya pointed at the room. 'What's in there?'

'The Great Hall.' Her voice was barely a whisper. 'It's where the Collective lives. Or lived.'

'Not anymore.'

Dom focused on her. 'What did you see?'

'About a hundred inactive Copies, but looking like they could be activated at any time.'

Dom dragged a hand down his face and looked around. 'We should search every inch of this place, leaving that room till last.'

He nodded at the Great Hall.

The Learning Center wasn't big. In fact, they checked it in five minutes flat. All they found were a few empty rooms, none of which led to the back of the Great Hall and the supposed corridor. Otherwise, there was just a locked door one down from the hall. Carissa confirmed it was a download room and likely to have Copies inside.

They approached the Great Hall with caution. It was the only place left to try. Dom opened the door to reveal the scene that had stolen Anya's breath away. The Copies were all in sentry mode, eyes open, as if waiting for a command. Anya spotted Julius and one of the blank-newborn foot soldiers who'd kidnapped Jerome and Alex.

She nudged Dom and pointed.

'At least we know where they are,' he said softly. 'Okay, let's see what happens when I enter the room.'

Her breathing turned shallow when Dom stepped inside. The second he did, the Copies activated. Their eyes trained on him. He stumbled back out of the room. The Copies went into deactivated mode.

'We can't go in there.'

Jacob looked down at Carissa. 'Can you try?' He explained to the others. 'They may be programmed to keep humans out, but they might not react to one of their own.'

Carissa nodded once. She licked her lips and opened the door, then stepped inside. The Copies didn't activate. She hesitated, looking at Jacob.

He encouraged her with a nod. 'Check the room, Carissa. Check for panels. You know it well.'

She looked unsure. 'I've only ever stood before the screens. I've never been allowed to do more than that.'

'Now's your chance.'

The girl turned back, her borrowed military boots squeaking on the white-tiled floor. She froze when she reached the first Copy, checked it visually, then walked the perimeter of the room. The taller Copies made keeping a visual on her small frame impossible. Anya heard the girl knock on the walls and press panels.

A hidden panel. Could that be their way out? Carissa arrived at a door, the one Anya had seen Dom's Copy guard leave through. She opened it, then closed it. She continued her search, arriving back at the screens, where she became visible once more. She hurried past the Copies to return to the start.

'There's a door, Jacob,' she breathed out. 'It leads to the outside. But there is another way out. I almost didn't see the panel. It's to the left of the screen. It appears to lead down.'

'That must be it!' said Dom. 'The way out of this city and to the Beyond.'

But Anya saw one hundred problems with that prospect. And they were all staring ahead of them.

18

Dom

Anya thumbed inside the room. 'How do we get past them?'

Dom studied the Copies, who were focusing ahead of them. He entered the room a second time, putting one foot inside the space. The second he did, the Copies blinked and refocused on him. He stepped back out and their faces and stares returned to their vacant state.

Their response to him lifted tightness in his chest that had been lodged there for days. He carried tech inside him belonging to the city, but it wasn't enough to trigger a response. That small test gave him hope that he was still human.

He pushed past the others in the corridor and returned to the foyer. The farther away from the room he got, the better. He turned to see all eyes were on him to solve another problem.

So far, he'd been useless as a leader.

Both Vanessa and Charlie looked concerned and he considered handing the reins over to them. They had more experience than him.

'Let's talk through the options,' said Anya.

Her soft voice snapped his focus to her. He noticed the group had gathered loosely around her. Carissa was sticking close to Jacob. Rover and his mate sat outside, their tongues lolling to one side as they watched the gathering inside.

'Can we destroy them?' asked one soldier.

Carissa shifted nervously, then drew nearer to Jacob.

'Can they be destroyed, Jacob?' Dom asked.

The old man rubbed his chin. 'I suppose so. I've never looked into it.'

Carissa fidgeted with the hem of her top. 'There's another way.' All eyes were on her. 'We can disable them.'

Thomas nodded. 'Of course. The Copies are basically computer programs. We might be able to hack them, disturb their most recent command somehow.'

Anya asked Carissa, 'Do you think they know about the secret passage?'

Carissa shook her head. 'The exit isn't on any maps I have—or had—access to.'

'So, why is there an army in that room?' asked Anya.

Carissa glanced back at the space. 'The Copies

might be there in case of an attack. It's hardwired into all Copy programming that the Collective must be protected at all costs.'

That gave Dom some encouragement. 'So we might be on the right track with disabling them?'

Carissa nodded.

Their priority was getting inside that room.

To Thomas, he said, 'How much do you know about computers?'

'Enough to deliver a hack.'

'How can we access the Copies' programming on a wider scale?'

Jacob answered, 'As long as their neuromorphic chips are working, the Copies retain a link to the city network. That means any console should give us access to them.'

Carissa clenched and unclenched her fists, as though the idea didn't sit well with her. Then, her eyes widened and she gasped. 'The tagging stations.'

Jacob frowned at her. 'What about them?'

'The Collective had the ability to terminate us from any location. The tagging stations or the upload consoles were its main routes to do so.' Her eyes flicked to the corridor. 'Wait...'

She raced halfway down and tried one door. It wouldn't budge.

She looked back. 'The download-upload rooms are in here. If we can get in here, we might be able to disrupt the programming.'

'You also said Copies could be waiting for us,'

said Jacob. 'Miss, I think we should try the tagging station first.'

Carissa gave up with a sigh. They walked outside, where Rover went from sitting to standing. He trotted over to Carissa, his head low. She patted the top of his head. His mate gave the group a low growl, as though she didn't trust them.

Anya took the lead. The others followed her, like she was their natural leader. Dom would follow her anywhere.

The nearest tagging station wasn't far, positioned between Zone A and Zone B. He had no recollection of this city. He'd been out of it for most of their escape.

Carissa ran to catch up with Anya. She pointed to an area; Anya nodded.

The group arrived at the station. Thomas muscled his way to the front and, with Jacob's help, got the panel off the station.

He peered inside and frowned. 'We're going to need some way to analyse the data.'

Jacob clicked his fingers. 'We can use the diagnostic machine in my lab.' He glanced back at the building. 'I'm going to need some strong men to get it up here.'

Dom volunteered. He flexed his good arm. 'Might as well put this to some use.'

Ten minutes later, he had hauled the machine out of Jacob's workshop and up the stairs. With Rover's help, they pushed the machine to the tagging station. His mate looked on curiously.

Jacob opened up the panel of the diagnostic machine and extended a set of wires connected to the back. He used them to connect the machine to the tag station console.

'The machine should be able to read the data.' He frowned at the screen, set low enough that he had to bend down. 'What kind of hack should we do?'

Carissa stepped forward. 'I have one.'

It worried Dom that the young Copy had been keeping back information about how to escape this city.

She stepped closer to the machine that Thomas and Jacob examined.

'All hacks are temporary,' she said, her eyes flicking between the pair. 'But you'll only be able to do it once.'

'What one should we try?'

She swallowed. 'An overload hack should do it. A DOS attack—denial of service.'

'How does it work?'

Her voice went quiet. 'It sends too much data to the Copies, burying their hardwired commands so deep that it will confuse them.'

'How long will the confusion last?'

Carissa shrugged, her eyes wide. 'I don't know.'

Jacob bent down to her height. 'Carissa, if you were still connected, you'd have attacked us already or you'd be in sentry mode, like the Copies in the

Great Hall.'

A look of relief washed over her face. Dom finally understood her hesitance to put forward ideas. Whatever damage they did to the Copies could risk disabling her systems, too.

'Jacob's right; you're not connected,' he said. 'Quintus knows that. It's why he's contacting you.'

Carissa nodded and took a quick breath. Then, she turned her attention to the diagnostic machine.

'Type in the following exactly as I say,' she said.

Thomas stepped aside. 'Do you want to do it?'

She shook her head. 'I'm not able to interfere with the Copies' programming. The system will deliver a shock to me. Hurry—we don't have much time.'

A bout of nerves hit Dom. He chewed on his thumb while Thomas typed in exactly what Carissa called out. A stream of information filled the tiny screen.

She stepped back. 'That should do it. We need to move before they figure out the hack.'

Dom motioned to the group. 'Everyone, back to the Great Hall.'

Frahlia was hiding behind June's leg, but she looked more curious than scared. He still didn't know what to make of the child, but he would save everyone who belonged to their group, rebel or city-made.

He ran ahead of the others and made it to the

Learning Center first. From there, he raced to the door to the Great Hall. Opening it a crack, he peered inside to see the Copies alert and looking disorientated. He stepped inside the room, but they didn't seem to notice him. It was like he was invisible.

'Hurry—we don't have much time.'

He ushered the others through the open door, pointing to their destination on the far side of the room.

Anya waited back with him. She grabbed his hand and together they dodged the alert Copies. His arm brushed one. It grabbed him, as if the action were an automatic response and not anything intentional.

Anya stopped to help him.

'Go on ahead,' he said. 'I can deal with it.'

He used his strong arm to peel the Copy's hand off him. The guard returned to its state of disorientation. Anya kept going, smashing herself into the walls and away from the outstretched limbs. She made it to the panel and Dom dodged and ducked new attempts to grab him to join her. To his relief, the others had gone on ahead. He peered through the newly open panel; it revealed a dark stairwell.

'Here goes nothing.'

He took Anya's hand and entered the stairwell. They eased the panel back into place behind them. If the guards came out of their disorientation, hopefully they wouldn't spot anything was amiss.

He concentrated on the way down. The

stairwell was dark, like the one leading to Jacob's workshop. He used the rough walls, made of cold, compacted earth to steady him. One floor down, the others had gathered in a larger area to the left. Ahead of them appeared to be a dead end with no obvious way out.

He relaxed his grip on Anya's hand.

'This can't be it,' he said to her.

Carissa was alone at the dead end, feeling the wall of compacted earth.

Anya walked up to it next. A blue light appeared out of nowhere and scanned her. She jumped back. Carissa, too. A grinding noise sounded in the wall.

Anya was panting. There was only one other place that produced such a noise: the third floor in Arcis, where a pair of cutting discs had killed Frank and injured Anya.

Her hands became fists as she waited. Dom stood closer to her, ready to pull her back. A scissor pattern appeared in the wall before them. The wall separated into two parts and disappeared partially inside the existing structure.

'Holy crap!' said Thomas.

Nobody moved. Not even Vanessa and Charlie. The gap showed a new tunnel excavated in the same rough way as the rest of the area.

'Is this the way out?' asked Vanessa cautiously.

'Let me test it.'

Dom inched forward, worried that the second

they passed through the door it would slice them in two. He stuck his strong arm in the gap. Nothing happened. He stepped through fully, keeping his arm in the entrance, just in case. The way stayed open, even when Carissa and Frahlia walked through. Although he suspected the child was more flesh, blood and bones than Carissa was.

The new opening hadn't responded negatively to Carissa.

This had to be it—the way out. It must have been programmed to disguise itself from any Copy attempts to open it. No wonder the Collective had found zero evidence of the Beyond before now.

The way ahead took them five hundred meters to another dead end. To the right was a large, steel door.

'What the hell's this doing here?' said Vanessa. She ran her hands over the smooth metal. It had no handle. 'It looks... modern.'

Dom stared at the possible exit to the Beyond.

Thomas checked Janet's book. 'The tunnels match the drawing.' He removed one of his maps and checked it. 'The map for this place shows the way out as far as the false wall.'

Carissa looked around her. 'This place wasn't on any maps I had access to.'

'Because the Collective never knew it existed, miss,' said Jacob.

Hope bloomed in Dom's chest. They'd found the way out. But a fear of the unknown rooted him to the spot. Every false door in Arcis came rushing back to him. This could be another trick. Another third-floor, gold door with the potential to kill whomever opened it.

A new, blue light coming from the top of the door scanned the group. Dom jumped back from it and pulled Anya out of its glow. June stepped up, allowing the scanner to check her. A loud click could be heard. It was coming from the other side of the wall. Some giant mechanism turned.

The door opened a crack.

'Everybody back!' Dom said.

He heaved the giant door open with his strong arm and peered inside. Ahead was a nondescript tunnel made of more compacted earth, with steel structures at intermittent points to keep the ceiling from caving in.

Dom pointed to the rebel soldiers, who stepped up first. The blue light scanned them, then turned off. They stepped through the door. Sheila and Imogen followed them, their guns raised.

June went next. No alarms sounded as the blue light turned her pale skin a ghostly blue. She smiled and held her hand out for Frahlia. The scanner bathed the child in blue and both of them crossed over the threshold. Alex followed next, then Jerome.

Anya shrugged at Dom and the others. 'Seems okay.'

He nodded for her to try. The blue light scanned Anya, then switched off. She walked through the door with him following. On the other side, he looked back at the remaining group: Carissa, Charlie, Vanessa, Jerome and Thomas.

'Come on, it's safe.'

Jacob pushed Carissa forward. She looked up at the scanner. It started out blue but flashed red suddenly. The door began to close.

'What the hell?'

Dom lunged at the door, catching the edges. He pulled back, but the weight of the door dragged his feet along the ground.

'Wait! We're not all inside,' shouted June down the corridor.

A shocked-looking Jacob yanked Carissa back from the entry before it trapped her.

Dom shouted, 'I'll find a way to open it again.'

Vanessa and Charlie nodded at him.

The last thing he heard was Charlie saying, 'Be careful, son...'

Dom tossed the Disruptor through the gap. 'Thomas, take it.'

He scrambled for the gun.

The door sucked shut, leaving a stunned Dom to stare at the metal.

Anya clawed at the handle visible on their side. 'We need to open it again.'

The familiar sound of guns being cocked and electricity whirring spun Dom round. His rebel soldiers had their guns up. Ahead of them was a group of armed soldiers, their guns pointed at his team.

A female soldier stepped forward and stood between their groups. 'Welcome to the Beyond.'

19

Carissa

Carissa stared at the door. 'What happened?'

The Inventor said, 'It closed on us.'

No, it had closed on *her* when she'd tried to go through. The blue scanner had flashed red.

She looked up at the Inventor. 'Why wouldn't it let me pass?'

He patted her on the shoulder, but his gaze was on the others. She'd spent enough time with him to know what that pitying look meant.

Carissa had trapped him, Vanessa, Charlie and Thomas on this side of the Beyond.

A new energy hummed. She felt pressure on her arms and legs as something new pushed her back.

Thomas cursed. 'They've erected a damn force field.'

'I don't feel comfortable being down here. We could be under surveillance,' said Vanessa with a shiver. 'We should return up top, work out a plan there.'

Charlie nodded. 'Let's do it fast before the Copy guards figure out the hack.'

The Inventor marched back to the stairs. His stiff posture and clenched fists told Carissa she should give him space. She trailed at the back of the group.

'Don't worry, Carissa,' said Thomas, turning, the Disruptor and Atomizer in his grasp. 'Jacob and I know a few things about force fields. We'll find another way through the door.'

She didn't know why the brown-haired young man was being nice to her, but his kindness soothed the frayed edges of her nerves. She managed a quick nod and a smile at him.

The Inventor reached the base of the stairs and anchored his hands on either side of the wall. He placed one foot on the first step.

Thomas muscled his way to the front.

'Wait here. I'll check,' Thomas said, easing the old man's hand from the wall.

Jacob relented with a sigh and the whisper of a smile.

'Me too,' said Carissa.

She had no idea how long a hack to the system would keep the guards in a confused state. A combination of her and Thomas' efforts should determine that fast enough.

At the top of the stairs, Thomas eased the door open with one gun. Carissa peered past him into the room to see the Copies still looked disorientated.

She huffed out a breath and said, 'I think they're still under. We need to hurry.'

Below, the Inventor started to climb. Charlie followed and Vanessa brought up the rear. She looked concerned for the two puffing, old men in front of her. Her arms were outstretched a small way, as though she expected them to topple back down.

Carissa said to Thomas, 'You need to check if they can see you.'

Thomas nodded and stepped into the room. The Collective's guards continued to mutter incoherently and shift on the spot, but they remained blind to the presence of a human. Quintus must have issued a central command to all units to protect the Great Hall. But the lack of additional security told Carissa that the Collective no longer resided here.

Thomas turned back to the others. 'They can't see me.'

'You should go,' Carissa said, pushing him out the door. 'I'll wait for the others.'

Thomas kept to the walls and away from the disorientated guards. Carissa saw their minds working to process the info dump she'd told Thomas to send to their connection. At least the same confusion didn't apply to her. Not for the first time, she was grateful to no longer be on the network.

When one of the Copies lunged at Thomas, she clutched at her throat. He skipped out of the guard's clutches and disappeared from view. When the far door opened and closed, she breathed out.

Carissa turned her attention to the next person.

Charlie looked inside the Great Hall. 'Did young Thomas make it?'

'Yes, but we need to hurr—'

A voice in her head cut her off. '173-C, what are you doing? Have you found the Beyond? I'm detecting confusion among the Copies in the Great Hall.'

Flicking her gaze to the trio in the stairwell, she answered only one of those questions. 'The Copies are malfunctioning, Quintus.'

'I can access their systems from here,' Quintus said. 'I will reset them.'

'No need to reset them, Quintus. I can fix them.'

She waved Charlie, Jacob and Vanessa ahead. They kept to the wall, like Thomas had.

A new silence from Quintus filled her with dread. 'Quintus, are you there? I said I can fix them.'

All three of them had reached the screens and the podium, hugging the wall that would take them to the door. The guards continued to lash out blindly, as if fighting off an unseen enemy.

Quintus said, 'I have performed an analysis. The Copies have been in this state for five full minutes. Why have you delayed fixing them?'

Carissa's part-organic heart pounded in her chest. She thought fast. 'I... thought they were running diagnostics.' She saw the trio were only halfway along the final wall. 'I'm not connected to the network so I couldn't check for myself.'

'Then how did you expect to fix them?'

'I... er...'

A Copy lunged for the Inventor.

Carissa gasped.

'What's wrong 173-C?' said Quintus. 'I cannot read your vital signs.'

She jogged into the room, pushing through the swell of Copies to get to the Inventor.

'Nothing's wrong, Quintus. I'm on my way to the Great Hall now to see if I can help.'

'No need, 173-C. I have accessed their systems. They appear to be under attack. Was it the rebels?' A moment's silence followed, then Quintus said, 'What have you allowed the humans to do?'

'Nothing, Quintus.'

She skidded to a stop next to the Copy that had the Inventor's arm in a tight grip. From the doorway, Thomas guided the others to safety. Making it out, she turned her attention to the guard who refused to let the Inventor go. The old man tried to free his arm.

Carissa jumped onto the guard's back. The guard startled and tried to twist around in the tight space. She slapped its ears. The Copy released the Inventor suddenly, then swung around with Carissa on his back. She slipped off and landed on the floor with a thud.

Several Copies rounded on her.

'I've reset their systems,' said Quintus.

Carissa breathed in and out fast. One of the guards reached down for her and picked her up by her top. He held her up at eye level.

'What are you doing?' the guard said, alert and no longer confused.

Carissa flicked her gaze over to the door. The Inventor slipped out but stayed by the entrance. He waved at her to come.

She concentrated on the gray eyes of the Copy; she knew him to be lower in status than her. 'I am 173-C. I command you to put me down.'

The guard ignored her.

'Quintus, one of the Copies won't let me go,' she said.

'He's under a new command,' he replied. 'Did you find the Beyond?'

'Yes, but I couldn't pass through to reach it.'

'Who made it through?'

She detected excitement in his voice.

'Most of the humans.'

'What about Jerome? Alex?'

'Yes, they did. Why?'

The guard holding her squeezed his eyes shut, then dropped her. A breath rushed out of her upon impact. Carissa crawled away from him and made it to the door. The Inventor and Vanessa pulled her through.

Leaving the hall behind, their group ran for the exit and out to the courtyard. An excited Rover greeted them.

Jacob patted the wolf's nose as he passed and commanded, 'Guard the entrance.'

The wolf went into sentry mode. He and his mate stood in the space between the workshop and the Learning Center.

They slipped into the stairwell. The cool air inside the tunnels settled Carissa's nerves. Only when they'd reached the Inventor's workshop did Carissa release her breath.

'We should be safe here for a while,' she managed to say. She explained for Charlie and Thomas, 'The Copies don't like dark spaces.'

Neither of them had spent time in the city.

The Inventor turned her to face him. 'What happened in the Great Hall? What did Quintus want to know?'

'He was asking if we'd found the Beyond, and who had made it through.'

'It seemed like the guard received a new command, right after you told him something. What was it?'

Carissa swallowed. 'He was asking about Jerome and Alex. When I said they'd made it, the Copy released me.'

The old man straightened up. Vanessa, Charlie and Thomas stepped in closer.

'What are you thinking, Jacob?' Vanessa asked.

He rubbed his chin. Carissa saw the worry in his eyes.

'Alex and Jerome were brought to this city,' he

said. 'We have no idea what happened to them during that time. I'm concerned one or both of them are not quite themselves.'

Carissa cleared space on the workshop counter and climbed up onto it. Thomas joined her while Jacob and Charlie took the only two seats. Vanessa paced the room, looking unsettled.

She turned suddenly. 'How are we going to get out of this one?' She pointed up through the hole in the roof. 'We could still leave the city. The defensive barrier is still down.'

'And go where?' said Charlie. 'Back to the camp and risk this place becoming impenetrable? Dom was right. We need to stay. We've found the Beyond, and it sounds like this Quintus character is happy about it. If Dom, Sheila and the others are in danger, we need to warn them.'

Vanessa stared at him. 'How? We've got a room full of violent Copies between us and freedom. Not to mention'—her eyes flicked to Carissa —'Carissa can't pass through the scanner.'

'We also don't know if the system will reset and open the door again,' said the Inventor.

'Most systems reboot or reset at some point,' suggested Thomas. 'What we experienced was probably a defensive capability. The door will lock down for a predetermined length of time. Then, after that time has lapsed, it should open up again.'

Carissa listened to the others debate their next move. She didn't see how they could succeed while the guards in the Great Hall remained. She needed to know what Quintus had planned.

'I think we should search the city properly,' she said.

All eyes turned to her but only one of the others spoke.

'Why?' said the Inventor.

'Maybe there are other humans here—'

The Inventor mumbled, 'Of course.'

'And other Copies.'

He shook his head at her. 'Why on earth would you want to find more?'

She had an idea. 'I knew some of them. One of them showed compassion to both Anya and Dom. 118-C was Anya's medic. If we can find her, she might help.'

Thomas perked up at that idea. 'I say we try. We could use all the help we can get. Plus, they might know how to disable the other guards in the Great Hall.'

Vanessa was folding her arms tightly and Charlie had his head in his hands. Neither of them looked happy with Carissa's idea.

But the Inventor seemed intrigued. He said to Carissa, 'I always suspected there were other Copies like you in this city, miss.'

Other Copies with a conscience and an interest in the humans? Not in the same way Quintus had an interest, but a more sociable one. It intrigued her, too.

She jumped down from the workbench, eager to

get started. 'We should begin our search now.'

The Inventor held up his hand. Her excitement wavered.

'Not so fast. We should wait until dark to go look. We're too visible in the daytime.'

'But we have Rover! And the other wolf—'

'It's not enough, miss.' He turned to the others. 'I vote we wait until nightfall.'

Charlie and Vanessa agreed.

Thomas muttered a quick *sorry* to Carissa, then said, 'Me too.'

She stared at him. 'I thought you'd be with me on this.'

He shrugged. 'Night time is safer. We can sneak around more.'

Carissa looked up at the broken roof, then at the entrance. She shivered, hoping she was right about the Copies not coming down here.

But after Quintus' reset, anything was possible.

20

Anya

'How many of you are out there?' the female soldier said.

She was dressed in a uniform with colors familiar to Anya. Black with gold trim on the sleeves and neck. The uniform of Essention. This soldier wore a short, black jacket and tapered trousers with heavy, military boots. Not quite the same. The other gun-toting soldiers wore similar garb.

Who cared what they wore? She must be in shock.

Dom pushed his way through to the front. 'Enough. Can you open the door?'

The female shook her head. 'It's on a twenty-four-hour lockdown.' She eyed the weapons. 'I'll take you to our commander. But first, leave your guns here.'

Anya glanced at Dom, who shrugged lightly.

How could he be so calm? They'd just found the Beyond, only a set of stairs and a hidden tunnel away from where the Collective lived.

Ironic. But really, really messed up.

Dom nudged her on, breaking her out of her daze. He tossed his gun through the gap. He ordered the others to do the same. The sound of clanging metal echoed through the tunnel. She added to the noise with her own weapon.

They'd come too far to go backward.

Their team of rebels followed the five armed men and women. Dom slipped back to where Anya was. Sheila and Imogen did the same. They walked slower than the rest of their group down the darkened tunnel, which had a modern feel to it in places.

Ahead of her, Jerome eyed the space. June smiled as she glanced down at her daughter. A relieved-looking Alex kept pace with them. Alex placed a hand on Frahlia's back. Anya noticed the girl flinch.

'Where are we, exactly?' whispered Anya.

She was free. She should be happy. But she'd been through too much to just accept that they were safe. She'd made that mistake once in Essention.

'The Beyond, I suppose,' said Sheila. Her eyes raked the smooth ceiling. 'It's not what I expected.'

'What did you expect?' whispered Imogen.

Sheila bit her bottom lip. 'I don't know. That's the problem.'

That was Anya's issue, too. They'd known of

the existence of the Beyond but not what it was. Nor that it would turn out to be so freaking close to the operational hub of Praesidium.

'Let's see what this commander has to say,' said Dom. 'Our priority is getting the door open and the others to safety.'

Seeing a shocked Carissa staring at the door—at her—had disturbed her. The Copy wasn't to blame for their predicament, but the Beyond obviously considered her presence to be a hostile act. Could the Beyond be the ultimate safe haven—free of both Copies and the Collective?

The soldiers led them down a long tunnel with doors on either side. Anya glanced into the rooms with open doors. People in white coats milled around what looked like a laboratory. It reminded her of the testing rooms in the medical facility.

Fear lodged in her throat. She forced her gaze ahead.

As though Dom's mind was tethered to hers, he said, 'What's wrong?'

'I saw labs, people in white coats...' She swallowed. 'It reminds me of the medical facility.' She looked up at him. 'What if these are Copies?'

He mulled it over for half a second. 'They can't be. Otherwise, Carissa would have been allowed to pass.'

That was true. She breathed out. Okay, maybe they weren't Copies. But the need for laboratories here put her on edge.

The tunnel ended and opened out into a large space. Steel beams carried the weight of a ceiling three times as tall as the tunnel. Trucks were parked in the area. Anya couldn't see an obvious route for them to get out. A set of steel stairs ahead of them led up to a second floor and what looked to be a lookout area.

The female soldier stopped at the bottom of the stairs. 'The leader only. Please step forward.'

The rebels looked at Dom, a move that caught the female soldier's attention. She gestured for him to come closer.

Dom grabbed Anya's hand and led her through the parting sea of rebel soldiers.

The woman's brow arched. 'You're both in charge?'

Dom nodded.

She didn't look convinced. 'Okay, follow me. The rest of you can wait here.'

She climbed the stairs. Dom followed with Anya behind him. Their collection of military boots hitting steel sent a clanging noise through the space. Anya counted fifty steps to the next level. They stepped onto a steel-weave platform next to a prefab. There, the woman knocked on the door.

'Enter!'

She opened it. Dom stepped in first. Anya's eyes grazed every inch of the space. She didn't want to forget anything.

The female soldier waited outside and closed

the door, instantly shutting out the noise below. Anya looked around the room. It was like an office. Two guest chairs sat opposite a desk. The walls were decorated with images of scenery she'd never seen before.

One image showed tall buildings with the words *San Francisco* underneath.

A dark-skinned woman aged around fifty years old sat behind the desk, watching them. Her outfit wasn't as formal as the soldiers' black uniforms. She wore a navy-blue suit with a white blouse.

She stood and came around to the other side of the desk, proffering her hand. Dom shook it, then Anya. The leader's skin felt warm and a little clammy, as though she were nervous.

She smiled at them. 'My name's Agatha. We're delighted to receive new guests to the Beyond. Please sit.' She gestured to the seats. 'And you two are?'

Dom hesitated before answering. 'Dom and Anya.' He looked around. 'Where are we? What is the Beyond?'

Anya sat in a chair. When Dom refused to sit, she pulled him down. He relented with a sigh.

Agatha returned to her seat. 'It's a holding area for refugees from the Region.'

Anya frowned. 'Region?'

She nodded. 'The place you came from.'

Anya had no name for where they'd come from. *Why?*

Her gaze went to the image behind Agatha's

head. 'Is this San Francisco?'

The woman laughed. 'No. It's an old photo. Bygone times.'

Dom leaned forward. 'Please. We got separated from our friends. We need you to open the door and let them in.'

Agatha shook her head. 'It's not possible. The door locks automatically for twenty-four hours. We won't be able to open it until the time has expired.'

'So they're stuck there?'

She nodded. 'A non-human life form attempted to pass through the door. It triggered the lockdown.'

'You mean a Copy?'

'I believe that's your term for the lower life forms the Collective has created.' She clasped her hands on the table. 'We've had others make it here before. They've filled us in on the evolution of events there.'

Anya thought of Janet, of Warren's parents—of other rebels who may have made it.

'Are they here? Can we speak to them?'

Agatha shook her head. 'Moved to another location. Sorry.' She leaned forward. 'What I'd like to know is why a Copy was attempting to cross the barrier. Were you being attacked?'

'No, Carissa was helping us,' said Anya.

'Carissa?'

'It's her name.'

Agatha sat back, eyes wide. 'Copies with feelings? I didn't think their evolution would get that far so fast.'

'Neither did we,' said Dom. 'Carissa is the exception.'

Agatha leaned forward again. 'So you would like me—us—to rescue her?'

'She deserves a chance to be free.'

Agatha clasped her hands tighter, turning her dark skin paler in places. 'What about the Collective? Is she still connected to it?'

'No. With her help, we successfully escaped Praesidium a few days ago,' said Anya. 'After, she broke her connection to the city.'

She left out the part about Quintus still talking to her.

Agatha nodded and waved one hand. 'Well, it doesn't matter right now. The door won't open.' She stood. 'Well, Dom and Anya, I expect you to keep your team in line while you're here. We also insist all refugees go through a physical. For your peace of mind as well as ours. We find those who arrive here unannounced are malnourished.'

Anya stood up fast. 'Is that it?'

Dom grabbed her hand, as if to calm her.

Agatha stared at her. 'What did you expect?'

She snapped her hand out of his grip. 'I don't know... a better explanation of where we are?'

She was supposed to find answers here, to turn her parents' and Jason's deaths from senseless into a cause worth fighting for. So far, she wasn't seeing it.

Agatha smiled and gestured to the door. 'All in

good time, Anya.'

Dom stood up and walked swiftly to the door.

She stayed put, not ready to leave. 'We have more questions.'

'And I promise to answer them soon. But for now, we have our rules. If you want to stay here, you must abide by them.'

Agatha opened the door. Outside, the soldier with the gun stood to attention.

'Take them to the infirmaries,' Agatha said to her. 'I want to make sure they're healthy.'

The soldier nodded, then signaled to the soldiers below.

Anya stepped out onto the high platform. A cross walk connected the prefab to a door on the same level. From the rock face opposite her, it looked like they were deep underground. The soldier led them back down to the level below. Anya saw other soldiers leading Sheila, June and the others down a new corridor leading farther into the heart of the Beyond.

At the bottom, a male soldier waited.

'Take him to the infirmary,' said the woman, nodding at Dom. 'I'll escort this one.'

Dom gave Anya a quick nod and whispered, 'I'll see you soon.'

Fear and anxiety set her hands shaking. It reminded her too much of the medical facility. And it felt too much like she was about to be experimented upon.

But with their weapons under the Beyond's control and with the way back locked down, she didn't see another choice but to comply.

21

Dom

The male soldier led Dom down a right-hand corridor that led to an area with a circle of doors. The soldier opened one room and told him to enter. Dom eyed the layout of steel benches. There was equipment he'd never seen before and too many cutting instruments for him to settle.

He hesitated by the door. The soldier gave him a gentle push inside.

'You have to complete a physical if you want to stay in the Beyond,' he said. 'It's for your own good.'

Dom understood the rules, but the layout of the room gave him pause. No way would he let them open him up again.

He shuffled inside. A man in a lab coat looked up from a microscope.

He took his glasses off and pocketed them. 'And you are?'

Dom cleared his throat. He was a leader. He needed to act like one.

'Dominic Pavesi. And you?'

'Not essential.'

The doctor, he presumed, picked up a small screen. He gestured to a reclining chair that reminded Dom too much of the ones in Arcis—except this one was black leather, not cream. Dom and the others had been forced to sit in front of screens on the seventh floor and answer questions. Their answers had determined their success moving on.

'I'll stand if that's all the same to you.'

'It's not. Sit or I'll make you.'

The soldier poked him on.

Dom slid into the chair, hands tightly clasped. 'What do you do here?'

The doctor waved his hand at him without looking up from the screen. 'Medical stuff.'

He pulled up a second chair next to Dom's and sat in it. 'I have some routine questions that I need you to answer. Okay?'

Dom nodded. At least he'd asked first.

'How old are you?'

'Nineteen.'

'And how long have you lived in the Region?'

'All my life.'

The doctor recorded something on screen. He looked up. 'Are you in good health?'

'Reasonably.'

'Explain.'

Dom shrugged. 'As well as can be expected.'

The doctor nodded. 'Have you been ill at all?'

He'd been operated on, given new tech and brought to the brink of death. But none of it had been naturally occurring.

He answered honestly. 'No.'

The doctor recorded something, then turned to Dom. 'Roll up your sleeve.'

He did, presenting the arm without tech in it. The doctor placed a blood pressure cuff on him. Pressure built up, then lessened.

He took it off. 'One twenty over eighty. Normal.'

Dom rolled his sleeve down.

Two new doctors dressed in white coats wheeled in a black machine big enough to stand in.

Panic flared in Dom's chest. He hopped up from the chair and back, instantly recognizing the design. 'What the hell's that doing here?'

The lead doctor looked intrigued. 'What do you think it is?'

Dom eyed the machine again. 'A copying machine.'

'Actually, no. It's a harmless body scanner.' He rubbed his chin. 'But I'm interested to hear about this other machine. What did it copy?'

Dom settled at hearing that. His pulse settled, too. But the man was too interested in his answer.

'Nothing important.'

The lead doctor gestured to the chair again.

'You seemed pretty rattled by it. What did it do?'

Dom sat down, not sure how much he should tell this stranger. He'd agreed to this examination as a way to see more of the place. But he still didn't know what this place was or who these people were.

Yet, they knew about Copies.

'It copied the Copies.'

The man lifted both brows. 'A copy of a copy produces an inferior product.'

Didn't he know it? Dom had been copied a few times. Each attempt had been marginally better than the first one.

He sighed, not wishing to see a repeat. 'Are we done here?'

The lead doctor slid his glasses on. 'No. I need to scan you. Head to toe.' He looked over the top of his glasses. 'Will I find anything unusual?'

Dom hesitated. 'I have machine tech inside me.'

The man's eyes widened briefly. He recorded something on his screen, then gestured for Dom to stand up and enter the machine.

Dom slowed his walk to it. The machine didn't look exactly like the one he'd seen in the medical facility. For a start, this one had four open sides. Nor did it have a container of biogel needed to make an actual Copy.

He released a quiet breath and entered it by the front, then stood facing the doctor. A blue scanner started from his feet and swept up and back down. The scanner didn't make his skin tingle. But neither had the machine in Arcis, right before his Copy had appeared.

'You can exit now,' said the doctor, frowning at the screen. 'According to the scan, you have one new lung, one kidney, a new liver and adjustments to your arm.' He looked up. 'What would you say if I asked to see the tech?'

'I'd say, over my dead body.' He inched closer to the exit. 'Are we done now?'

'Not quite.'

The man nodded at the entrance. Dom turned to see the two spare doctors were now blocking the open door. Three soldiers appeared in the gap outside. The blockade parted suddenly and a frowning Agatha walked through.

'Mr Pavesi,' she said and the blockade closed again. 'It appears you've been lying to us.'

'How so?'

'You fooled our scanners, brought unknown tech through to this side.'

'You never asked.'

'How many of you have this tech in you?'

'Just me.'

Alex was human, as was Frahlia. And Jerome was more biogel than anything else. Carissa's neuromorphic chip must have triggered the alarm, not any organs she might have received.

'No matter. The physical exams of your followers should determine that.' She stepped closer. 'Your presence creates a dilemma, Dom. One I hope you can help us with.'

'Help?'

'Yes. We created this place to keep the machines out.' Her hands disappeared behind her back. 'But the fact that you fooled our systems tells us the machines have found a way to circumvent our controls. It means they pose a threat to our haven. Do you understand?'

'Not really. Your scanner stopped the only Copy among us.'

Agatha paused. 'The scanner we use separates humans from the Collective's synthetic designs through a specific frequency the Copies put out. Humans emit a natural low frequency, but machines... they run on a network. Theirs is more of a vibration.'

Dom guessed Carissa's self-repairing NMC emitted that vibration.

She brought her arms to the front and folded them. 'We need to study the tech in you to determine why our scanners allowed you to pass.'

His blood ran cold. His pulse thundered in his veins.

Dom forced a smile. 'Can we do this later? I'm starving.'

Agatha pursed her lips, then nodded at one of the soldiers. 'Take him to the dining hall.'

One armed soldier led Dom out and away from the circle of doors, back down the corridor and into a wider one that ran beneath Agatha's elevated prefab. It bothered him that he was being taken farther away from the Region, as Agatha had called it. Charlie and the others were still trapped there. He didn't want anyone here to forget about them.

Despite his dilemma, any decision making would be sharper on a full stomach and a little sleep.

The soldier dropped him off at an entrance to a large room. Inside, tables and chairs were laid out in rows, with an aisle separating the rows into sections at intervals. Other Beyond soldiers looked up at him when he entered.

One pointed to a counter at the back wall.

'Go there,' he snapped and resumed eating.

Dom increased his step to the counter, partly to escape his armed escort, partly to see what food was on offer. He'd been living on rations for too long.

His mouth watered as he saw the display of fruit, an assortment of meats, pre-packed sandwiches and water. There were even bottles of beer. He grabbed a tray and loaded it up with a selection of food. He eyed the beer, but decided against it. Last thing he needed was a fuzzy head.

Dom sat at a table and ate his sandwich in record time. It tasted normal, not sweet like Arcis food could be. He chased it down with a long pull of water.

Anya walked in with Sheila, Imogen and Jerome. He waved at them. Anya's gaze roamed the space, as though this were a place to fear. It might well be, but at least the food tasted good.

She neared the table, a question in her eyes.

'Get some food and we'll talk,' he said.

She nodded and collected a tray. The others regarded the space quietly. They followed Anya to the counter. One by one, they returned with food and sat down at Dom's table.

Dom eyed Anya's selection. She had picked a sandwich, one piece of fruit and a cup of water. Similar to what she'd eaten while in Arcis.

She took a cautious bite, then sighed. Some of the tension lifted from her shoulders. 'This is good.'

To the others, he said, 'Eat what you can. We don't know if this will be a regular thing.'

None of them talked. They'd all been weakened by the rations in the camp. With the threat over temporarily, they could concentrate on other things.

'How did the medical go?' Dom asked.

'Passed with flying colors,' said Anya.

Sheila and Imogen replied the same thing.

'Jerome? What about you?'

The newborn shrugged. 'They say I'm fine, but I don't know if they know what I am.'

Anya leaned toward Dom. 'What did they say to you?'

He sighed. 'They found my tech. They want to study me.'

She leaned back in her chair and looked around. Dom frowned. He'd thought she'd have something more to say on the matter.

'We should get a good night's sleep and ask tomorrow about bringing the others across,' he said

209

and drank more water.

Anya nodded, but she didn't seem enthused by the idea.

She traded an odd look with Sheila and Jerome. A look that was reciprocated. Imogen was too busy eating to notice.

He put his bottle of water down. 'Okay, what's up with you?'

Anya's eyes had widened slightly. 'This place... it's just odd.'

'Odd, how?'

She studied the ceiling, the layout. 'It reminds me of somewhere.'

'Thank God you said it,' muttered Sheila.

Imogen flashed her a curious look. Jerome looked as relieved as the pair.

Okay, now Dom's curiosity was piqued. 'Where?'

Anya leaned in closer. 'You really don't see it, Dom?'

'See what?'

'The food, the layout?'

He frowned at her.

'The size is different and the food choices are more abundant but'—Anya shivered—'right now, we could be sitting in any one of the dining halls in Arcis.'

22

Carissa

Carissa's leg bounced while she watched the Inventor and Thomas work out how to get past the Copies in the Great Hall. Vanessa and Charlie stood huddled in a different corner of the workshop talking about something.

She hated the secrecy, the separation. It felt like it had when she'd severed her NMC and lost her link to the city. Not knowing if or when Quintus might contact her again made her leg shake more.

The Inventor looked up from his discussion and frowned at her. 'Are you sure Quintus hasn't been in contact again, miss?'

She nodded, wishing she could be more useful.

'And it wouldn't work to try the hack on the guards a second time?'

'They've already learned from the attack. Their defenses will be harder to breach. It won't work a second time.'

One side of his mouth curled up into a smile, but the tension on his face said he was not happy with her answer. Neither was she. They were stuck in Praesidium and it was all her fault. If she hadn't tried to enter the Beyond, the door wouldn't have closed on them. A lump settled in her throat at the thought that her friends might perish here.

But a part of her was glad they hadn't made it through. Carissa hated being alone.

She tuned into the conversation between Thomas and the Inventor.

'Is there another way past the Great Hall, I wonder?' said the old man.

Thomas glanced between the hand-drawn map and the screen of the diagnostic machine, which still displayed the collection of Carissa's cached maps. Thomas and Vanessa had dragged the machine off the streets and down the stairs. The Inventor didn't want to leave it up there in the open. They'd also gone on a run to grab bags of food from the remaining trucks.

Thomas shook his head. 'I wish there was. Only one tunnel was mentioned in Janet's book. I doubt there's more.'

'How did they get past the Great Hall to reach it?'

Thomas shrugged. 'Maybe the machines sleep.'

Carissa knew. It was mentioned in Janet's book. It was how they'd escaped the city. 'The system reboots periodically in downtime periods, to patch security issues.'

The Inventor's eyes widened. 'You mean we can get past the guards if we hit the hall at a certain time?'

Carissa shook her head. 'It won't work. The Copies are in sentry mode. All downtime has been suspended.'

Charlie and Vanessa rejoined the group. Vanessa had folded her arms tightly. Carissa recognized the stance; she was about to suggest something.

'I'm sorry to sound like a broken record here, but Charlie and I think we should leave the city. For real.'

'Leave, why?' said the Inventor.

'There's no extra food here, and the Collective and its army could arrive back at any time.' She shivered and glanced up at the hole in the roof. 'This place gives me the creeps. The camp is our territory. We can rally more troops.'

'What's to say the camp isn't riddled with Copies right now?' said the Inventor.

'Or the second we leave, the barriers restore around this city,' said Thomas. 'Then we'd struggle to get back in.'

Vanessa gestured at Carissa. 'What about her? She got us out once before. She could get us back in.'

The Inventor rubbed his chin in thought. 'I don't think it would work, not without her NMC chip aligned to the system. She knew the frequency of the barrier then because she was still connected.'

Vanessa released her arms. 'What then? We're sitting ducks here.'

The Inventor sighed. 'We're sitting ducks if we go back to the camp. The Collective abandoned this city for a reason.' He looked at Carissa. 'Any idea why the Ten vanished and only Quintus is in touch?'

She wished she knew. Ever since Quintus had contacted her, she'd wondered if it really was just him, or if the Collective had been listening.

'Jacob's right,' she announced. 'There is no guarantee the barrier would open up for me a second time. We can't risk leaving.'

Charlie said, 'So what do we do? We can't get past the army in the Great Hall. And Carissa can't pass into the Beyond. The only way to leave is to leave her behind.' He looked at her. 'I'm sorry.'

Her heart sank at Charlie's words. She'd feared this new friendship arrangement would be temporary.

'No!' The Inventor's sharp voice startled her. 'We all came here together. We all leave together. We find a way through the force field, then we disable the scanner so it can't detect her NMC, or biogel—or whatever the Beyond has programmed it to look for.'

Both Vanessa and Charlie agreed with a reluctant nod.

Carissa's hope lifted for the first time since arriving at this city. She needed to be—she would be —useful.

214

But the Collective's absence from a city that still had guards in sentry mode bothered her.

'I think we should search the city again,' she said. 'The Collective would never leave Praesidium. It's a part of the Ten. They have nowhere else to go.'

The Inventor furrowed his brow. 'What do you suggest?'

'While we figure out how to get back to the tunnel and the door to the Beyond, we should do our own research. This city is empty. The Collective is apparently gone, but Quintus still talks to me so that means he's here. He wanted to know where the Beyond was. In fact, that's all he wanted to know.'

Charlie nodded. 'If we search the city some more, maybe we'll get answers.'

The Inventor frowned deeply. 'Dom's Copy guard is gone.' He looked down at Carissa. 'Can you get us into the locked buildings?'

She didn't think so. 'There may be other Copies who can help, others who aren't in sentry mode.'

Vanessa paced. 'No guns, no way for us to keep them under control.' She stopped. 'We can't take the risk.'

The Inventor said, 'You're all we have, miss. You'll have to talk them round.'

Thomas added, 'I can try picking the locks or hacking the system. You know, the old fashioned way.'

Ω

They stepped over rubble in the courtyard. Rover waddled over to them as soon as they emerged, his bum wiggling with excitement. His mate, not programmed by the Inventor, cocked her head in silent wonder. The Inventor patted his nose and walked along the empty street leading from the central Zone A to Zone B.

The wolves acted like chaperones and their company settled Carissa's pounding pulse. She glanced at Rover, who was more proof the machines could evolve beyond their original design. Maybe there was hope for her yet.

They arrived at the buildings in Zone B. Their only stop there was the school for both Copies and Originals. Classes had been conducted in separate sections of the same building. The setting sun cast an orange and red glow over the building. She walked up to the door of the school she'd been in many times. Here, her level of empathy had been tested to determine if she was becoming more than her design. This was where she'd fooled the teachers into thinking she had not developed in any meaningful way.

She tried the door to find it locked. Without a chip to open it, she couldn't do much. Carissa looked back at Thomas. He stepped up to the door, removing what looked like a series of picks from a black sleeve of fabric.

'I never travel without these,' he said with a

wink.

Thomas removed the panel and fiddled around with the electronics. But after ten minutes of fiddling, he couldn't get the door open.

'What if we break a window?' asked Vanessa.

Carissa shook her head. 'The glass is tempered. You'd need something with a lot of force.'

Vanessa pointed at Rover.

'Not even him.'

'What about one of the trucks? We could put a battering ram on the front.'

Charlie shrugged. 'It's worth a try.'

The group returned to Zone A while Thomas ran to get one of the trucks. Carissa helped Charlie, the Inventor and Vanessa collect one of the steel girders from the courtyard rubble that had been holding up the workshop roof. Rover pushed the girder along the ground with his nose. Thomas drove back to Zone B. Together, they popped out the window of the truck and secured the girder against one of the chairs.

Thomas lined up the truck with the front of the school and floored it. A wide-eyed Carissa chewed on her thumb. The girder hit the glass of the door but bounced the truck backward. Carissa popped her thumb out of her mouth.

'You okay, Thomas?' shouted Vanessa.

Thomas shook his head in a dazed way. 'Fine. I'm going to try again.'

He backed the truck up, then aimed for the

same spot.

The edge of the girder marked the glass. He backed up again and punched a hole on his third attempt.

Carissa ran up to the door and fed her arm through. She felt for the lock and released it.

Not waiting for the others, she slipped inside the school, entering a short corridor that led to two classrooms on the left. If there were Copies here, she should greet them first. The first room was for the younger Copies, the second for the older ones. A separate structure with its own controlled entrance taught the Originals next door. But if there were Copies, they would be in this part of the school.

She looked around the space as if it was her first time. She'd always headed straight for the second room. She'd never looked beyond the classroom she was in. Carissa noticed a corridor behind the two classrooms. She pressed her toes lightly into the tiled floor and found two more rooms down the new passageway.

The Inventor came to her side. 'What's down here?'

She didn't know. 'I've only ever seen the one classroom.'

She opened the first door and looked inside. She did a double take.

Behind her, Vanessa said, 'What the hell...?'

Carissa widened the opening and walked into the room. It looked like a nursery, similar to the

Perspex boxes in Arcis on the eighth floor. Toys dotted the floor, making it look like someone had been playing here recently. But the thin layer of dust told her whomever had been here was long gone. She backed out of the room and tried the second door. Inside was an empty room, except for a two-way mirror looking inside the first room, and a computer console.

Carissa stepped up to the console and tried it. The display sprang into life. Permutations scrolled on screen, too fast for her to read.

'Let me see,' said Thomas, nudging her out of the way. She stood back. Thomas nodded at the screen. 'It's computer code. Do you recognize any of it, Carissa?'

'Should I?'

'Well, yeah. It's a part of you. This would have formed part of your original programming, I guess.'

Carissa frowned at the screen, stepping closer. She put her hand out and the words that scrolled by slowed down. She pulled her hand away and they sped up again.

She blinked. 'Why is it doing that?'

'It's responding to you, miss,' said the Inventor. 'Try again.'

She looked back at the screen, this time holding her hand out for longer.

The words slowed until she could read them. It was a list of downloads from the Copies. Each one had a designation beside it. She recognized a few numbers, including her own—173-C. Carissa searched for other codes, namely those belonging to the Collective, one through to ten. She found nothing lower than eleven. She searched for the medics instead, focusing on data that had been created after they escaped the city.

One number stood out: 118-C. Anya's medic, who had helped them to escape. She was still alive and, according to this, in the download room inside the Learning Center.

Her hands shook as she checked more data on 118-C. According to the console, she'd had contact with both Jerome and Alex. Julius had been put into stasis and was currently guarding the Great Hall. Interviews had been conducted with both Alex and Jerome. Quintus was listed as having ordered them.

She searched for more details as to what happened after but none were forthcoming.

'What does it say?' said Charlie.

Carissa looked up at them. 'Quintus... his name is listed here... he interviewed Alex and Jerome.'

'What did he do to them?' asked Vanessa.

'It doesn't say. Nothing possibly.'

The Inventor shook her shoulder. 'We need more information, miss.'

'I don't have it.' She glanced around at the disappointed faces. 'But I know someone who might.'

23

Anya

The Beyond sent a deep chill through Anya. It reminded her too much of parts of Praesidium. She'd only been in this supposed sanctuary six hours and already she wanted to leave.

Three hours ago, Agatha's soldiers had shown them to a dorm, a large space with a concrete floor and dozens of beds lining both of the rockface walls. The rebel soldiers took one side of the room while Anya, Dom, Sheila, Jerome and Imogen occupied the other side. Farther back, June, Alex and Frahlia sat huddled together, looking like the nuclear family they'd become in a matter of hours. Frahlia's gaze scoured the room. She hadn't said anything since she'd been born, but her eyes held a mix of confusion and fear. Anya had felt that same way when she'd woken up in Alex's room, with no idea where she was or what had happened.

While Alex spoke to June, Frahlia looked from one guardian to the other. Anya wondered what was going through the child's mind.

Then Alex looked around at the rebels opposite them, at the walls, at the door. His eyes narrowed slightly as if searching for something. His gaze found Anya's. The former Breeder nodded at her and looked away.

Anya copied Alex. She studied the structure of the walls and the ceiling, looking for the telltale gap between the two that might hint this area was staged. Dom was on the bed next to her, arms resting on the tops of his legs. He was making his own assessments of the space. His brow had barely lifted since Anya had pointed out to him the similarities between this place and Arcis.

Dom looked at her suddenly and flashed her a weak smile. She wished she could do something, say something, to make that frown go away.

'Tomorrow,' she said.

Dom blinked. 'What?'

'Tomorrow. That's when Agatha says the door will unlock. We can rescue the others then.'

He nodded, looking as if he'd forgotten about the rest of their team. Of course he hadn't, but Dom worried too much. Over-thought everything. It was typical of him to take everything on himself.

She touched his hand. He startled and blinked again.

'It's going to be okay,' she said.

'Is it?'

'I hope so.' His lips thinned at her reply. 'What is it?'

'I can't help thinking about what you said about Arcis. I'm seeing the similarities now. I'm worried I've led us all into a trap.'

'We can't know for sure where we are,' said Sheila. 'But it has to be better than where we've just been.'

'We were trapped in the city and the camp,' said Jerome. 'We would have died.'

'And we needed to get Frahlia to safety,' added June.

Dom nodded hesitantly.

'I promised to keep everyone safe.' He looked at each of them in his row. 'Vanessa and Charlie wanted us to return to the camp and I said no. Maybe we should have left when we had the chance.'

Anya shifted closer to him. 'They were wrong. They were making that decision based on the fact we hadn't found the Beyond yet. I'm guessing they're on the other side, trying to work out how to get the door open.'

Sheila nodded in agreement and turned to Dom. 'I'm sorry for taking their side. I should have trusted you.'

'Should you?'

Sheila glared at him. 'Of course, Dom. It's always been you and me. You've never been wrong.'

Dom sighed heavily. 'There's always a first

time.'

Anya worried for him and the stress he was putting himself under. She took his hand, weaving her fingers between his. 'We're in this together. It's a democracy and we all made the decision to cross.'

Dom nodded tightly. He squeezed her hand in response and released a soft breath.

She looked into his eyes. 'Okay?'

'Okay.'

Ω

An hour later, the lights were turned off. Anya had no idea what time it was; she assumed it must be late evening. Dom crashed out on the bed next to her, exhausted. The other rebel soldiers did the same. Nobody had slept properly since the attack outside their camp. It was natural that everyone would want to sleep.

Anya managed a quick nap. She woke some time later and rubbed her eyes. The dorm was quiet, almost zen-like. She looked around her, seeing only shadows and the outline of bodies in beds. She sat up, feeling somewhat rested, but her mind still refused to settle.

With everyone else sleeping, she got out of bed. Now was the perfect time to explore this base and find out why it felt familiar to her.

She hung a left outside the door and walked along a dimly lit corridor leading farther inside the base. The corridor carried on for a while before it opened into a new section that was more modern than the last. Gone were the bare, rock walls. In their place were rendered walls painted in bright colors. It looked almost homely. She looked inside one room. It had sofas and a large screen on one wall. In front of the screen was a couple of black, leather gaming chairs. A memory hit her of the fourth floor in Arcis, where the sexes had been separated. The boy's dorm room had had a section just like this: bright and airy with a screen and an area for VR game play.

She backed out of the room and checked the other rooms in the vicinity. She found a well-stocked kitchen in one and an area with showers in another. Another memory hit her, this time of the third floor with the maze and three sections, one black with a gold door. It didn't look exactly the same, but the place triggered enough bad feelings to unsettle her.

She crept through the section, discovering a door that said *Authorized entry only*. The door was open. Inside was a control room with a collection of black screens on one wall and a glossy, black console beneath it.

Worried someone might catch her, Anya hurried back the way she had come. But before she reached the door to the dorm, someone pulled her into a dark corridor.

What the—?'

A warm hand clamped over her mouth that smelled of lemons.

Sheila turned her around; she had one finger to her lips. Anya nodded and she released her.

'What are you doing, Sheila?' she whispered.

'Same as you, checking this place out. I think we should do a little exploring.'

Sheila pulled her out of the corridor and dragged her back to the modern section. Anya wanted to explore more but not alone. When they heard a noise, Sheila pulled her inside the room with the sofas and the screen.

Anya peeked out to see Alex pass by the door.

She turned to tell Sheila it was only Alex, but Sheila pressed a finger to her lips. Anya tracked Alex again and saw him disappear down a corridor she hadn't explored yet.

Sheila whispered, 'We can't trust anyone.'

'Not even Alex?'

'Especially not him or Jerome. We have no idea what was done to them in the city.'

Anya wanted to say she felt odd around Alex, that she thought his reaction to Frahlia was over the top.

Sheila glared at her. 'What is it?'

'I don't know... don't you think Alex is being too full on with Frahlia?'

Sheila folded her arms and raised a perfect brow. 'Remember the eighth floor and the babies?'

Like it was yesterday.

Anya hadn't known what to do or understood the others' reaction to them. 'Okay, I get your point.

Are you saying I'm worrying over nothing?'

'No, not nothing. But this place has me more worried than Alex's obsession with Frahlia. When you went for your examination, what did they tell you about it?'

'Other than what Agatha had told me and Dom in the office, nothing.'

Sheila uncrossed her arms. 'Dom's not trusting his gut. If Max were here, the pressure would be off and Dom would be all over this. But as leader, he's worried about messing it up for everyone else.'

Anya felt that way, too. 'So, what do we do about it?'

'We make him see sense. This place is sending out serious vibes of déjà vu and we need to understand why.' Sheila shivered and looked back at the room they were in. 'This one reminds me of the boy's dorm room on the fourth floor.'

So she wasn't imagining it.

'Yes!' Sheila shushed her and Anya lowered her voice. 'What do we do?'

'Agatha says the door will open tomorrow. We wait for that to happen, get the others across, and see what to do then. We should try to bring the wolf over, you know, for protection.'

Having Rover here would shift the balance in their favor.

'What happened at your medical?'

Sheila shrugged. 'Nothing much. They took my temperature, blood pressure, heart rate. Then they scanned me and found nothing. You?'

'Same. They found Dom's tech.'

Sheila checked the corridor. 'We need to keep an eye on him.' She looked back. 'Make sure he doesn't become their newest experiment.'

Anya nodded.

Sheila checked the corridor a second time. 'We should get back. You coming?'

'In a minute. I want to check one thing out first.'

Sheila slipped out the door as quietly as she had entered it.

Anya crept back to the control room. Maybe it would give her some insight into how this place operated. She froze at the door when she saw the screens had been activated and Alex was hitting something on the console.

'What are you doing?' she whispered.

Alex startled. He yanked his hands back as if something had electrocuted them.

'I... was seeing if there was a way to release the door.'

She checked behind her and stepped inside the room. The screen showed security details. It looked like Alex was searching for the security access.

'And is there?'

'Nothing I can see.' His eyes shifted. 'Go back to bed. I won't be long.'

She took a step closer. 'Maybe I can help.'

Alex stepped in front of the console, blocking

the screen.

'Why aren't there any guards in here?' she asked.

'The system is a sentient one. It runs on its own schedule after hours.'

'Did you find anything?'

He shook his head and shifted to the left. She caught a glimpse of something on screen. Override command codes.

She hadn't spoken to Alex properly since the Collective had taken him prisoner. Frahlia's birth had pushed that conversation further away.

'I need to talk to you,' she said.

'Can't it wait?'

'No.'

Alex hit something on the console and the screens went black.

She walked out of the control room and led him back down the corridor to the start of the more basic designed area.

'We haven't spoken since... you know.'

'Yeah.'

'What happened when Julius took you and Jerome to the city?'

Alex shrugged. 'They separated us. Then you found us.'

Anya frowned. 'Nothing else?'

'Like what?'

She didn't know. 'Did they try to experiment on you? Did anyone talk to you?' She gripped his sleeve.

'You and I spent a week together and they barely left us alone.'

Alex eased his sleeve away. 'It wasn't like the last time. I guess my Breeder status meant something only when there were females to pair up with me.'

Anya shivered, thinking how clinical it all sounded. 'I guess.' She paused, bit her lip. 'Are you and June doing okay?'

He shrugged again. 'Sure. We're fine.'

'And Frahlia?'

His eyes lit up and he beamed. 'She's perfect. I couldn't believe it when I saw her. I never knew how perfect children could be until she came along. She's something, isn't she?'

The child with the strange eyes, less than a day old, was certainly something.

'She is perfect.' It was the only way Anya could think to describe her. 'But her eyes, they're a little bright, don't you think?'

His smile dropped away. 'Do they give her away?'

She understood his worry. If Agatha discovered what Frahlia was, she could be experimented upon for the rest of her life.

She smiled. 'No, they're fine.'

The way Alex looked at her, the way he switched from a quiet energy to a nervous one, bothered her.

She rubbed her arms. 'I'm gonna head back to the dorm. See you back there?'

Alex nodded. 'I'm going to take a look around.'

Anya watched him go. A hand on her arm startled her. She spun around to see it was June.

'What are you doing here, Anya?'

'I... was talking to Alex about his time in the city.'

'Sounds like you were interrogating him. And asking about Frahlia. Do you have a problem with her?'

Her mouth flapped open. 'No... I... we were just talking.'

June's eyes had hardened. 'I will do anything to protect her, so don't get in our way.'

'I wouldn't...'

'And leave Alex alone. You had your time together in the medical facility. He doesn't want you; he wants me.'

'I'm not interested in Alex.'

It was true.

'Stay away from him. Leave him alone.'

'Fine. I'm gone.'

Anya turned and walked back to the dorm.

24

Carissa

Carissa marched on ahead of the others, out of the school and toward the Learning Center.

She heard a set of steps behind her hurrying to catch up.

The Inventor reached her and put a hand on her shoulder. 'Where are you going, miss?'

'Back to the Learning Center.'

She resumed her walk but the Inventor stopped her again. 'To do what?'

Carissa caught the looks on the others' faces. Both Vanessa and Charlie were concerned, but Thomas was curious. She'd forgotten the Originals needed more detail to make decisions. They could not hear her thoughts or gauge her response in the blink of an eye.

'There's a download-upload room in the Learning Center.' She looked from one to the next. 'I used to provide my daily uploads there. The console says there's someone in that room who might be able to help us.'

The Inventor's eyes widened in fear. 'More Copies?'

She shook her head. 'Not like the ones in the Great Hall.'

She didn't explain further.

The old man released her arm and she hurried on, keen to see if the Copy she needed to find was actually there.

Rover was sitting in the middle of the courtyard amid the broken bricks, his tongue lolling out the side of his mouth. His mate was lying beside him, head nestled in her paws. Rover stood when Carissa approached; the second wolf lifted her head with apathy. Carissa rewarded Rover with a pat on the nose as she passed.

The entrance was still unlocked. She hurried inside and down the corridor leading to the Great Hall, stopping outside the door just before it.

The Inventor caught up with her a second time. 'Are you sure, Carissa?'

She stilled at the Inventor's formal use of her name. Not miss, but Carissa.

She nodded. 'I'm sure.'

Truth was she had no idea what she would find. Her connection to the Collective, meaning her connection to other Copies, no longer existed. Anything she did now came from a gut feeling.

She tried the handle but the door was still locked. Thomas got out his lock-picking set and worked his magic on it. Carissa pushed the handle down again. The door clicked open to reveal a dozen upright pods lining both sides of the room. The familiar connectors hung down from the ceiling over each pod. Carissa shivered at the sight of the room, a place she had been expected to upload her experiences to the Collective. Her NMC had been disabled, but Quintus could still contact her. Could she still use one of these?

She shook the thought from her mind. A collective gasp from the others pushed her on. Of the two dozen pods, only half were connected. She walked along the right-hand row, checking the occupants there. She stopped at one, the Copy she'd wanted to find, the same one who'd helped Anya to escape.

The medic's eyes were closed. But her lids betrayed no rapid movement to indicate an upload was in progress.

The Inventor came to her side. 'Do you think the units were shut down mid-upload?'

'It's possible.' She looked up at him and pointed to the connectors. 'I can't reach. Please disconnect this Copy from the pod's connector.'

The old man reached up and pulled the connector away from the Copy's NMC disc. Her eyes remained closed.

Carissa waited for the medic to reboot. Within a

minute, the Copy's eyes fluttered open.

She flashed a nervous look at the Inventor, her spine straightening. 'What are you doing here?'

118-C stepped out of her pod and a fearful Inventor stepped back.

Carissa placed her hand on the Copy's chest, breaking her fixation on him. 'I asked him to disconnect you.'

118-C blinked and refocused on Carissa. Her eyes narrowed.

'173-C,' she said. Carissa nodded. 'Why can't I sense you?'

'I'm no longer connected to the network. Do you remember the last time you saw me?'

The medic blinked, her pupils sharpening to fine points.

They dilated and she gasped. 'The escape! Did you make it?'

Carissa nodded. 'Thanks to you. What happened after we left?'

118-C frowned at the floor. 'I was captured and taken here.' She looked at Carissa. 'Then you woke me up.'

'I don't have time to explain, but the Collective has abandoned the city.'

The medic frowned. 'Abandoned, why?' She closed her eyes, and Carissa knew she was attempting to assess the situation. 118-C opened her eyes with a sigh. 'I can't sense anyone. Can the Collective leave?'

'I don't know, but I need to know where they

went. Also, do the names Alex and Jerome mean anything to you?'

The medic frowned deeper and shook her head. 'I don't know anyone by those names.'

'Hidden data says you were the last to speak with them.'

118-C paced a small area. The others kept well back.

'They must have deleted my memories of that interaction.' She stopped pacing, looking unsure. 'How can I help?'

Carissa cut her eyes to the Inventor.

The old man stepped forward. 'Do you know who I am?'

118-C nodded nervously. 'The Inventor. You disable Copies. I thought you were here to disable me.'

The old man shuddered. 'Correct. But no, I'm not here to disable you. I have a diagnostic machine that will help to read the data from your memories. With your permission, I'd like to use it to read your mind.'

118-C eyed him, then the others.

Last, she cut her eyes to Carissa. 'Is he a friend?'

'Yes, and also of Anya and Dom.'

'They're alive?'

'And well.'

A look of relief crossed 118-C's face. 'I'm glad I helped them.' She straightened up, her expression growing stern. 'We must try.'

Ω

They regrouped in the Inventor's workshop. Carissa stood back while 118-C sat in a chair. The Inventor had attached magnetic discs from the machine to her NMC and communication discs. The old man turned the machine on; it whirred low. Both he and Thomas checked the screen.

The Inventor called Carissa over. 'Miss, tell me what you're seeing.'

He stepped back as she stepped closer. A stream of green code was displayed on the black screen. Carissa recognized the jumbled-up words as an encryption. She memorized the out-of-order words and closed her eyes to reorder them.

New words came into focus. She opened her eyes and committed more jumbled-up text to memory. A pattern unfolded in the data that would be impossible for either the Inventor or Thomas—or any human—to decipher. Alex and Jerome's names popped up several times in the medic's memory. Except their names had been replaced with a Praesidium designation that only the Copies would recognize.

118-C turned sharply in her chair. 'What do you see?'

She knocked the connection loose and the data vanished.

The Inventor turned her back and reconnected the discs. 'I need you to sit still.'

118-C did as she was told. The data displayed on screen again. Carissa found mention of the battle and Alex and Jerome's capture. She continued her search for new mentions of the pair—designation or otherwise. But when Quintus' name popped up, she switched her focus to all mention of him.

A hidden message between the Collective members was buried deep in the encryption.

She frowned at 118-C. 'Were you called to the Great Hall in the last couple of days?'

The only way 118-C would have had access to the Collective's thoughts and conversations was if she'd been touching the podium.

118-C blinked. 'I don't remember.'

Carissa looked at the data once more. Before her was a transcript of what the Collective had discussed while she'd been connected.

They were arguing over 118-C's proposed punishment for helping the prisoners to escape. Then the conversation veered to a new topic.

A sentence stopped her cold.

We may have found a way to replicate Julius' success.

It was from Septimus to Quintus. She read on.

Yes, the newborn proved to be not only useful, but controllable.

And the new prisoners?

One is a newborn, lost from the city. The other,

one of our Breeders.

How soon before we can fit the behavior modifier? asked Unos.

Quintus replied, *Soon.*

The Originals will be coming for them. We must leave.

Our success with Julius will give us a way out...

Carissa stepped back, feeling sick.

She swayed. The Inventor's hand on her arm steadied her.

'What is it, miss?'

118-C was staring at her, too. 'What did you find?'

Carissa swallowed and focused on the Inventor. 'The Collective mentioned a behavior modifier it used on Julius and plans to replicate that success elsewhere.'

The Inventor's eyes widened. 'You're saying someone else may be under the Collective's control? Jerome or Alex?'

With no mention of surgery in 118-C's memory banks, she wasn't sure he'd had time to do anything. 'Ever since the others escaped through the door, I haven't heard from Quintus.'

'Silence doesn't mean anything bad,' said the Inventor. 'It's possible he failed and went into hiding.'

But 118-C's stare unsettled her. 'The Collective cannot survive outside of the system.'

'If the Ten aren't here, where did they go?'

asked Charlie.

Carissa wished she knew.

Vanessa said what Carissa was thinking. 'They must have found another way.'

25

Anya

Anya woke to the sound of gentle snoring beside her. Sheila's long mane of hair covered her face. She grunted, then swiped at something imaginary in her sleep. Anya suppressed a giggle and turned to Dom. He was awake, sitting up, fully dressed.

Ready for action.

Anya had slept in her clothes last night, despite Agatha leaving her a pair of pajamas on the end of her bed. From a look around the room and its twenty-four beds, some had opted for the new clothing. Many had not.

She sat up and rubbed her eyes. But when she saw the worry on Dom's face, her spine stiffened. 'What's the matter?'

Dom's eyes flickered to her, then away. 'Nothing. I couldn't sleep.'

Neither could she at the start, but exhausted

with grief at losing Jason and full from her meal last night, she'd eventually conked out. Things weren't right here, but at least she'd slept a little after her confrontation with June. In the cold light of the dorm room, she knew what had to be done.

She pulled on a hoodie, also from Agatha's stash, with the words *New San Francisco* emblazoned across it. Similar to the poster in Agatha's office.

The name sounded familiar, but not enough to evoke any specific memory of it.

Anya stood. It prompted Dom to do the same.

'We need to get that door open,' she said.

'Just what I was thinking.'

Dom strode out of the room; Anya chased after him. The others slept on.

He followed the corridor back to open-plan area that Agatha's elevated office overlooked. He crossed the space with trucks to the corridor that led back to the door and the Region.

Nearing the place where the Collective ruled slowed Anya's walk. It wasn't like she was going back, but it still made her skin prickle with fear. She imagined the others trapped with a small army of Copies. The thought spurred her on and she overtook Dom.

'Wait up!' he said.

Their weapons were gone, exchanged for safety.

She slowed when the door came into view. Two of Agatha's soldiers were guarding the exit.

'How soon before the door opens?' she asked them.

One soldier looked at her like she was crazy.

Dom repeated the question.

The soldier said, 'The door isn't opening again.'

Not what they'd been told.

'Agatha said it was on a twenty-four-hour timer,' said Anya.

The soldier shrugged. 'It's not opening again.'

'Then why are you here?'

'Agatha doesn't want anyone leaving. The Region cannot be accessed again.'

Anya looked to Dom, who wore a deep frown. He turned and marched back to Agatha's office. She followed him up the steel stairs and he knocked on the door.

There was no answer. He tried the handle. The door was locked. Next to it was a flat plate, like in Arcis. Like in Praesidium.

'Where is she?' he asked, his voice rising in anger.

'We should check the rest of the base.'

Anya crossed the walkway and tried the door on the same level. It was also locked. She returned to the ground level and began her checks in the rooms closest to the area, needing to do something. Many of them refused to open. The ones that did were occupied by doctors or lab technicians. This military base—that's what it felt like—was feeling stranger by the minute.

'Maybe it's too early.'

She wished she knew what time it was. Jason's watch, the one she'd borrowed and taken to Arcis, was still there.

Dom's lips turned thin and white. 'I'm responsible for them. Charlie, Vanessa, Thomas, Jacob—even Carissa.'

Anya touched his arm. 'It will be okay. Let's keep looking.'

They continued their search, ending up outside the control room where Anya had caught Alex snooping last night. It was closed. She hadn't told Dom about it or her chat with Sheila—or June. She didn't want to worry him.

Another corridor led into an area she had yet to explore. Three guards appeared from a hidden room and stopped them from going any farther.

'You don't have permission to be in this area,' one said.

Dom stepped forward. 'We need to speak with Agatha.'

'She's sleeping.'

'I don't care. Wake her up.'

'Go back to your dorm room.'

'Why isn't the door to the Region opening again?'

The soldier glanced at his colleagues. 'Wait outside her office. She'll be with you shortly.'

Anya and Dom returned in silence to the place they'd just come from. They climbed the stairs and sat on the top one. The area was void of life, the trucks below idle.

'What's going on here, Dom?'

'I don't know, but Agatha has some questions to answer.'

Five minutes later, a noise carried from across the walkway on the same level as Agatha's office. They both stood as the leader exited through the door and crossed the walkway. Agatha was dressed in an electric-blue pant suit and looked fresh, not like she'd been woken from a sleep.

She walked past them and opened her office by pressing a chip in her wrist to a flat plate. Just like in Arcis. Just like in Praesidium.

Agatha entered the room first. Dom went next. Anya closed the door and took the remaining seat next to Dom. Agatha sat down in her chair opposite them.

Dom wasted no time. 'When is the door to the Region opening, Agatha? Your guards seem to think it's not.'

Agatha clasped her hands on the table. Her eyes were downcast. A sick feeling swirled in Anya's stomach.

'You never planned to open it, did you?' she whispered.

Agatha looked up at her. 'No.'

Anya's chest heaved from the unfairness. 'Why? There are people trapped on the other side.'

'There are also synthetics on that side that cam

harm us.'

Anya stood, too angry to sit. She would not lose another person to that place.

She pointed at the woman before her. 'Open the door, Agatha. Or I'll...'

Agatha eyed her. 'Or you'll what?'

'I'll open it myself.'

Agatha laughed. 'The door is on a timer—that's no lie—but I control it. You won't open it without my authorization.'

Anya folded her arms. 'We came here believing this place was a sanctuary. But it feels to militaristic for that. What is this place for, Agatha?'

The woman's expression darkened. She gestured for Anya to sit, which she did, but perched on the edge of her chair.

'What do you two know about the Beyond?'

Dom said, 'That it's a place the Collective doesn't control.'

'And what do you know about the Collective?'

'It's a group of ten artificial beings who control Praesidium,' he said.

Agatha lifted a brow. 'Nothing else?'

Dom and Anya shook their heads at the same time.

'Should we know more?' asked Anya.

Agatha unclasped her hands and leaned back in her chair. 'The Collective is just one individual, an artificial being gone rogue. Quintus—the Latin word for "fifth."' She released a hard breath. 'It appears

Quintus found a way to clone himself. From people who started arriving here, we learned that he created nine others, and that those others helped him to run the city called Praesidium.'

Quintus had contacted Carissa. Never the others. It made sense he would be the ringleader in all this. But something didn't make sense.

'How do you know he's just one and not ten?'

Agatha's lips thinned. 'Because we created him.'

Anya's mouth dropped open but no words came.

Dom had no trouble speaking. 'Excuse me?'

Agatha stood and rounded the desk. In the space between them and the exit she paced, before stopping and turning to face them.

'The Beyond is a military facility. I'm guessing you've already figured that out. Eighteen months ago we created Quintus to run this facility—an autonomous program, if you will. Except Quintus turned on us and locked us out of key systems. We struggled to rein him in; we had the best programmers working round the clock to hack his system. But he knew how everything worked. Only one choice remained.'

'And that was?'

'To contain him.'

Anya's chest tightened.

'In the Region?' she whispered. Agatha nodded. 'Where we live?'

Agatha's gaze shifted to the floor a second time.

Anya wanted to be sick. 'There's more?'

Agatha walked back to her desk. But instead of sitting, she perched on the edge next to Dom. 'The Region was designed to control him. We wiped his program as best as we could. But the Region had to look foolproof to give Quintus a purpose. So we sent families to live there.'

Anya stood up too fast, knocking over her chair. 'That's bull. It was our home for years. I was born there. Alex, the Breeder in our group, told me he'd been created twenty months ago. How is that possible if we were only there for twelve?'

'Time became skewed for the people living there.'

Dom got to his feet. 'Enough of your lies. Open the door or we will.'

'It's not a lie, Dom. It's the truth.'

He laughed. 'How can the Region be fake if we remember our lives there?'

'In the same way that a group of teenagers had their memories wiped by a machine in Arcis.'

Bile rose in Anya's throat. She swallowed it back down. 'You're saying... the people who lived in the Region... had their memories wiped?'

'Not quite.' Agatha held her hands up. 'Let me explain.'

Dom was shaking. Anya tried to calm him with a touch, but it was she who needed calming.

He sat down, looking too stiff to be

comfortable. 'Explain.'

Anya remained standing. She gripped the back of her chair keep from crumpling to the floor.

'We banished Quintus to the Region or, more precisely, to a city that existed before he did. We limited his access to technology by creating towns that neither had nor needed tech to survive. The city and Quintus' presence were both meant to help the volunteers adapt.'

Anya snorted.

Agatha continued, 'To live a good life. The volunteers agreed to the mind regression because they knew it was the only way to stop Quintus. If they didn't remember this place, then Quintus couldn't gain access to it. But when Quintus found a way to override the safety protocols in his program, it spawned a rebellion. The shock of events in the Region knocked loose some memories that hadn't been buried deep enough. Some volunteers suddenly remembered how to access their true home, which they designated the Beyond.'

Anya shook her head. This was too much.

Agatha said, 'We created as real an environment as possible and gave people false memories to make sure the sentient program didn't suspect anything. It was only supposed to be for a few months. By that time, Quintus was meant to be subdued and we could safely remove him.'

'But,' Dom prompted.

'But Quintus found his way out of the hard

reset, designed to remove his knowledge, and multiplied himself. He remembered how to make technology he had access to here. He replicated it, including a cruder version of the memory regression machine we'd used on the volunteers.'

That would explain why this place felt so familiar. But Anya wasn't ready to believe Agatha's farfetched story just yet.

'He used us to learn more about humans,' Anya said.

Agatha nodded. 'His goal became to leave the Region and return here. In his current, evolved state, we cannot let that happen.'

Dom grunted. 'If this is all true, let our friends come through to this side. We have people who can help you.'

Agatha shook her head. 'They have a Copy with them. Copies are built to follow commands, and any sentient being that was connected to the Collective will have a little bit of Quintus in their programming.'

'So you're going to let the volunteers die?'

Agatha's lips thinned. 'We can't risk opening the door again.'

Dom stood up roughly, knocking over his chair. 'We're not going to let them die.'

'They won't die. They have resources.'

'You have no idea what that place has become.'

Agatha smiled sadly. 'I have an idea. We lost good people when Quintus took over this base. He got control of the weapons system. People died trying to protect this place.'

'And people have died in the Region trying to get us away from the Collective.' Anya's lower lip wobbled. 'My parents and my brother died in their attempts to keep us safe. Don't let their sacrifice be for nothing.'

Agatha's gaze sharpened. 'So you understand more than most why we can never open up access to the Region again.'

That wasn't what she meant. She needed Agatha to see reason. 'Not all the Copies listen to Quintus. Some have developed independent thoughts.'

'Like Quintus did.'

'Copies who've rebelled against him. A couple of them helped us to escape Praesidium.'

Agatha's eyes widened a fraction. But then she shook her head. 'We can't take that risk. If we expose our systems to him again, we risk losing not only the military base but the entire city on this side.'

This couldn't be the end.

Anya stared at Agatha, hoping to see some remorse. Her hardened gaze told her all she needed to know.

'What are you saying?'

The commander said, 'Mourn your friends and be grateful you made it this far.'

26

Carissa

The sound of soft whimpering woke Carissa. She bolted upright and rubbed her eyes. As a Copy sleep was sporadic, but ever since she'd left the city she'd found herself falling into a regular sleeping habit.

She'd had the strangest dream. The Inventor had been waving at her as he walked away. She'd run after him, but the harder she'd tried to catch up, the farther away he'd gotten. She shook the feeling of abandonment away with a shiver.

118-C, sitting on the floor next to the workbench, watched her curiously. She wore her medic uniform—white tunic and trousers with red trim on the collar and cuffs—and had her feet pulled under her.

Carissa blinked. 'How long was I out for?'

'It's morning,' said the medic.

She looked around. 'I heard whimpering.'

'It came from you.' 118-C stared at her. 'How can you sleep?'

'It's what the humans do, so I do, too.'

118-C touched the discs in her head. 'The upload rooms are all I know. I don't know how to exist without them.'

That's what Carissa had thought, too, when they'd escaped the city. She smiled and repeated what the Inventor had said to her. 'Don't worry. I'll help you.'

Remembering her dream, she scanned the workshop for the Inventor, breathing out when she saw him and Thomas sitting in one corner. Thomas had his pencil and paper out and was showing him something. Vanessa and Charlie sat in another corner, looking tired and ready to try a new idea. But this remained their best chance at escape.

The last thing Carissa remembered was seeing the Inventor and Thomas hooking 118-C up to the monitoring machine a second time. She must have fallen asleep during it.

'Did they find anything new about where Quintus went?'

118-C shook her head. 'But it's possible one of the Copies downloaded him and the other nine, and is keeping them safe until we leave. That's probably why the Great Hall is under protection, for when they return.'

The thought hadn't occurred to Carissa. Knowing Quintus could still be on this side filled her with relief. 'We can't let him upload in this city again.'

'I agree. He's always had too much control over the Collective.'

'Over all of us.'

The Inventor let out a deep, frustrated sigh. Carissa had become attuned to his noises and what each one meant.

She got to her feet and walked over to him. 'What did you find out?'

'Not much, miss. 118-C's recollections have been interfered with.'

'By whom? The Collective?'

'Who else could it be?' He sighed again. 'I'm afraid I can't shed light on where the Collective is hiding out, or find information on the Beyond.'

Carissa's dream of abandonment hit her again. Her heart pumped fast and set her hands shaking. This was it. Everything that had happened—that was happening—would push her away from the Inventor.

But perhaps, for this plan to work, it demanded that Carissa let him go. Perhaps, to get out of this mess, she needed to make a sacrifice. A sacrifice could work. And that terrified her.

But the Collective's unknown whereabouts still bothered her.

She turned to 118-C. 'What happened in the days after our escape?'

118-C frowned at the ground, then at her. 'I don't remember.'

'I've been hearing Quintus in my head these last few days. Is there a way he could be on a separate network?'

118-C considered it, then shook her head slowly. 'I'm not sure.'

Carissa turned to the Inventor next, refusing to give up. 'What about the frequencies? Could we determine where Quintus is hiding from those? Maybe he can lead us to the rest of the Collective.'

The Inventor nodded slowly, like the idea might work. 'We could try.'

He gestured for Carissa to sit in the seat next to the diagnostic machine.

She did and he hooked her up to the machine. She settled back in the worn, leather chair and huffed out a breath. 'There must be some trail his communications have left that can lead us to him. We can't leave this place without knowing where he is.'

The Inventor and Thomas crowded around her. Vanessa and Charlie joined them. The presence of all four plunged her into deep shadow. 118-C got to her feet but stood back, looking uneasy about the new attention on Carissa. In some strange way, their proximity made Carissa feel safe—loved, even. And for that, she would do anything she could to protect them.

Thomas jabbed his finger at the screen. 'Look, there's a second frequency showing up. One is yours. I assume the other belongs to Quintus.'

'Only one?' Carissa asked, leaning forward.

The Inventor double-checked and nodded.

Her hope deflated. 'That means Quintus has found a way to separate himself from the other nine.'

She sat back with a sigh. They had run out of time to find them.

118-C drew nearer to the machine. 'Are you saying the others are gone?'

'It's possible.' The Inventor frowned at the machine. 'The frequency trail went cold some time yesterday.'

That information tied in with when Carissa had stopped hearing him. 'I thought he might attempt reconnection, but I've heard nothing.'

The Inventor drew back from the machine in alarm.

Carissa's part-organic heart thundered loudly in her chest. 'What is it?'

He slid his eyes to her. 'Communication stopped around the time we attempted to cross over to the Beyond.'

Vanessa said, 'I don't understand. Do you think the scanner above the door might have disabled his connection to Carissa?'

'It's possible,' said Charlie.

No, that's not what the Inventor was saying. Her hands shook and her breathing quickened.

'Miss?'

She turned away from him, not ready to believe it. Her stomach churned. Her skin burned with a sudden fever. This was just... like... a panic attack.

The Inventor gripped her arm. 'What's wrong, miss?'

She looked up at him, eyes wide. Her mouth opened and closed but no words came.

She swallowed. 'I think... I know where Quintus is.'

'Where?'

Her voice was barely a whisper. 'H-he found a way to cross. Using me.'

The Inventor straightened up. 'There's no evidence to say he's left the city. It's more possible the scanner disabled him as he attempted to hitch a ride on your connection.'

Carissa swayed as she stood. She gripped the back of the chair. 'You don't understand what he's capable of. He's... obsessed with the Originals. He ordered extra testing on Dom... when the other nine didn't want to. H-he pushed the boundaries of learning so he could understand human behavior.'

Vanessa said, 'It's still possible he never made it across and he was disabled.'

Carissa marched over to 118-C, pulled her over to the chair and sat her down in it. 'She'll know.'

118-C blinked. 'But I don't remember anything.'

'We have Quintus' frequency. We can use it to see what activities he had an interest in and what he ignored. The Collective talked about behavior modifications. It was successful with Julius. I don't know if the Ten had time to modify anyone else.'

The Inventor shrugged at the medic. 'It can't hurt.'

118-C allowed him to hook her up to the machine again.

He squinted at the screen. 'I can see his signature. He checked in when you visited one of the labs in the medical facility.'

118-C nodded. 'The labs are used for surgical procedures.'

'Maybe he was removing information from Julius,' said Charlie. 'He spent months with Max and me. He amassed a lot of knowledge.'

'Wait, there's a snippet of transcript here,' said the Inventor.

'What does it say?'

'He's asking, "Is it done?" And you replied, "Yes."'

118-C frowned at the floor. 'I don't remember speaking with him.'

Carissa worried the procedure hadn't been completed on another Copy, but on someone closer to home. 'His signature disappeared when the others passed into the Beyond. Only two people from that group could have been in surgery that day. Jerome or Alex.'

The others stared at her.

'What are you saying?' asked the Inventor.

'That Quintus successfully inserted a behavior modification in either Jerome or Alex, and that he hijacked it.' She pushed past 118-C on the chair. 'We have to open the door to the Beyond, now!'

The Inventor pulled her back. 'Don't work yourself up, miss. We can't reach it, not while the Copies occupy the Great Hall.'

Carissa stared at 118-C, who was busy looking at nothing. She'd thought she'd have at least one solution.

Carissa shoved her shoulder. 'How do we get past the Copies in the Great Hall without disabling them?'

118-C lifted her gaze. 'I don't know.'

Anger swelled in her chest. She marched to the exit, but didn't leave. Quintus was her problem. He had contacted her while she was in the camp. Maybe if she'd spoken up earlier, Julius wouldn't have had time to communicate from the camp back to the Collective. Maybe Max and Jason would still be alive and Alex and Jerome wouldn't have been kidnapped.

She stood by the entrance, looking out into the dark corridor that smelled of damp, and rested her head on the cool rock.

A hand on her back spun her around.

The Inventor leaned over her. 'What is it, miss?'

She looked up at him, her eyes wide. 'It's all my fault.'

'Why do you say that?'

'If it wasn't for me, you all could have exited into the Beyond.'

The Inventor shook his head. 'If it wasn't for

259

you, we wouldn't have made it that far, or we'd still be stuck down there with no way to get past the Copies.'

'Quintus contacted me. He wanted me to help him.' She sniffed. Biogel leaked out of her nose and eyes; she wiped it away with the back of her hand. 'I made it possible for him to escape.'

The old man shook her shoulder. 'No, miss. Even if Alex and Jerome hadn't been taken, it sounds like Quintus would have inserted the behavior modification in someone else—someone we may have rescued and brought with us anyway.'

She looked up at him. 'Really?'

'Yes, really.' He straightened up and looked back at the others. 'We still need to figure out how to get past the door that leads into the Beyond. If we can't, it won't matter if we disable the Copies or not.'

Thomas cleared his throat, catching everyone's attention. 'If the force field on the door is similar to the one that surrounded this city, I might be able to use the Atomizer to punch a hole in the field. Max used it to get inside Arcis. I'm assuming the energy and composition is the same.'

Vanessa said, 'You think it's possible?'

Thomas nodded to 118-C. 'If she's still connected, she may have access to the security files and the frequency the field uses.'

118-C said, 'Of course. I'll help whatever way I can.'

At least they had a partial plan.

'But that still doesn't solve our problem with the guards in the Great Hall,' said Charlie. 'Carissa said the hack wouldn't work a second time.'

Carissa twisted her hands together. She flicked her gaze toward 118-C. 'I have another idea, one that will ensure the Collective or Quintus can never return to this city.' All eyes settled on Carissa, except for 118-C's. 'We can disable the Copies permanently.'

'Is that even possible?' asked Charlie.

Carissa nodded. 'An electromagnetic pulse. It will kill all connections. It's built into our security protocol in case we're ever taken over. A blast of energy will shut everything down, including the network.'

An angry Charlie stepped forward. 'Why didn't you say anything before? We've been stuck down here without a plan.'

118-C said, 'Because it kills the Copies, too.' She glanced at Carissa. 'All of us.'

27

Carissa

'Hold on, let's talk about this for a moment.' The Inventor fanned his hands. 'How do we disable the Copies without hurting Carissa or 118-C?'

Carissa's pulse pounded in her throat. 'We don't.'

The old man strode to the other side of the room. She heard Rover whining through the hole in the retractable roof. He must have heard the raised voices.

The Inventor turned and walked back, fists on hips. 'No, this isn't happening.' He looked at Thomas. 'Can't we try the hack again? All we need is for them to be disorientated long enough for us to slip past.'

118-C's next answer turned the biogel in Carissa's veins to ice. 'My system sensed the hack. There's already a patch in place for the breach. It wouldn't work a second time.'

Carissa clutched to thin hope, but there was only one permanent solution. 'The EMP is the only option left, Jacob.'

The Inventor bent down to her. 'I hear you, miss, but it's not the human way to sacrifice others to save ourselves.'

That was the opposite of what Quintus had taught her: sacrifice was sometimes necessary.

She stared into his pale blue eyes. 'You're not sacrificing me; I'm volunteering. Anya went first through the machine on the ninth floor of Arcis to save Jason and Max. Max gave his life to save others. Warren tried to save Jason.'

The Inventor's lips thinned. 'I don't want you to die, miss.'

She managed a smile, despite the wobble in her lower lip. 'I need to do this. Quintus used me to get to you. I need to make this right.'

'It wasn't your fault.'

'I know.' She wiped her expression clean and looked at 118-C. 'Are you in or out?'

The Copy, who once would have had superiority over her, nodded. 'In.'

Carissa looked at the others: Vanessa, who had always been kind to her; Thomas, who spoke to her like they were equals; Charlie, who had protected Anya and was a friend to Dom and Sheila. She would miss them all.

'Okay, we need to find something that will

deliver an EMP blast, and a place to receive it.'

Thomas pointed up through the gaping hole. 'The tag machines—they're connected to the network. We could deliver a surge to the machine, fry the connection.'

Why did the ideas with the most carnage always deliver the best solution?

'Okay, that's one problem sorted.'

A possible solution to the EMP carrier came to mind. She looked at 118-C and pointed to the chair. 'We need the frequency, the one that controls the energy of the barrier. If we can activate it, we may be able to redirect a surge to the nearest tag station.'

This was the Inventor's space, but today he was unusually quiet. Charlie and Vanessa looked on like a couple of spectators.

With a shake of his head, Charlie moved to stand next to Thomas. 'What can I do?'

'Nothing for now. We just need the frequency.'

'What about using one of the Copies?' 118-C said from the chair. 'Dump an electrical charge into the system to create a feedback loop inside the Copy. It should max out the charge and fry the system.'

Vanessa looked unconvinced. 'Do the Copies have enough amps to blow the city's entire grid?'

So did the Inventor. 'An army of them might, as long as they dump it simultaneously, but it's too risky. We should consider Carissa's idea about the barrier.'

118-C sat back in the chair while the Inventor

fixed the wired discs to her connection points. Carissa stayed by his shoulder, searching the on-screen data for the latest frequency code for the barrier. While she did, she wondered what dying felt like. All her short life she'd wanted to be human. And humans sacrificed themselves for their friends. In the test on the seventh floor of Arcis, Quintus had asked Anya to choose one person to die: Jason or Dom. She'd said neither and picked herself.

Anya's selfless act inspired Carissa now.

'I've located the security file,' said the Inventor.

Carissa checked the numbers on screen. 'Three different codes were used in the last three days.' She pointed to the last one on the list. 'This one should get us access.'

Vanessa frowned. 'If we have the frequency, can't we just reverse the command for the Copies' sentry mode in the Great Hall?'

Carissa wished it were possible. 'The Collective's commands are isolated on a separate network. Quintus didn't trust the Copies.'

Vanessa snorted. 'Figures.'

Thomas jotted down the code on his hand. 'If I can align the Atomizer Gun with the frequency code, it might also work on the force field protecting the door to the Beyond.'

'It's all connected, so it's possible,' said Charlie with a nod.

'Come on,' said Carissa. 'First thing we need to do is reactivate the barrier. Then we need to shoot at it.'

Thomas picked up one of the Electro Guns. 'Will this work?'

'It has a range of about half a kilometer, so no. The barrier is about twice that high up.'

Thomas put the gun down and picked up the Disruptor that Dom had left him. 'This has twice that again.'

'Where do we reactivate the barrier from?' asked Vanessa.

'The tag station should work.' Carissa pointed at the diagnostic machine. 'But we'll need that to issue the command.'

118-C, Vanessa and Thomas dragged the machine up the stairs and to the nearest tag station. The panel was still off from when they'd inserted the hack. With the diagnostic machine connected, it didn't take Carissa long to find the controls for the barrier. She keyed in the frequency and typed in 'yes' when asked if she'd like to reactivate it. A shimmering, translucent barrier slid up the sides of the outer zone and over, meeting in the middle overhead.

'It's up.'

She squinted against the new brightness. It gave the city an artificial look that she hated.

'What now, miss?' said the Inventor.

'When Thomas blasts it, we need to force the energy to loop back on itself. We'll need to disable the safety protocols first. With them in place, the barrier will only absorb any energy burst. It must be allowed to build up to create a surge that will hopefully strike the tag station.'

She keyed in a new command and looked up. The electricity in the barrier bounced around, unrestrained.

'No better time than now, I suppose,' said the Inventor.

He glanced back at Rover and his mate. Both were sitting and watching, their mouths closed, their heads slightly cocked at the sky.

'What will happen to them?' asked Vanessa.

'I don't know,' said the Inventor. His gaze found Carissa briefly. 'They might not survive it.'

Thomas stepped back and drew energy from the tag machine into the Disruptor gun. It shook with new power.

He pointed it up and muttered, 'I hope this works,' before releasing a pulse of energy into the sky.

The blast hit the barrier and created pockets of unstable energy. A strike of lightning shot down from above and pierced the ground.

'Stand back!' warned Thomas.

They took shelter closer to the Learning Center —the tallest building in Praesidium. If a bolt struck, it should hit the building first. Uncontrollable bolts of energy snapped down from the skin of the barrier, striking at random. Then one hit the machine. A crackle from the machine plus a reduction in the brightness drew Carissa's eyes up. The barrier was retreating. A loud pop from the tag machine followed. Smoke billowed out from the panel.

118-C dropped to the ground like a stone. A deep whining came from Rover. Carissa and the Inventor looked back. Rover's mate was down and he was nuzzling her leg.

A pain started in Carissa's head, in the area where she knew her NMC was located. It had repaired enough for her to feel the effects of the surge.

She stumbled back, surprised to still be standing. She must be more separated from the system than she'd thought, unlike 118-C.

The Inventor grabbed her. 'Miss, are you okay?'

She looked up at him and nodded. 'We need to bring the medic with us.'

'It's not possible,' said Vanessa. 'She's still one of them.'

'She sacrificed herself for us. She comes!'

The Inventor looked down at the deactivated medic. 'If we make it to the Beyond, I might be able to fix her.'

Had that idea occurred to him when Carissa had offered herself up as a sacrifice?

He commanded Rover to lie down. Thomas, Vanessa and Charlie dragged 118-C over to him and hoisted her up on his back. Rover stood up, looking restless. He continued to whine for his dead mate.

'Can he fit in the tunnels?' asked Thomas.

'We'll make him fit,' said the Inventor. 'I'm not leaving him here. He won't survive this place alone.'

They crashed through the doors of the Learning Center. A wave of sickness hit Carissa. She hid it with a cough.

The Inventor eyed her. 'Are you sure you're okay?'

She managed a smile. 'Yes.'

They approached the Great Hall, where they discovered a hundred Copies in a heap on the floor.

'Quickly, in case they're not really out.'

Their group picked their way across the bodies and made it to the hidden stairwell. Thomas and Vanessa pulled 118-C off Rover's back; with her as a passenger, there was no way the wolf would fit. They carried 118-C down the stairs.

Carissa's head swam and everything went dark. She steadied herself against the rough wall. A gasp escaped her lips.

'What is it, miss?'

'I can't see.'

She groped for the walls, finding the cool rock first, followed by something warm and steady.

'Take my arm.'

Her breathing became more labored with each step.

'The wolf won't fit,' said Charlie.

'Boy, make yourself smaller,' the Inventor instructed.

Rover whined behind her as Carissa made her way slowly down the steps.

'It's working,' said Charlie.

Carissa concentrated on what was ahead. Her organic heart hammered her ribs. Something wasn't right. A new pain ripped through her skull and brought her to her knees.

'Miss! Hold on.'

Someone lifted her up—the Inventor, she presumed—and carried her. He no longer smelled of grease and oil, but of lemon soap.

'Thomas, get started on bypassing that damn force field.'

'On it,' shouted Thomas from below.

Carissa heard sounds all around her. Her breaths shortened in the Inventor's arms.

In a whisper, she said, 'Put me down, please?'

The wolf whined behind her. Her feet found flat ground. Rover nudged her on with his nose. At least he'd made it here, wherever *here* was in the tunnel.

'I can feel the barrier,' said Thomas, sounding close.

The air crackled as he fired at something. The Atomizer, she presumed, that would punch a hole in the defense wall.

Carissa heard a *clink clunk* and a large door open.

'That wasn't me,' said Thomas sounding panicked.

Carissa's heart pounded harder. They were

coming for them. This time, her friends would make it.

'How did you get the door open?' said the Inventor.

Another surge of electricity hit her NMC connector and made her hands shake.

This was it. The end.

'Goodbye, Jacob,' she whispered.

All noises drifted away.

28

Dom

Agatha's confession rocked Dom to the core. In a haze of numbness, he shuffled back to the dorm with Anya. She was biting her nails, looking as calm as he felt.

He pulled her to a stop. 'It's not true. It can't be.'

She popped one finger out of her mouth. 'I... don't know.'

His failure to lead returned to haunt him again. He'd insisted they find this place. Now, their group was separated and Agatha was feeding them a pack of lies to keep their people apart.

He combed his fingers through the longer section of hair on the top of his head. Charlie had styled his hair a few days ago.

His throat tightened. Charlie. And Vanessa. Both stuck in the Region dealing with who knew what.

'What do we do?'

He searched Anya's eyes for the answer, and to borrow some of her strength. The fire in them had died a little after Agatha's chat.

'I don't know, Dom,' she said, meeting his gaze hesitantly. His hope flittered away. 'I... don't know what to think right now.'

'Should I tell the others?'

'Yeah. You have to.'

He took her hand. Her grip was weak, unsure. But when he looked down at their hands she gripped harder, as if she didn't want him to know she was struggling.

'Let's go,' she said.

They entered the dorm they'd left twenty minutes ago. Everyone was still asleep. Anya closed the door softly.

'We need to wake them,' she whispered in the dark. 'This news can't wait.'

'Agreed.'

Anya flicked on the light and they went around the room, gently rocking the others awake. Dom woke Sheila last.

She groaned and looked up at him through two slits. 'What are you doing?'

'Sheila, I need you to get up.'

'Get up?' She nestled deeper under the covers. 'Leave me alone, ass munch.'

He ripped the covers from her. She bolted

upright. 'Hey! I could be naked under here.'

She wore her clothes from the day before; the pair of borrowed pajamas was still folded on the end of her bed.

'Please, Sheila. This is important.'

Sheila huffed and sat up properly. Imogen, in the bed next to her, became alert.

The others shook off their lethargy with collective groans. Dom saw some of the younger soldiers had opted for the borrowed clothes. It must have given them a sense of normality to wear something other than rebel gear. Seeing everyone enjoying their newfound freedom ripped his heart in half. He wished he had better news to share, that he and Anya weren't about to shatter their hopes.

'What's going on?' asked June.

She had Frahlia in the bed with her. The strange, little girl stirred and stretched. She made no sounds, not even a whimper or a cry. He wondered if Agatha knew the truth about her.

Alex stirred in the next bed. Jerome was on the last bed at the end of their row. He sat up with a frown.

All eyes were on Dom; it quickened his pulse. He had no idea how to do this. Anya stood in the middle of the room. Her hands were two fists, as though she were using them to keep her true emotions back. When he rejoined her, her fists unclenched and her hard look softened.

How had Max managed to do this, to speak to a

room full of people relying on him to keep them safe?

Dom cleared his throat. 'We had a chat with Agatha just now.'

Jerome stood up. 'And? What did she say?'

Dom told them what the Beyond and the Region were, according to Agatha.

Jerome frowned. 'What does that even mean?'

'It means she could be lying to keep us here.' said Anya. 'Or she could be telling us the truth.'

June said, 'What's wrong with staying here? Why would we want to go back to the Region anyway? The machines were trying to kill us.'

Sheila had that look on her face, the one that said she didn't trust people. 'And Agatha just blurted it out?'

'Yeah.'

'Why?'

Dom blinked. 'I don't know.'

Anya said, 'She told us after we demanded she open the door and bring the others across.'

June frowned at Anya. 'I don't understand. She promised it would open today.'

'And she said just now it wouldn't be opening again. That it was too risky.'

Alex stood and jabbed a finger at the room. 'That's bull. We have to open it again!'

Dom looked at Frahlia. The little girl was staring at Alex, slightly pulled back from him.

A hardened soldier stood up. 'What do we do?'

Dom shoved his hands into his pockets and

answered honestly. 'I don't know.'

'You can't leave them in the Region. We barely got out alive.'

'It's possible they haven't survived,' said one of the younger soldiers.

'So we leave them to die without knowing for sure?' Sheila growled at him. She turned to Dom. 'We have to get that door open. You know we do.'

'I'm with Sheila,' said Jerome.

He'd been quiet up until now, not offering much of an opinion.

Dom sat on the edge of the bed and buried his face in his hands. Around him, the others discussed their predicament. Their strained voices made it hard to focus. The bed dipped beside him. A familiar, warm hand on his calmed his racing heart.

Anya bent her neck and looked into his eyes. 'It's going to be okay, Dom.'

Her beautiful, blue eyes. Their time at Arcis came rushing back to him. The tests, the trials. The battle in the landscape. They'd almost died. But they hadn't. Against the odds, they'd survived. Max had given his life to save them. Jason had, too. Their deaths had not been in vain. They'd found the Beyond. But they hadn't all made it. And that was on him.

'Charlie and Vanessa doubted I could do this. Maybe they were right.'

She shifted round to face him. 'Charlie and Vanessa are stuck on the other side. They're relying

276

on you to help them.'

He kissed her lips, needing to feel more than her hand. She sagged against him.

Pulling away, she said, 'You've got this, Dom. You always have.'

With a nod, he stood. 'We need to find a way to open the door.'

Alex smiled. 'I might be able to disable the security in this place. I found a backdoor into their program last night.'

They could do with all the help they could get.

'Do it.'

Anya's brief nod at Dom gave him the reassurance he needed. This was the right call, despite what Agatha had said. For all he knew, she could be lying. And one thing was certain: He would not leave the others to die.

Ω

Before Alex had slipped out of the room, he'd told Dom that disabling the security wouldn't take long. Dom had sent one of the soldiers with him.

But it did take long. An hour longer than Dom had been prepared to wait.

The soldier had returned ten minutes ago, but without Alex. He'd said Alex was right behind him, but when the Breeder didn't show, Dom readied to go after him.

Preparing to leave, he told the others to wait. At

the door, he'd barely touched the handle when it moved on its own and the door opened.

Finally.

Except it was one of Agatha's men.

'This room is on lockdown.'

Anya stood up sharply. 'Why?'

Dom backed up to the bed and caught her wrist.

'One of you was caught trying to disable the security system,' said the base soldier.

Alex.

'That makes all of you a threat.'

Anya pulled out of Dom's grip. 'Please, let us speak to Agatha. We can straighten this out.'

'No.'

The soldier closed the door. Dom heard the *clunk clink* of a lock being turned. Anya rushed to try the handle. The door wouldn't open.

Dom rounded on the soldier who'd made it back. 'What the hell happened?'

His eyes were wide, his face flushed. 'Alex was in the control room. I-I was keeping guard. He told me to head back, that he was right behind me. He must have triggered an alarm.'

A worried June pleaded with Dom. 'Do something. He was trying to help us.'

He squeezed her arm. 'I will. I promise.'

But Anya had an odd look on her face.

'What is it?'

She looked up at him before her gaze flicked to June, then away. 'I saw Alex last night. He was in the

278

control room doing the same thing he said he would today. Except, then, he didn't trigger any alarms.'

'They must have different security during the day, that's all,' said June hotly.

Her cheeks flushed red. 'I guess that's it.'

The door opened again and an irate Agatha entered the room. Her furious gaze landed on Dom.

'You and you'—she pointed at Anya—'come with me.'

Dom took Anya's hand. He glanced back to see June was glaring at Anya. Dom gave her a reassuring smile.

They followed Agatha and her soldiers out and into the corridor. All he could hear was the beat of his heart and the thick, echoing thud of military-grade boots pounding the concrete floor. The sounds changed to sharp clanging when those boots hit the steel stairs leading to Agatha's office.

Agatha entered the room first, but one of the soldiers stopped Dom from following.

'When she's ready, not before.'

After a minute, Agatha called out, 'Send them in.'

They entered the room. A visibly distraught Agatha paced the room.

She stopped at the desk and turned to face them. 'What the hell have you people done?'

'What are you talking about? We've done nothing.'

'We've just had a security breach.'

He played dumb. 'I'm not sure what that has to do with—'

'The one called Alex?' Agatha glared at him. 'He was in the control room. At your insistence, I presume?'

Dom said nothing.

Anya spoke up. 'If something's happened, it's your fault. We told you we needed to open the door to the Region. We have people trapped on the other side.'

Agatha folded her arms. Her lips thinned. 'You don't understand what's happening here, do you? A security breach is a big deal in this place.'

Anya smiled. 'Open the door and we promise not to touch your security again.'

'You're not listening to me, girl. You never were good at listening. Your *Alex* has uploaded something extra into our systems.'

'What?'

'A virus.' Agatha perched on the desk's edge. 'You brought something back with you, something that could destroy this base and our city.'

'Alex did that?' said Dom.

Other than Frahlia acting strange around him, he'd seen nothing odd about the former Breeder.

But when Anya fell quiet, his blood ran cold.

'What is it?' he asked.

She looked up at him with round eyes and he suddenly felt sick.

'When Thomas and I freed Alex in the medical

facility, I thought there was something off about him. Then Frahlia didn't take to him.'

His breath caught in his throat. 'In what way was he off?'

'He was too excited by Frahlia. I put it down to my not knowing him all that well. I'm sorry. I should have said something.'

He rubbed her back. 'It's okay.'

'No, it's not,' said Agatha. 'None of this is okay.'

There had to be a way to fix this. 'What can we do?'

Agatha pushed off from the desk. 'We need to evacuate the base, cut the systems off from the rest of the network. Find a way to fight this enemy again.'

Enemy? Again?

His stomach flipped. 'You think it's Quintus?'

'I know it is.'

'Let us open the door. We have people on the other side that can help. We have the man who was the Inventor for Praesidium. Please.'

'No, it's too dangerous.'

'At least let us try. We didn't bring Quintus across willingly.'

Agatha pursed her lips. 'The damage is done. The one entity we wanted to keep out is now here. We can't risk rebooting the security to open the door.'

Dom had another idea. He held up his arm. 'If you agree to it, we may not need to reboot your system.'

Agatha's eyes widened. 'What are you going to do?'

'You wanted to study my tech? Well, here's your first chance. I'm going to open the door with it.'

But Agatha looked unconvinced. 'Then what?'

'You let the others pass and you can ask me whatever you want. Study me however you want.'

Anya turned sharply. 'Dom, no!'

He smiled at her. 'It's okay. I'm not afraid anymore.' He looked at Agatha. 'What do you say?'

'Do you really have someone who can help?'

He nodded.

Her expression relaxed. She strode over to the door and opened it, to speak to the soldiers. 'Get a team to the door. We're going to try opening it.'

'But it's on lockdown,' said the wide-eyed soldier.

'I know. Just do it.'

She turned back to Dom. 'Let's see your tech in action.'

Agatha led the way and Dom followed, taking the stairs two at a time to the ground floor. He heard Anya's lighter, hesitant steps behind him.

This would work. He would use Quintus' technology against him.

Agatha moved fast and he was tempted to outrun her and reach the door first. But he stayed back; he couldn't risk losing this opportunity.

They arrived at the heavy, steel door. Five armed soldiers guarded it. They parted when Agatha approached them.

She turned to Dom. 'The door is shut tight. You're going to need all the power you can muster.'

Behind him, more soldiers filled the area. One held a grappling hook. He glanced back and saw the wire led back to the bay area. Probably attached to one of the trucks there.

'If you can get the door open partially, the grappling hook and truck will do the rest,' said Agatha. She paused. 'Are you sure you can do this?'

Dom held up his arm. He hadn't tested the strength all that much, but he couldn't think of a better reason to use it.

'No, but I'm going to try.'

He tugged on the handle of the door and leaned back into it. His body quivered with the force. The door groaned, but he felt it shift, if only a few millimeters. A pain radiated up into his shoulder socket and lit his muscles on fire.

'Dom, you don't have to do this,' said Anya.

'I'm okay.'

He kept tugging, because his body was all he really had control over. If Quintus was here, Dom would make him pay for everything he'd done to him.

The door loosened a little more. One of the soldiers wedged the hook in the crack. The slack wire snapped tight and instantly lightened the load. Despite the blaze in his muscles, Dom continued to add his effort to it. With one last heave, the door creaked open.

On the other side was the Inventor. His white hair was disheveled and he had a wild look in his eyes. He held Carissa in his arms.

'How did you get the door open?' Jacob said.

Dom stared at an unconscious Carissa. 'What the hell happened?'

'She sacrificed herself to save us.'

Agatha blocked the new gap, which was getting wider.

Dom said, 'He can help you.'

'But he's holding a Copy.'

Dom readied to shove her back if necessary. 'If you want to solve your problem, this Copy and this man are the answer. But first, we need to help her.'

Agatha stepped back with a huff.

Jacob rushed forward through the gap and into the Beyond. Charlie followed. Vanessa and Thomas carried a medic Dom hadn't seen before. Last, Rover poked his nose in.

'No, absolutely not!' said Agatha.

Dom said, 'It's all of them or none.'

She pursed her lips, then waved her team back. Rover pushed his shoulder against the door to widen it. The soldiers in the corridor cringed back from the beast that squeezed into the corridor. Rover growled and assessed the strangers. Jacob said something to him and he whined.

Agatha blinked in surprise.

'He controls the beast,' said Anya.

'How?'

'He built him.'

All eyes were on Jacob and Carissa.

The Inventor looked like he was losing his grip on her. 'I need to get her help.'

Agatha resumed command. 'Dom tells me you're the only one who can help us with our problem.'

'What problem?'

'Quintus is here.'

Jacob looked down at the limp body in his arms. 'She can speak to him.'

Agatha ordered her soldiers to alert the doctors. 'In that case, follow me.'

The wire for the hook slackened. Dom heard the door suck shut behind him.

Jacob carried Carissa while Thomas and Vanessa followed with the second Copy. Dom took her from them and slung her over his shoulder.

Anya gasped. 'It's my medic. The one who helped us to escape.'

'She helped us to kill the Copies,' said Vanessa. 'We owe her and Carissa our lives.'

'All of them?' he asked, wondering about his former Copy guard.

'As good as dead,' said Vanessa.

Dom carried the female medic down a corridor and into a room that Agatha gestured to, setting her down on a bed. It was the same room he'd been in for his examination with the doctor. Men and women in lab coats watched nervously as the new group took over.

Agatha clicked her fingers at the doctors, pointing to Jacob. 'Give this man what he needs.'

The people in lab coats rushed over to the table with Carissa on it. 'What can we do?'

Jacob looked frazzled, as though he didn't know where to start. 'Get me a diagnostic machine. I need to see what's going on in her brain.'

'Does she have an NMC?'

He nodded. 'It's been disabled. But it could still be working.'

One of the men pulled a machine over. Dom stood back, not wanting to get in the way.

Anya slipped her hand into his. 'It's going to be okay. They'll get her working and she'll help to fight Quintus.'

Dom shook his head. 'I should have picked up on what Alex had planned.'

'I spent a week with him. I knew him better than most. The second I picked up on his odd behavior, I should have said something.'

Dom didn't want to think about Anya's week with the Breeder. It had been an intimate one. But he understood they had both been under the influence of Rapture, a powerful attraction drug. And none of that mattered now.

He turned his attention to the table, stepping closer. A new machine was beside the bed. Wires from it had been connected to Carissa's discs. He released Anya's hand. 'Will she be okay?'

Thomas stood by Jacob's shoulder. 'Anything I can do...?'

Jacob didn't answer either of them. He squinted at the data on the machine's screen, one fist on his hip, the other on the table.

'Her NMC is fried and it's interfering with her circuitry.' He backed away from the table. 'I don't know how to reactivate her.'

One of the lab people stepped forward. 'We can replace it.'

Jacob looked up sharply. 'With what?'

'A new NMC.'

Jacob blinked. 'How? You don't even know what you're dealing with.'

Agatha said, 'We do. The NMCs came from here. As did Quintus.'

Vanessa pressed a hand to her mouth.

Charlie gasped. 'How is that possible?'

Dom looked at the pair. 'I'll explain later. Right now we have a serious problem and Carissa might be the only one who can help.'

But as the team worked on Carissa, he couldn't be sure she'd ever wake up.

29

Carissa

Warmth spread through her head. Her ocular implants began to water. A deep surge of pain hit her NMC and she screamed, but no sound came. Carissa had never experienced death before, but at least it contained familiar sounds and feelings.

She thought she heard the Inventor say, 'We need you, miss,' but it must have been a residual memory.

It surprised her that death hurt so much.

She fluttered her eyes open, seeing a brightness that instantly reduced them to two slits. This must be Copy heaven; it reminded her of Praesidium. A low hum of voices reached her ears. Just mumbles with no clarity.

Carissa blinked away the confusion. A group of people dressed in white stood in a huddle next to her. Copies. They had to be. But a familiar, old man was with them with his back to her.

A residual memory. That's all it was

'Inv—' She cleared her throat and tried again. 'Inventor.'

The vision of her friend turned and pushed the people in white away. He was grinning. The pleasant memory warmed her biogel. Although, she didn't remember him smiling that widely before.

'I thought I told you to call me Jacob.'

His voice came through clearer now. All their voices did.

Her part-organic heart thrummed in her chest as she realized. 'I... I'm alive?'

The Inventor nodded.

She licked her lips. Last thing she remembered was passing out at the door. 'Did... we make it?'

He nodded. Her eyes found the others. She saw them clearer now. Men and women dressed in white lab coats stared at her, their expressions serious. None of them were any Copies she'd seen before.

She blinked at the Inventor. 'What's going on?'

The old man's smile dropped away; he drew his brows forward. 'Quintus is here and he's in the control systems.'

She sat up so fast her head spun.

The Inventor grabbed her. 'Easy, miss.'

She swung her legs over the edge of the bed. 'I have to stop him.'

His smile was back. 'That's what I was hoping you'd say.'

Carissa touched the connection point to her NMC. A familiar buzz sounded in her head that made her heart beat faster. 'Is my NMC fixed?'

'Yes. Agatha's team were able to fix it.'

'Agatha?'

Dom stepped forward. 'There's no time to lose, Jacob. We need to get to work.'

She hadn't even seen him in the room. Anya was with him. A dark-skinned person stood next to the pair, wearing an electric-blue pant suit.

She stepped forward and thrust out her hand. 'I'm Agatha. Nice to meet you.'

Carissa shook her hand tentatively, uncomfortable about the attention her death—and resurrection—had caused. But all she could think was that Quintus was here.

He'd followed her somehow.

It was time to silence him once and for all.

She jumped off the bed. 'Tell me what I need to do.'

Agatha clasped her hands together. 'Jacob tells me you spoke to him through your NMC, more than the other Copies did.'

She nodded. For some reason, Quintus was fixated with her. 'He found a way to communicate with me separately.'

'Well, he's here inside my compound, and we need to stop him.'

Carissa didn't know how exactly. She looked up at Jacob. 'Should I try talking to him using my

NMC?'

'That would be a good start, miss.'

She closed her eyes, but opened them just as fast. 'What should I say?'

'Ask him where he is,' said Agatha.

She closed her eyes again and reopened them. 'Then what?'

'Concentrate, miss. You know how to speak to him.'

Carissa closed her eyes once more. The second she tried her NMC, she sensed him. The connection sent a shiver through her.

'173-C,' Quintus said. 'Where have you been? I've been looking for you.'

'I've been... busy.'

'Trying to escape?'

'Yes, trying to help my friends to escape.'

'I can feel you. You made it to the Beyond.'

Carissa opened her eyes and held her breath. Agatha had a walkie talkie in her hand.

She whispered to Carissa, 'Distract him.'

She kept her eyes open and focused on the Inventor. He had his arms folded and a worried look on his face. It didn't matter what Agatha had planned for her later; only her success mattered now.

'Where are you, Quintus?'

The ethereal voice said, 'I'm everywhere.'

'Where are the other Collective?'

Quintus laughed lightly. 'There was only ever me.'

She looked at Agatha, who rolled her hand to keep going. She flashed her eyes to the Inventor. His lips were pursed.

'Only you? I don't understand.'

'I controlled it all, 173-C. The Ten were not separate voices, but personalities I created to help me control Praesidium and the Region. The Collective ten was my protection. If the Copies knew there was only me, it would have diluted the power I had over them.'

Agatha mumbled something into her walkie talkie. She scribbled something down in her notebook and waved her hand at Carissa, to get her attention.

She held up the notebook. It read: *He's in all the primary systems. We need him in a secondary one. We can create a firewall around him there.*

Carissa nodded.

Quintus spoke. 'Are they using you to distract me?'

She answered honestly. 'Yes.'

'I have control of their base now. I used to live here. They tried to take it from me once, but not again.'

'What do you plan to do with it?'

'Make it my new Praesidium.'

She didn't see how that was possible. 'It won't be like the city, Quintus. There are no Copies here.'

The Inventor scribbled a message on a notepad and held it up. It read: *What is he planning?*

Quintus answered her. 'I don't need Copies,

173-C. I can control the humans through the environmental controls.'

'They can leave.'

'I control the doors, too.'

She grabbed the notepad and scribbled: *new city.*

The Inventor's eyes widened when he read it. He showed it to Agatha, who spoke immediately to the people on the other end of her walkie talkie.

'Why are you doing this, Quintus?'

She heard a laugh. 'You used to follow my direction once. It's actually a good thing that you've made it to the Beyond. I can also sense 118-C. Follow me again, 173-C. The three of us can make this compound ours.'

Agatha grabbed the notepad and scribbled something down.

Carissa said, 'I want to stay with my friends.'

'Your friends can stay here,' Quintus replied.

'That's not what I meant...'

Agatha shoved the notepad under her nose with a note that read: *Get him to environmental controls.*

She mouthed, *How?*

Agatha pretended to choke then jabbed her finger at Carissa.

'173-C, are you there? What are the humans asking you to do?'

'Quintus... what are you doing to the air? I-I can't breathe.'

She faked a panic attack, similar to the ones she

had when something upset her.

The Inventor watched her closely. Others did, too, but she saw only two people.

A frowning Agatha rolled her hand at her.

Carissa's voice grew louder. 'Quintus, please... I can't... breathe.'

'I am not doing anything to the environmental controls. Breathe, 173-C. You are simply having one of your panic attacks.'

Quintus would have seen her panicked moments in the Inventor's workshop through her downloaded memories. She glanced at the Inventor. He lifted both hands, as if to tell her to do more.

'Quintus! There's something... wrong.' Her voice rose in pitch. 'The humans, they've collapsed around me. My... lungs...'

She sucked in a new breath, but rattled it out.

A silence followed, as though Quintus had gone to check something.

Carissa dropped to the floor for dramatic effect. The Inventor lunged for her.

She waved him away. 'Quintus! Hurry! The air...'

Agatha whispered into her walkie talkie.

Quintus came back online. 'The environmental controls are operating as normal. Oxygen levels are normal. What's happening there, 173-C?'

Carissa waved her hand at Agatha.

'Go,' she hissed into the walkie talkie.

A moment passed, then Quintus said, 'What are

you doing, 173-C? Why can't I get out?'

The Inventor helped her to her feet.

Carissa brushed non-existent dirt from her clothes and spoke to the entity who had acted like her father in her early months. 'It's for your own good.'

'No, 173-C. What are you doing? Tell them to let me out.' He shouted in her head. 'Let me out!'

A warm buzz started in her mind. It made her feel lightheaded.

'Tell them to stop what they're doing,' said Quintus. He sounded panicked. 'Or I'll kill you.'

The dizziness in her head became worse and she dropped to her knees. 'I can't.'

The Inventor went to help her, but Agatha stopped him. Carissa looked up at the pair through her tears.

'The antiviral attack needs time to work on all entities connected to Quintus,' Agatha said to the Inventor. 'That means her.'

Carissa's eyes grew heavy. 'Jacob...'

He knelt down and held her hand. 'It's okay, miss. I'm here.'

'Am I dying?'

'I don't know, miss.' He released a hard breath. 'Is Quintus gone?'

She reached out for their connection. 'I can't hear him anymore.'

Agatha spoke into the walkie talkie before turning back to them. 'The antiviral attack has completed on his original, hard-coded files, but we need to do the same on any start-up routine to prevent his program from enabling again.'

'How long will that take?'

'As long as necessary.'

The dizziness in her head swelled and she slumped against the Inventor's chest. His arms pressed against her back.

'I'm sorry,' she whispered.

His voice rumbled in her ear. 'For what?'

'For trusting Quintus. For not helping you to escape the city sooner.'

He pushed her away and smiled through tears of his own. 'It's not your fault.' He looked up and growled, 'Do something. Help her.'

Agatha bent down. 'We can reverse the effects of the memory purge but she won't be the same.'

Carissa's heart slowed to a beat every few seconds. 'Jacob?'

'Yes, miss?'

'I love you.'

He smiled down at her. 'I love you, too.'

Unfamiliar warmth flooded through her. Death wasn't all that bad. She closed her eyes and allowed the hand of death to carry her to the next plane.

30

Anya

The tension in the compound deflated like a balloon. For the first time since they arrived, Anya didn't feel like a prisoner. Agatha had come to get them an hour ago. She'd taken Anya and Dom on a tour of the compound, which wasn't as big as she'd first thought. While they walked, they passed by more rooms that were being used for testing. She'd come to think of this base as a testing facility.

'What are you going to do with Frahlia?'

'My medical team has deemed her to be no threat. She was never connected. Neither was Jerome. I see no reason to keep either of them here for the long term.'

That surprised Anya. 'I thought you'd jump at the chance to study them.'

Agatha just smiled, as if there was more to the story.

'And Carissa, and the Copy medic?'

'Once we're certain Quintus is no longer an issue, we will initiate a hard reset on both of them. It will wipe their knowledge, including whatever deep-program commands Quintus gave them. We have synthetics living in the city, so they can be programmed with new personalities and given new lives that have no connection to the network.'

Another mystery.

'So they won't die?'

'They won't be who they were before, so in a way they do die, but are reborn anew.'

They walked on farther. Agatha ended the tour at a large, closed door spanning at least twenty feet up and ten across.

'What's past there?'

Agatha hesitated. 'The Sect.'

'A city?'

Agatha nodded. Anya waited for her to show them, but she said, 'I'll show you soon, I promise. But first, we need to talk.'

'When?'

'After we've reset the Copies.'

The Sect. The Beyond. The Region. Agatha had only shared snippets of what had happened to create the latter. The Region had been her life. Did she really want to know how she'd ended up there?

But the commander's veiled hints at her former life intrigued her. 'I'd like to see the Sect now, if that's okay.'

Agatha slid her hands in the front pockets of her trousers. She wore a royal-blue suit, a color that exactly matched the jumpsuits the workers had to wear in the food factories in Essention. Where Jason used to work.

A lump lodged in her throat.

'Later. The Sect is not what you will be expecting.' Agatha walked away from the door. 'Come on. I'll take you back.'

Anya and Dom followed her back into the compound. Anya tried to remember the positives. Her friends were okay; that's all that mattered.

But she wanted to know the whereabouts of two people in particular.

'Did two people arrive here, last name Hunt?'

Agatha looked back at her and nodded. 'About four months ago. Why?'

She glanced up at Dom. 'We knew their son.'

Agatha smiled. 'They'll be glad to hear. Not many who cross still have family alive.'

'He didn't make it.'

Dom rubbed small circles on her back. She felt the tension in his hand.

Agatha said softly, 'I'll tell them.'

'Can you also tell them something else?'

Agatha stopped and looked at her.

The words wouldn't come. What did she want to say about the boy who'd been so desperate to succeed he'd tried to rape her? His parents abandoning him had damaged him psychologically;

he'd used everyone around him. She could see that now.

Agatha waited for her answer.

'Tell them he died a hero and they should have trusted him with the truth.'

Anything else was in the past, where it belonged.

Dom leaned closer to her ear. 'You're a bigger person than me.'

Agatha gave a tight nod. 'I've got some work to do. You two okay on your own?'

It wasn't like there were many places to venture in the Beyond. But there was one place she wanted to go.

'Is Alex being released soon?'

'I hope so. We're taking precautions at the moment. He was able to pass through the door undetected because our scanners did not pick up the chip implant in his head that Quintus had hijacked. We want to make sure Quintus is fully gone.'

'I'd like to see him.'

'That can be arranged.' Agatha lifted her wrist and spoke into it. 'Please give Anya Macklin access to the prisoner.'

She nodded at the pair and walked away, leaving Anya and Dom alone in an echo-filled space.

Dom's deep-brown eyes were filled with worry. 'Do you want me to come with you?'

They were no longer in danger, but she sensed Dom was still unsettled. So was she. Maybe when they left the base for the new city she'd feel different.

Anya shook her head. 'I need to talk to him alone. Do you mind?'

He crooked a smile. 'I'll catch up with Sheila and June.'

Anya placed a hand on his chest. His heart beat was steady, but she felt a slight shake in his body. 'Hey, you got us here to safety. Things are good.'

Dom smiled at her, but it didn't reach his eyes. 'See you soon.'

He walked away.

Anya followed the corridor to a split and took the left turn. It led her to a new area she had only seen with Agatha as part of their tour. It appeared no place was off limits to her now. That put her mind at ease.

She arrived at a room. Outside, two guards were posted.

One said to her, 'Agatha said ten minutes.'

He opened the door and she entered a room that held a single bed and a bedside locker. In one corner was a metal chair. The room was as sparse as the dorms in Arcis had been. The gray blanket on the bed and the white walls reminded her of the unit she and Jason had occupied in Essention.

Alex was sitting on the edge of his bed. He looked up when she entered.

His mouth curved up on one side. 'Hey.'

'Hey, back.' She closed the door and pulled the chair over to the bed. 'How are you feeling?'

Alex smiled sadly. 'Stupid. I almost got

everyone killed.'

She sat down. 'It wasn't your fault. Quintus was using you.'

'I felt him in my head, but I couldn't do anything about it.' He looked at his hands, turned them over. 'He was controlling my thoughts and actions.' He looked at her. 'It was like when we were on Rapture.'

Anya shivered at the memory. 'Carissa sacrificed herself to save us. To save you.'

'What's going to happen to her?'

'Agatha says they're going to wipe her mind and reboot her.'

'Any chance she'll remember us?'

Anya smiled sadly. 'I hope so.'

She had managed to regain her own memories after the machine in Arcis had wiped them. Maybe Carissa's memories would come back to her in the same way.

She nudged his leg with her foot. 'Hey, Agatha says you can leave soon.'

Alex looked around his room with a sigh. 'It may not be the fancy room we had in Praesidium, but it still feels like I'm a damn prisoner.'

'Only while they make sure Quintus is gone.'

'Sure.'

'Agatha says I might have been born in this city, not in Praesidium. That it was impossible to have been born twenty months ago in the Region. That Quintus may have taken me as a boy—teen, I

302

don't know—and turned me into a Breeder.'

'She must have a record of you entering the Region.'

He shook his head. 'She says I may have already been in there when the Region was being set up.'

Anya changed the subject. 'Did June come to see you?'

Alex nodded, looking anywhere but at her. She sensed something was up, that June's visit had not gone as planned.

'What are you three planning after?'

He released a sigh. 'I don't know. Quintus was the one who was happy to see Frahlia, not me. I don't even know if I want kids.'

'And what does June think?'

Alex looked up at her. His eyes glistened with unshed tears. 'There's no question. She wants to keep her, even though, biologically, she's not hers. What should I do?'

It wasn't a decision she could help him with.

'Do what's right for you. Whatever way you choose, I'm sure June will understand.'

Alex blew out a breath. 'I really like June, but I'm also new to this. To the idea of freedom.' He laughed bitterly. 'All I've ever known is my short life in Praesidium. And according to what they told me, I'm not much older than Frahlia or Carissa.'

That was true. Alex had been under the impression he'd matured rapidly using the same growth machine in the medical facility. Without any memories to the contrary, by normal standards, he had barely lived.

She shifted from the chair to sit on the bed next to him, and pulled him into a hug. 'Choose what's right for you.'

He nodded into her hair but pulled back quickly, as if the moment was too much for him.

She stood. 'See you in twenty-four hours.'

Alex grinned, looking more like his old, cheeky self. 'Looking forward to it.'

She left the room with heaviness in her heart. The physical fight might be over but the battle was not yet won. It wasn't a physical battle they faced now, but a psychological one. One that required them to choose what life they wanted. Each of them had been ripped from the only life they'd known and was facing a new future, with new choices.

She walked away from the guards, worried about what the new city might hold. Agatha was delaying its reveal on purpose.

Maybe it was bad. Maybe there was no city and this base was all that remained.

But the prospect of a functioning city and a new life worried Anya more. Because it would force her to face a future she wasn't ready for.

31

Dom

Pain radiated up Dom's arm and into his shoulder. He rotated his arm slowly, still blazing from having pulled open the heavy door to the Region.

Would he do it again? Definitely.

What was the point in having this damn tech if he couldn't put it to good use? All the experiments on him, all the torture the Collective put him through—meaning Quintus—would not be for nothing.

He stood in one of the labs next to Anya, who had her arms folded. Her eyes had narrowed and she was eyeing everything the lab technicians were doing.

Set on two gurneys before them were the Copy medic and Carissa. Both were out, or disabled. Dom wasn't sure which. The technicians hovered around the pair. Jacob barked at one to be careful when he went to move Carissa into a new position.

Dom moved closer, seeing the blank look on

both their faces. It reminded him of the guards in sentry mode in the Great Hall.

Agatha stood next to the lead technician. They chatted in hushed tones.

'We're ready,' said the lead technician finally.

Jacob looked back at him, his brows pulled forward in worry. 'Are you sure she won't feel anything?'

The man in the white coat shook his head. 'It will feel just like waking up.'

He stepped forward and motioned for another to bring a machine over. The second man wheeled it into place. It had a set of wires attached to it, which the doctor connected magnetically to the Copy medic's connection point. He set the machine running. Dom heard a low hum building in intensity, until there was a *snap*. The Copy jolted hard on the table.

Jacob glared at Agatha. 'What's happening?'

'They have their new NMCs. We need to deliver a blast of energy to wake the chips up.'

The Copy medic stirred, her eyes fluttering open. She looked around, clearly startled by the room full of people. She jerked up into a seated position, but the lead technician stopped her.

'Take it easy. Just lie down for a moment.'

The Copy medic did as she was told.

The technician removed the wires and copied the procedure with Carissa. Jacob chewed on his thumb as the energy inside the machine built up and reached a fine point that jolted Carissa's body.

Jacob grabbed her hand, one eye on the machine, the other on Carissa. Carissa opened her eyes, blinking hard against the new light. She looked around.

Jacob lifted her hand and pressed it to his chest. 'Miss, are you okay?'

'I... think so.' She blinked again and looked around at the others. 'Where am I?'

The old man smiled and breathed out. 'You're safe, miss.'

She tried to sit up. The technician stopped her, pulled the wires off her, and she tried again. Jacob helped her to sit.

Dom watched as the girl, dazed and disorientated, took in her surroundings. The Copy medic also sat up and perched on the edge of the gurney. One of the technicians shone a light in both their eyes and asked them basic questions.

'What do you two remember about Praesidium?'

Both of them frowned and Dom saw their eyes move rapidly, as if processing.

The Copy medic answered first. 'I have no memories of such a place existing.'

Carissa answered next. 'Neither do I.'

The lead technician waved a wand over their heads and checked a diagnostic machine. He gave a quick nod.

Agatha seemed to relax.

Dom asked her, 'What's next for them?'

'Now, we give them new programming, which will give them a new life. We need to take them to the upload room.'

Jacob helped Carissa down from the gurney while one of the technicians helped the Copy medic.

'Will she remember anything?' said Jacob to Agatha as one of the technicians took control of Carissa.

'No, I'm sorry. She is a blank, a newborn.'

Jacob's shoulders slumped a little.

Carissa looked up at Jacob and frowned. 'Why are you sad?'

Jacob attempted a smile. 'I'm not sad, miss. I'm happy you're well.'

Dom couldn't bear to look. Before him was a man who had lost a daughter, even if that daughter *had* been a Copy.

Carissa's eyes narrowed at him. 'Why do you call me miss?'

'It's... it used to be your name.'

She cocked her head. 'Like a nickname?'

Jacob nodded.

She nodded back, as if she'd decided something. 'I like it. And I will call you... I will call you...'

She frowned as if stuck on a name.

'You can call me Jacob.'

She smiled. 'Jacob. Nice to meet you.'

The technicians led the pair of Copies out of the room and Jacob went with them. Dom and Anya stayed back with Agatha and two more technicians.

'Will she be okay?' asked Dom.

'Time will tell. She may want to learn about her old life, or she may start anew.'

Agatha looked like she wanted to ask him something.

'What is it?'

'Your tech. Your body is riddled with it.'

Anya slid her hand around his waist. In that moment, he was glad for her support.

'It is.'

'I was wondering if you wanted us to remove it.'

He widened his eyes. 'You can do that?'

Agatha nodded. 'We can do anything here. All the tech that existed in the Region came from here. From Quintus' mind. He learned about it here and replicated it in there.'

Dom had made his peace with it. Agatha had been surprised to see his tech, so he must have had the surgery after he entered the Region, a year ago, and not at age seven. But now she was telling him he could get rid of the tech?

'And replace it with what?'

'Donated human organs. The tech in your arm might be tricky to remove but we can do it, if it's what you want.'

Dom looked down at Anya. 'What do you think?'

She stared up at him with her cobalt-blue eyes.

Their beauty always calmed him, no matter what mood he was in. 'It's not my decision, Dom.'

He took a deep breath and cut his eyes to Agatha. His tech was a reminder of what his father had done, how he'd sold him to Quintus for money. Whatever the real story, it was his last tie to the man.

'Take the tech out.'

'And your arm?'

Dom looked down at it. He flexed it. His shoulder still hurt but other than that, it gave him no trouble.

'I'll keep it.'

32

Anya

A bout of nerves hit Anya in the stomach. She clutched it, in an attempt to settle them. Dom, on the other hand, looked cool. And it wasn't because of his green shirt and black tie. He was a walking refrigerator. She, on the other hand, felt like she'd just jumped from two floors up and landed in a heap.

Sheila entered the dorm room with Imogen. Both of them were laughing and chatting. Sheila's eyes slid to Dom in his suit and she did a double take.

'Well, well, don't you look nice? Where are you off to?'

Dom fussed with his tie. Sheila clucked her tongue and strode over to him. 'You never were good at fixing ties, Dom. Let the expert handle things.'

She redid the knot and fixed it into place. Imogen watched her, a soft smile on her face.

Sheila's gaze flicked from Dom to Anya. She

gave her a long look that did nothing for Anya's nerves. The summer dress with the floral pattern was a gift from Agatha. Anya pulled on the edges of the dress, which didn't quite make it past her knees. At least she had a soft cardigan to cover her bare shoulders.

'Why do you both look like you're off on a date?' Her eyes widened. 'Are you off on your first date?'

Anya blushed. She and Dom were past first-date anything. *Although, it would be nice...*

'Agatha has invited us to dinner,' said Dom.

Her eyes lit up. 'Oh? Is that an open invite?' She glanced back at Imogen. 'Because we could do with a good feed.'

'No, just me and Anya. She wants to talk to us about what happens when we leave this place.'

Sheila's expression darkened. 'It can't be good things if they haven't allowed us to leave yet. They're preparing us for the worst.'

'Or everything's fine and we'll be okay.'

Sheila folded her arms. 'Not what Charlie says.'

'None of us know anything, Sheila. Let me and Anya talk to Agatha first. Then we'll report back. Where are the others, by the way?'

'Some are having dinner, others are relaxing in the lounge area.' They shared the area kitted out with sofas and TVs with Agatha's team. She pointed at him. 'Make sure you report back. And bring Imogen and me back a doggy bag.'

'Every word. And no promises.' He looked down at Anya.' Ready?'

She took his hand. 'No.'

They arrived at the base of the stairs leading to Agatha's office. It was where Agatha had told them to come once they'd changed into their outfits. A soldier waited at the bottom of the stairs.

'Follow me,' he said, climbing the metal steps. Both of them followed him to the top. Anya had expected them to go to Agatha's office, but the soldier crossed the walkway leading to the only other door on that level.

Anya frowned. 'Where are we going?'

'To the commander's private quarters.'

On the other side, he opened the door. Anya entered after the soldier, Dom behind her. She stepped into a dark corridor covered in concrete panels. To the left were three closed doors. Ahead was another door. The soldier stopped and knocked on it.

Agatha opened it and smiled at the pair. 'Right on time.' She turned to the soldier. 'Thank you, Enright.'

The soldier nodded and left.

'Come in,' said Agatha, opening the door wider.

Anya entered the space. It had the same concrete-walled panels and the ground was made of the same smooth concrete, but there were rugs on the floor. Agatha led them down a short corridor that opened out into a large room.

Anya stopped and gasped. One wall was covered in floor-to-ceiling glass. It was dark, as though the world outside was the same. In one section of the open-plan room, three black-leather sofas sat, arranged in a C formation. Next to them was a small table dressed for dinner. Anya smelled food and instantly forgot about her nerves.

'Drink?'

Agatha walked over to the table, which held an open bottle of wine. She poured three glasses and handed one each to Dom and Anya.

Anya walked around the room, unsure what to make of this place. 'Is this your living room?'

'These are my private quarters.'

That's when Anya noticed a level above them, accessible by a set of stairs. Underneath it was a kitchen made of sleek, black granite.

'Where do you sleep?'

Agatha pointed upstairs and lifted her glass. 'Here's to new beginnings.'

Anya and Dom clinked their glasses. Anya took a small sip of the wine, trying not to grimace at its bitter flavors. She'd had wine once, when the controllers of the medical facility had brought it to her and Alex—one of many aphrodisiacs to get them to breed.

The thought of new beginnings made her hands sweat. She walked over to the three sofas and set her glass down on the glass coffee table in the middle.

'Hungry?' Agatha asked. 'I've replicated a few things. I wasn't sure what you liked.'

Anya folded her arms. 'Actually, I'd rather know what's waiting for us out there.'

She nodded at the blackened windows.

Dom moved closer to her and set his glass down beside hers. She could see the same question in his eyes, except he was being more polite than she was.

Agatha abandoned her glass and walked over to the window. She keyed a code into a control panel and the tint on the windows reduced. Colored lights twinkled in the distance but the dark hadn't lifted outside.

She keyed in another code and the door slid open to reveal a balcony. Cool air rushed in and made Anya shiver. But despite the cold, she walked outside. Ahead of her was an array of tall towers, each with a sprinkling of lights. The hum of life drifted up from below. A lone road surrounded the compound. They were up high, as though the Beyond had been built into the side of a mountain.

'What is this place?'

Agatha slid in beside her. 'New San Francisco.'

'Like the poster on your wall?'

'Sort of. Since the war, this Sect has been part of the Colonies. The west colony to be precise.'

Dom came to Anya's other side. She looked up at him. His wide-eyed expression told her he was both shocked at and in awe of the view.

'What's down there?' he asked.

'Life. Both human and synthetic.'

Dom shook his head, as if he hadn't heard her correctly. 'I don't understand. You have Copies living in your city? And you had a problem with ours?'

Agatha nodded. 'They're a vital commodity and help the four colonies thrive. Unlike your Copies.'

Anya's stomach swirled. She stepped back from the edge as a wave of vertigo hit her. She hit the sliding door.

Dom grabbed her. 'Are you okay?'

She swallowed and blinked. 'This is not what I was expecting.'

'What were you expecting?' asked Agatha.

'Destruction. A city in ruins. A reason for the existence of the Region.'

'There was a good reason.'

'To keep one of your rogue sentient programs contained is not a good enough reason.'

'It was the only way we could fool Quintus, if we gave him a city to command.' She clasped her hands together. 'Maybe we should have some dinner and talk about it.'

Anya walked forward, eager to get off the balcony. They returned to the living room and sat down. On the table were a bowl of spaghetti carbonara and a bowl of bread. She was starving, but the knot in her stomach refused to let her enjoy it.

Agatha helped herself. Dom scooped food onto his plate and, when Anya didn't move, he dished out a portion for her.

She stared at Agatha. 'I think you need to start from the beginning.'

Agatha chewed and swallowed her mouthful. 'The Region was to keep Quintus under control. It was supposed to be a short-term arrangement, but our sensors monitoring the situation stopped working. Maybe Quintus disabled them somehow, but without eyes there, we couldn't assess the situation properly. And we certainly couldn't open the door and risk him getting out.'

'How did we end up in there?'

'There are thousands of people in the Region—families mostly. We needed Quintus to think he was living in the real world and not trapped inside a program, which was our fallback option if this didn't work. The families entered willingly, but part of the agreement was that they would not retain memories of this place. We couldn't risk Quintus learning about this place from them.

'We held a consultation with representatives as to how the Region should operate. They voted for self-sustaining towns and a city with medical equipment, should the need arise to use it. So we designed the Region around an existing military testing base, which you knew as Praesidium. That was part of the agreement to enter: full consultation.'

'And why did they volunteer?' Anya said with a shake of her head. 'Why would they leave this behind if they didn't have to?'

Agatha smiled. 'The people who volunteered

were in low-paying jobs and looking for a fresh start. Some with specific skills were promised a good pay-out to enter—the rest were promised better work after this was over. The Region was a second chance for them. All entrants had their memories of this city repressed and received a new set of a life lived in the Region. Many were also trained in specific skills prior to entry—farming, engineering, hunting skills— that would make their time there more believable. Everyone received training of some kind, to make the towns sustainable and everything run smoothly.'

Anya clasped her hands together. No, twisted them was more like it. 'Are you saying my family was poor before we went in there? Dom's family?'

Agatha nodded. 'Dom's, yes, but your family entered for a different reason.'

'What?'

'To help someone close to you. This isn't the first time we've met, Anya. And I'm not surprised to find you in the group that found the Beyond.'

'We've met?' Her head swam with the lies. 'And I don't remember agreeing to your little social experiment.'

'Yes, you did. Everyone who entered had to sign an agreement.'

'I don't believe you.'

Agatha got up and picked up a tablet from a table nearby. She turned it on and swiped until she came to a page.

She showed it to Anya. 'You signed this. The

agreement was one month in the Region.'

Anya squinted at it. It could be her signature. She didn't remember what hers looked like. 'That could be anyone's scrawl.'

Agatha returned to the desk and opened the drawer. She pulled out a piece of paper and a pen.

She placed it in front of Anya. 'Sign your name.'

She did. Agatha showed her the signatures. They were identical.

'You could have forged my signature. That doesn't mean anything.'

'We also have your DNA signature on file.'

Anya looked at Dom, who was staring down at his plate. 'Do you believe her?'

He didn't answer, grabbing the page and pen and signing his name.

To Agatha, he said, 'Show me mine.'

She swiped a few times and showed him his signature. Again, identical.

'We agreed to the Region?' said Dom softly.

'Yes, you did. In your case, it was your father who pushed for it.'

'And the payment for it?'

'Sitting in an account with your name on it, ready to be claimed.'

'And my parents?'

'If they're dead, their payment is passed on to you.'

She flicked to a new page on screen and showed

a figure to them.

Anya had no clue about the value of currency in this city, but there were lots of zeros. 'Is that a lot?'

'Enough to buy you a nice life here. Quintus risked the entire operating system of New San Francisco. If he ever spread beyond this city, he could have gained control over the west colony. Believe me, we would have paid double to lock his ass down.'

Dom lifted his brows at Anya. 'Looks like we're rich.'

33

Carissa

Carissa sat inside a gray-walled room with only a single bed and a bedside locker for company. The way out was made of solid steel, except for a small viewing window two-thirds up. This place felt familiar to her, even though she'd never been there before. After Carissa had stepped out of a large machine an hour ago, a woman in a white coat had brought her to this room. She'd said it would help Carissa to adjust to her new life.

A face appeared at the viewing window. It belonged to the dark-skinned woman who ran this base. That much she knew; she'd been there when Carissa had exited the machine. The old man with the white hair had also been there. The door clicked open and Carissa—the old man kept calling her that—sat up straighter. Agatha entered the room first, followed by Jacob. Although, she sensed he had a different name.

She frowned at the pair, one smiling the other not. She flicked her gaze between them.

They remained near the open door, having a conversation that did not include Carissa.

'Will you consider staying on this side, Jacob? We could use someone with your expertise.'

Jacob's eyes flicked to Carissa. 'What will happen to her?'

'She may live as she pleases once she passes our cognitive tests to check her emotional responses.'

'Responses?'

'Humans and synths can live together in this city, but only after synths prove they can recognize the difference between right and wrong.'

Carissa wondered what that had to do with her.

'How much longer do I have to stay in here?' Her words snapped both sets of eyes to her. 'I feel fine. I'd like to leave now.'

She'd felt okay after stepping out of the machine and had told Agatha so, but the commander hadn't listened to her.

Agatha rarely smiled—an oddity she'd noticed about her. But the old man, Jacob... his eyes were crinkled and his mouth had softened into a smile. She focused on him and his stance. The familiarity of him nagged at her.

Agatha stepped forward. 'I thought you'd like a tour of the base. But I also have someone I'd like you to meet.'

Carissa stood and checked with Jacob, who smiled and nodded at her. She took a deep breath, smoothed down the front of her borrowed jeans and long-sleeved shirt and stepped closer to the exit.

Agatha walked on but Carissa hesitated a moment. The room felt safe, but the uncertainties of what freedom entailed worried her.

Jacob steered her out of the room. 'Come on, miss.'

She jerked at his touch and he withdrew his hand. 'I'm sorry. I didn't mean to frighten you.'

He gestured for her to follow Agatha.

It wasn't his touch that had alarmed her; it was something he'd said. Something that she should know...

Carissa hurried to catch up with Agatha, who had stopped at the end of the corridor. They resumed their walk and Agatha pointed inside rooms as they went. Carissa glanced inside them, barely hearing anything Agatha said. The commander stopped at the base of a set of metal stairs in the middle of a bay, trucks parked around it. The stairs led up to a prefab perched above the space.

'Follow me. There's someone I want you to meet.'

Agatha climbed the stairs.

Carissa hesitated and looked back at Jacob. 'Are you coming?'

He smiled. 'If you want me to.'

She nodded and he gestured for her to go on up.

She arrived at the top of the stairs, where Agatha waited by a door to the prefab. When Jacob made it to the same level, Agatha opened the door and stepped inside.

Carissa gripped her left arm. What did Agatha need her to see inside a tiny space?

A hand on her back soothed her. 'It's okay, Carissa. Trust me.'

She looked up into the watery eyes of the old man. She did trust him. Why, when she'd never met him before?

With a nod, she walked inside the room. A woman with curly, blonde hair waited there. She wore a beautiful, black suit that was perfectly tailored to her body. She looked important.

Agatha gestured to the woman. 'Carissa, I want you to meet Genevieve. She's in charge of security in this Sect.'

Genevieve offered her hand. 'Pleased to meet you, Carissa.'

Carissa shook her hand. It felt warm. But something about her felt off.

She stepped back. 'Who are you?'

Agatha said, 'Genevieve is one of our synthetics.'

Carissa's pulse went from a mild thud to an excited frenzy. She stared at the woman. 'A-are you real?'

Genevieve laughed. 'As much as you are. Please'—she gestured to a chair—'let's talk.'

Carissa sat down and listened while Genevieve explained her position in the Sect and that synthetics lived side by side with humans.

She couldn't believe it. 'Are you saying I can have a life, out there?'

Agatha nodded. 'Synthetics have the same rights as humans.'

'As long as they pass your test.'

It's what Agatha had said to Jacob.

Genevieve laughed. 'Yes, I'm afraid we must comply with the rules. Mandatory monthly testing as part of our upload cycle, to make sure we haven't gone rogue.'

Carissa's mind reeled with questions, with the possibilities of what a life in the Sect might look like. She glanced back at the old man who was leaning against the door.

'Would I live alone?'

'If you wanted to.'

She sensed she had never been alone, that there was more to her story than she'd been told. After exiting the machine, the doctor had said she was a reborn, not a newborn—a term that sounded familiar.

She looked at Jacob. He had his arms folded now. Tension lived there.

'Where will you live?'

He uncrossed his arms. 'In the Sect, like you. Like the others. Charlie, Vanessa, Sheila, June, Jerome. We will all have our own accommodation.'

He spoke to her like she was supposed to know

325

those people. But there was only one person she truly knew.

She turned to Agatha and said, 'I'd like to live with the Inventor.'

She heard a gasp behind her.

Agatha's eyes widened a fraction. 'What did you say?'

Carissa frowned and combed over her last words. Genevieve looked as confused by Agatha's reaction as Carissa was.

'I said I would like to live with the Inventor.' She looked back at him, surprised to see tears in his eyes. 'Is that okay?'

He strode forward and pressed his hands into the tops of his thighs. 'I never thought I'd hear you call me that again.' He shook her shoulder gently. 'I would be delighted with the company, miss.'

34

Anya

2 weeks later

Anya settled into the warm-brown leather sofa. Her gaze roamed the office. Pictures of a family were mounted on the wall, alongside three framed certificates.

A woman dressed in a light-blue blouse and black trousers sat opposite her on a chair that matched the sofa. She had her legs crossed and balanced a screen on one knee.

'You didn't answer my question,' she said.

Anya blinked. 'What?'

'I asked you if you've settled in yet?'

She'd been in the new city for two weeks. The shock of being surrounded by so much technology had freaked her out; she hadn't left the base for the first three days. Agatha had arranged for her and the others to receive psychotherapy, to help to adjust to the change. Or to readjust to their old life, as Agatha had put it. According to Agatha, it was too soon—and would be too traumatic—to simply reverse the deeply repressed memories of New San Francisco. Given her current feelings about the Sect, Anya was in no hurry.

The psychologist waited.

'Uh, fine.'

Anya smiled in an attempt to end this session sooner, but the woman didn't look like she was buying it. This was her tenth session—one per day. The others had been forced to undergo similar sessions to gauge their mental stability.

'I mean, I'm getting used to it.'

The woman nodded. 'It takes time to adjust from the poverty you had to a city with endless possibilities.'

This psychologist was calling the Region poor but Anya had never felt that way about it. Sure, Praesidium had boasted better tech than the towns, but trade and barter, plus the ability to grow their own food, had not left the townspeople destitute.

Although, one command from the Collective—meaning Quintus—and everything could have changed in an instant. She realized that now.

'The bright lights—I'm still not used to them. The noise of the Sect gives me a headache.'

It was the constant hum of cars traveling on the roads above her that bothered her the most. It created a buzzing in her ears.

The therapist nodded. 'It's common to feel like that. Your system is in shock.'

'I suppose that's what it is.' She smiled again, done with talking about it. 'I'm sure I'll get used to it.'

'Have you come to terms with what Quintus did to you?'

'Sure.'

'You said he had a fixation on you in particular.'

Carissa had told her that. Quintus had decided Anya was the ideal candidate for the Breeder program. That was before he'd found a way out, using Alex.

'I'm over it.'

The therapist paused, looking unconvinced. 'Agatha wants to schedule your mind repression reversal treatment soon, if you want it. That should help this city to feel familiar again.'

'Why not now?'

'You've all been through a trauma and the process is lengthy. The memories are buried too deep for conventional methods to reach them.'

That must have been why the memory reversal machine the Inventor, Thomas and Jason had built had only unlocked memories from the Region.

She'd lived a lifetime in New San Francisco but she remembered none of it. This city did not feel like home. While she had only been in the Region for a year, her memories of Jason and her parents were the most precious to her. And by gaining her other memories back, she would learn why she'd entered the Region in the first place, and what she and her family had left behind. That scared her.

She anchored her hands on the arm rests, ready to get up. Only ten minutes remained of the session and the therapist was repeating the same, tired material.

'Can we end the session early?'

The therapist cocked her head a little. 'I heard you spoke to your Copy medic, the one who helped you to escape the medical facility where you were kept prisoner.'

Anya sighed. Okay, they weren't done.

'I did.'

'How did it go?'

'She didn't recognize me.'

The Copy formerly called 118-C had been wiped and implanted with a new personality. Gone were her hard edges, replaced with a softer, chattier version laden with apologies for whatever she'd done in the past. Trouble was she couldn't remember it. Not her help and defiance against the city. Not her help getting Jacob, Charlie, Vanessa, Thomas and Carissa through to the Beyond.

But Anya had thanked her anyway, because doing so felt like concluding that traumatic part of her life.

'Do you feel at peace with it—with your time in the medical facility?'

She did. 'I'm ready to move on, to put that place behind me.'

The therapist eyed her. 'Including the Region?'

Anya hesitated. Was she done with it? She smiled and nodded.

The therapist uncrossed her legs and stood up. 'That concludes our sessions, Anya.'

She proffered a hand and Anya shook it slowly from her seat.

'We're done?'

She nodded. 'I see no reason to keep you here.'

Anya stood. Had her agreement to turn her back on the Region ended her sessions? If only she'd known that ten days ago.

'Thanks for your time,' she said to the therapist.

'Good luck with everything.'

A crash against the wall of the next room startled her, as if someone had thrown something. The therapist rushed to the door and opened it. Anya followed to see a smiling Sheila coming out of the next room. Her therapist, an older woman, was glaring at her.

'You are the most frustrating...' The older woman tugged on her hair. 'I don't want to see you back here again.'

'Fine by me,' said Sheila. She gave her a short wave. 'Buh bye then.'

Anya's therapist went to check on the older woman. Anya saw shattered glass on the floor. Sheila's eyes crinkled when she saw Anya. She hooked arms with her and walked her out of the building fast.

'Come on, before they haul my ass off to some lab.'

'What the hell happened, Sheila?'

'Oh that?' She waved her hand in the air. 'I may have tried reverse therapy on my therapist.'

Anya blinked. 'What?'

'When she asked me how I was coping with my parental loss and this place, I asked her why she was hiding her kinky fetish for dressing up like a school mistress and whipping her lovers.'

Anya pulled her to a stop outside. 'You said what?'

Sheila squeaked. 'How was I supposed to know I got it right?'

Imogen waited outside. Sheila unhooked her arm and went to her, planting a sweet kiss on her lips.

'I see you've been up to no good again,' said Imogen.

Sheila glanced back at the building. 'I think my sessions might be over.' She sighed. 'I blame my psychologist parents for teaching me so well.'

'Hey, Anya,' said Imogen. 'Do you and Dom want to come over for dinner tonight?'

Anya smiled. 'Thanks for the offer, but we've got plans. Tomorrow, though?'

'Yeah, let's do it.'

Sheila added. 'We should get everyone back together. You know, the whole gang. It's been too long since I've seen everyone.'

After leaving the base, their group had been split up and sent to different accommodations in different parts of the Sect.

'Yeah, I'd like that. I know Dom would, too.'

Sheila's head turned. 'Speaking of which... lover boy is here.'

Anya's heart kicked up when she saw Dom approach. He was dressed in plain, black trousers and a plum-colored shirt. His hair had been cut recently—by Charlie, she assumed—and he wore the sexiest smile.

'Hey,' he said, planting a soft kiss on her lips.

'Hey back.' A feeling stirred low in her belly. 'Hungry?'

'Sure. How did your session go?'

'I'm done. You?'

'Yeah. I guess I'm not certified crazy.'

'So, I know a little place, just off Chinatown...'

'Actually'—Dom held up a silver card—'I got the keys to our new place.'

'What?' Agatha had promised them a new apartment, but the place had been occupied. 'It's ready?'

'Yep. Wanna go see it?'

Ω

Dom opened the door with a brushed-silver card that reminded Anya of the ones used to operate the lift in

Arcis. She wondered how much tech Quintus had borrowed and recreated in the Region.

He opened the door and her eyes widened.

'Oh my God...' She turned around in the space. 'It's huge!'

A large window covered one wall, offering them a view of the Sect and the darkness that was befalling it. Multicolored lights twinkled softly in the distance. A large, white sofa sat with its back to the huge window. A bed was positioned in one corner of the space. There was no privacy. But with only the two of them living there, she didn't mind.

'What do you think?'

Dom's brow held a crease. Anya realized it might be a permanent one that could never be erased.

She wandered away from him, running her hand over the smooth, metal counter in the kitchenette, seeing more than a little resemblance to the unit in Essention with its gray-and-white scheme. She shivered, then hugged herself.

'You don't like it?'

She turned. 'No, I do. It's just...'

He stepped closer to her. 'Just what?'

'I never expected this to be our lives. I couldn't see past the Beyond.' She smiled. 'It will take some getting used to.'

Dom slid his hands around her waist, craning his neck down to look into her eyes. He grinned suddenly and it elicited one in response.

'What?'

'What do you say we christen this place?'

Her eyes flicked to the bed, then back to him. 'What did you have in mind?'

Dom kept hold of her hand and led her over to the bed. Her stomach coiled tight with excited anticipation.

There, he turned and faced her, sweeping a lock of hair off her face. Anya stood on tiptoes and brushed her lips against his. The windows had no covering but they were far back enough that the shadows in the room hid them.

Dom groaned against her mouth; the sound pushed her to explore him deeper.

He pulled back, removed his shirt and went back to kissing her. 'I've been dying to get you alone for ages.'

She smiled against his lips. 'Me too.'

They'd been living in the dorm on base before being moved to separate temporary accommodation while they completed their psychological assessments. All she'd had for two weeks were stolen looks and kisses during the times they could meet.

Her need for him consumed her so much, she thought she might die. He was her air. Without him she felt like she might suffocate. And from the way he was kissing her, deep and hungrily, she sensed he felt the same way.

Anya stepped back and removed her clothes to stand there in her underwear.

Dom smiled at her, his gaze lingering on the

places where she was still covered. 'Beautiful.'

He peeled off his T-shirt with his strong arm, slightly ripping the fabric as he went. His stomach no longer had a scar running across it. Agatha had kept her promise and removed his internal tech, replacing it with donated organs. But he retained the tech in his arm that had nothing to do with his father.

She ran her fingers across his belly, where his scar used to be, feeling him tense there. 'Do you miss it?'

He said in a low, throaty growl, 'No.'

She looked up at him. His brown eyes caught her off guard, like they always did when she looked into them. The intensity there made her blush.

'What now?'

A smile spread across his lips and he eased her onto the bed.

The feel of him pressed up against her, every part of him hard, turned her legs to jelly. She shivered from loving this man so much.

'You cold?' he asked.

She shook her head. His body warmth was enough. She widened her legs to allow his weight to rest there. He kissed her harder, careful not to crush her. She didn't care if he did, or if his weight killed her. She could think of worse ways to die than in the arms of the man who literally stole her breath away.

35

Anya

The next morning, Anya got up for a shower. She spent longer there than usual. The water slicked down her body, making her feel whole again. She was sore in places she'd forgotten existed. The heat of the water soothed her aches away.

She touched the gray tiles, wondering if Quintus had drawn inspiration for Essention from this city alone, or if he'd used his imagination. The thought made her shiver.

Anya toweled off and emerged from the bathroom. Dom was draped across the bed, one arm resting over his eyes. He peeked out from under it when she neared him.

'How was the shower?' he asked.

'Delicious! You should try it.'

He sat up, a wicked grin on his face. 'Maybe next time, I'll join you.'

'I'd like that.'

She sat down on the bed with a sigh.

'What's wrong?'

'I suppose this good feeling can't last forever.'

'What do you mean?'

'I mean we can't live like kings indefinitely. We'll have to join society at some point. You know, get a job.'

Dom nodded slowly. 'Agatha didn't say, but, yeah, I presume so.'

She got to her feet, holding the towel in place. 'I don't know where my place is here. I don't even know what this city is about. All I remember are the towns. I know the memory reverse will allow me to remember, but I'm not ready to.'

He stood up with her and wrapped his arms around her waist. 'Maybe it's time Agatha answered some of our questions. What I want to know is what's going to happen to the Region. Are they going to keep it locked away indefinitely?'

'Yeah, I'd like to know that, too.'

Ω

They dressed and met with Agatha in a small café not far from the base. Agatha paid at the counter and carried three coffees to the table.

Today, she wore a black trouser suit with a white blouse and a pair of red-rimmed glasses. Her black hair was pulled back from her face. Anya couldn't tell whether she'd come from a meeting or from her private quarters in the base.

Agatha sipped on her coffee then looked up. 'How are you two settling into your new place? You got the keys last night, correct?'

'How did you know...?'

Anya sighed. There wasn't any point in asking how anyone knew anything. Agatha seemed to have eyes and ears everywhere.

'Fine,' said Dom. 'It's nice.'

'Nice?' Agatha raised a brow. 'That apartment has the best view of the New San Francisco Sect.'

'It's great,' Dom added with a clipped smile. 'But we're not here to discuss views.'

Agatha lifted her cup to her lips again. 'I didn't think you were.' She took a sip and placed the cup back down, then clasped her hands on the table. 'You're here because of the Region.'

Dom nodded. 'We left a lot of people behind. We want to know what's going to happen to them.'

'The Region is still off limits. We haven't lifted the quarantine.'

'Why not?' asked Anya. 'Quintus is gone. There is no threat.'

'It's not locked down because of that. The people there don't know anything more than you did when you crossed. To open up this side would do more psychological damage.'

'What was your original exit strategy?'

'Bring people back in batches and restore their

memories. But they were only supposed to be there a few months, not twelve. Two weeks later, and you two are still coming to terms with this side. There are thousands still living there who will be traumatized if we let them out.'

'Thousands living in fear of a threat that no longer exists,' said Anya. 'Worried that Praesidium is still active and will send teams to their towns to remove them by force. That's what happened before the radiation attack. That's what they fear will happen again.'

'Yes, the radiation attack. Our teams have assessed the towns after dark and decontaminated the soil. There's no issue with growing crops there.'

She lifted her cup to her lips again.

'But they don't know that,' said Dom. 'We were almost out of food when we left. The tech the city uses to speed up growth is offline. With the current tech in the towns, the food will grow too slowly to keep up with demand.'

The cup clinked against the saucer as Agatha put it down. 'What are you suggesting? That we open up the two sides and traumatize thousands of people in one go?'

Dom leaned forward. 'I'm saying we need to give them a choice.'

Agatha sat back, her lips thinned, not looking happy with that outcome. 'I don't think—'

'How is food manufactured on this side?' Anya interrupted.

Agatha cut her eyes to her. 'What do you mean?'

'I mean, what's the food situation like?'

The Commander shrugged. 'We have food processing plants...'

'Like the towns, but on a smaller scale?' Agatha nodded. 'Then turn the Region into a live-in food manufacturing base.'

Agatha rubbed her chin, as though she were considering it. 'How much food did you grow there?'

'Not enough to feed a city this size, but with the right equipment we could double, triple, times-ten our production.'

Dom squeezed her leg under the table. A sign of his agreement.

'So what do you say, Agatha?' he said. 'Turn the Region into an extension of New San Francisco's Sect?'

'A live-in one?' said Agatha, eyeing the pair.

'Yes,' said Anya. 'If people want to stay, they should be allowed to.'

She guessed some wouldn't want to live on this side.

Agatha drained her cup. 'Let me think about it.' She stood up. 'I'll be in touch.'

Several soldiers Anya hadn't seen fell into line as she exited the café.

She released a sigh of relief. 'Do you think she'll go for it?'

Dom removed a communication device from

his back pocket and slotted it into his ear. 'I hope so.'

'Who are you calling?'

'Sheila. She invited us over for dinner tonight. You ready to catch up with the old gang?'

Anya nodded.

36

Dom

The time was hitting 7pm when Dom and Anya arrived at Sheila's new place. Five doors without numbers filled the corridor on the top floor, but Dom knew exactly which one was Sheila's.

A low, thumping noise permeated through the wooden door ahead of him. He knocked and Sheila opened the door, releasing a torrent of music into the hall.

'Dom Juan! Welcome to mi casa!'

She stepped back and gestured for them to enter.

He grinned at her. 'I just had a flashback moment to our unit in Essention.'

He'd arrived back from his shift in Arcis to discover Sheila blaring music in their apartment.

Sheila looked away. 'Oh yeah. I was a bit of a brat then, huh?'

Except now, the music didn't fill him with dread. 'Still are.'

Sheila stuck her tongue out at him. Beside him, Anya giggled, her hand in his. It was a warm, comforting reminder that they had all the time in the world to explore their new relationship.

He couldn't wait.

Anya held a container. She thrust it at Sheila, as if she couldn't wait to be rid of it. 'I made these. Brownies. Or rather, I tried.'

Sheila plucked the container from her. 'Perfect. I forgot about dessert.'

Dom led Anya inside the apartment, decorated in warm tones. He heard a collection of hushed voices coming from the other room and a child's voice.

The corridor opened into a space that was smaller than his and Anya's open-plan apartment. The walls of Sheila and Imogen's place had been painted in a mix of red rust and warm-orange colors. He could smell the paint.

'I like what you've done to the place,' said Anya, looking around.

'Yeah, the black, white-and-gray scheme wasn't doing it for me,' said Sheila.

Dom saw old faces in the room. Charlie and Vanessa. Jacob and Carissa. Thomas. Jerome. June had brought Frahlia with her. The child had not grown any further since the medical facility. She was still a six-year-old, in appearance only. But she had lost that curious, quiet look in her eyes. Now, she acted more her age, hiding behind June's legs when someone tried to talk to her. But one person she allowed near was Carissa. Dom had heard Rover was helping Agatha's team with logistics and loving his new role.

Dom didn't see Alex in the room. Anya had told him about their conversation and his hesitation to become a father. Nobody could blame the former Breeder. The situation they'd all found themselves in was messed up.

Charlie called him over. Dom smiled as he shook the old man's hand. It warmed him to see Charlie happy—well, as happy as he could be without Max.

'I heard you moved into your new place yesterday. How is it?' asked Charlie.

'Good.'

He lifted a brow at him. 'Really?'

'Yeah.' His eyes flicked to Anya. 'Things are great. How are you settling in?'

Charlie chuckled. 'I have all the money I could want and nothing to spend it on. It's not a life I envisioned for myself.'

'How much did you get?'

'Enough. Turns out, I was one of the first to enter the Region. That honor attracted a healthy pay check.' Sadness clouded his eyes. 'I'm just sorry Max couldn't be here to see all this, see how we're doing now.'

Dom clapped him on the arm. 'Max agreed to

enter the Region. We all did.' His mother, Mariella, too. 'He would be happy to see you well.'

Charlie nodded and looked around at the others. 'I'm glad we're all safe.' He slid his gaze to Dom. 'But this city...'

'It doesn't feel like we belong, does it?'

Charlie shook his head. 'Even though this was our home once.'

Sheila called everyone to dinner. Dom took a seat next to Anya.

'It's nothing fancy, just tuna casserole,' said Sheila.

Dom couldn't keep the shock from his voice. 'Since when do you cook, Sheila Kouris?'

Sheila lowered her eyes, as if embarrassed. 'Actually, it was all Imogen.'

'You helped to cut up the vegetables.' Imogen squeezed her shoulder. 'That was like cooking.'

Everyone laughed, even Sheila.

Dom held out his plate. 'In that case, load me up.'

Sheila stuck out her tongue at him again.

The mood was light and jovial. Everyone talked about anything but the place they'd come from, or the memory reversal treatment that would return the Sect's familiarity to them. Some, like Charlie, had opted for the treatment—to begin next week. Others were still undecided. No matter what memories people had or didn't, Dom sensed a mood change in the group, like they were at a crossroads similar to him and Anya.

After dinner, he couldn't avoid the off-limit topic any longer. He and Anya shared their discussion with Agatha and their proposal to open up the Region.

'She's considering it,' said Anya.

'But what will that mean for the Region and the people living there?' asked Vanessa.

'They will become part of this city's future, with the option to have their old lifestyle back.'

Charlie rubbed his chin. 'It's an intriguing idea. Do you think she'll go for it?'

Dom had no idea, and he told them so. 'We'll just have to wait and see.'

'And do you think you'll go back?'

Dom looked at Anya. They hadn't discussed it but he was sure they would, if only to help set up the Region.

'I admit I like this apartment,' said Sheila, looking around, 'but I'm restless, and I'm not sure I want to know who I was before now.'

'Me too,' said Imogen. 'All I've known is a rebel life.'

Getting the old memories back didn't guarantee a sense of belonging.

'So, who wants to volunteer?'

Sheila, Imogen, Jerome and Thomas put their hands up.

June said, 'I have Frahlia to think of now. I need to get her settled.'

'And Alex?' asked Dom.

'He's not going to be a part of our lives. But Carissa and Jacob have been helping with her.' She smiled. 'I'll be fine.'

He believed she would. According to Jacob, Carissa had slowly been remembering her past life. That must have been difficult for her, to live two lives simultaneously. But as rebel leader, Dom couldn't think about his former life now. Max was gone. His commander had fought to protect the people in the Region. Dom still felt responsible for those who'd been left behind.

'I'm hoping Agatha will give us an answer soon.'

37

Anya

Agatha made them wait two agonizing days before she came back with her answer. Her bosses agreed that converting the Region into a manufacturing hub would be the best use for it.

For the last ten days, new supplies had been brought steadily into the Region through a large gate that had been cloaked from the residents. It turned out the invisible gate hadn't been far from their camp. The operation was overseen by people dressed in green military garb pretending to be rebels. It took time to get the people to trust the newcomers, but slowly the Region became unrecognizable. The towns were kitted out and Praesidium was reclaimed and turned into an operational hub.

Agatha stood by her vehicle at the entrance to the city that Quintus had once controlled. 'This facility used to be part of the Sect, but we gave it over to Quintus because it had the right controls to keep him in place.'

'Except he used it to grow his empire,' said Anya.

'We couldn't have foreseen he'd find a way around our controls.'

'Where there's a will, there's always a way,' said Dom.

Agatha nodded, as if she was done explaining. 'What will you two do now?'

Dom looked at Anya.

There was only one place she wanted to go. 'We have somewhere to be. We'll see you soon.'

Agatha nodded and climbed into her car. The driver returned her to the Sect side.

Anya took Dom's hand. 'You ready?'

He nodded and they got into a vehicle Agatha had given them.

Anya's nerves hit her as they approached the entrance to Brookfield. The last time she'd been here the place had been emptied out. Copies from Praesidium had taken her and the other residents to Essention. Now, the town buzzed with new life. Those who'd been ousted had returned to begin anew. In the distance, several new vertical farms were being built, just beyond the perimeter of the towns. Brookfield would be responsible for the collective farms, reporting to Praesidium. Other towns would be responsible for their own farms. The Region had lots of space and plenty of room to grow.

She approached her old cottage on foot. She hadn't seen it in nearly five months and thought she'd never see it again.

Anya opened the door; it squeaked and a lump rose to her throat. She wished Jason were here, to see things play out for the better.

Dom slid his hands around her waist and nestled his chin on her shoulder. 'Are you sure you want to do this?'

She nodded against him, then stepped forward. He released her but kept hold of her hand. The first thing she saw was the dried blood on the floor. Anya turned away from the spot where her parents had been killed, from where she and Jason had collapsed with radiation sickness. She took a deep breath and released Dom, walking farther into her former home. Dom closed the door behind them.

The red sofa made her smile. Many evenings had been spent there playing games as a family. She no longer hated her mother. Both her parents had been trying to keep her safe. She wondered if they'd regained their memories of what Quintus was and why he'd been locked up in the first place.

Dom stayed by the door. She returned to him and grabbed his hand, pulling him into each room. She showed him the kitchen, where Jason used to sit for hours and do his electronic work. Then into the bedroom—hers—with the primrose-painted walls and the marks on the floor close to the hidden space behind the wall.

Dom was quiet behind her. She turned and wrapped her arms around his waist. 'I miss them.'

He stroked her hair. 'I miss my mother.'

She looked up at him. 'Do you want to visit your house next?'

'That's not home for me anymore. Is this place home for you?'

Breathing deeply, Anya looked around. 'More than our apartment is.'

Dom took both her hands and led her back to the living room. 'If we push the sofas back, we can fit a dining table in here.'

Her eyes widened and her pulse raced. 'What are you saying?'

'I'd like to do some good in the Region. But I don't want any of it unless you're with me.'

Anya rested her cheek on his chest. 'I can feel my family here.'

'So it's settled then.'

She smiled into his shirt. They were home.

Ω

Thank you for reading THE BEYOND.

Coming in December 2021

THE SECT (Standalone and Prequel to *The Facility*)

CAN'T WAIT THAT LONG?

Check out THE REBELS, BOOK 5 next. It's a companion story to *The Facility* retold from Dom and Warren's perspective. Find out what really motivated this pair.

DON'T WANT TO MISS A THING?

Sign up to my newsletter at www.elizagreenbooks.com to hear about new releases in this series and receive a free gift!

The Beyond

Other Eliza Green Books
Genesis Code

THE GENESIS SERIES
(adult series, adult language, moderate violence)

A hunter seeking revenge. An alien dying to stop him. Could a government conspiracy put them both six feet under?

Bill fiddled with his earpiece. 'Caldwell, Page. State your position now.'

An occasional crackle greeted him.

His body twitched from the stimulants in his system. Nervous energy and palpitations replaced his recent lethargy. He sat down and fussed with his ear piece as he waited for a response.

For a moment he considered joining the pursuit, but everything was happening too fast.

Bill pulled the thin microphone closer to his mouth. 'Caldwell? I know you're out there and I know you can hear me. Where the fuck are you?'

A heavy silence hung in the air. His heart pounded against his ribs, forcing him to pull in a sharp breath. Both hands quivered from a mixture of agitation and stimulants. He was sick of this shit, following Gilchrist's insane instructions not to intervene. Why weren't they capturing the alien?

'Jesus, come on...'

A voice broke through the air and startled him.

'Caldwell here. Sorry for the silence earlier. It was necessary. Over.'

'What the hell is happening down there? Where are you?'

'Page and I are keeping our distance. It appears the alien is headed for the Maglev station, in New Victoria district. Over.'

He slammed his fist down on his leg. 'You'd better not lose him. Where is he now?'

Caldwell grunted. Annoyed or out of breath? Bill didn't care.

'The alien is closing on the main entrance. He already had a strong head start. The crowds are thick here. They might slow him down. Over.'

Bill warned Caldwell, 'Make sure he doesn't see you. We need the meeting to happen next week.' When he got no reply, Bill added, 'Understood?'

'Sure, sure. Gotta go.'

Get *Genesis Code*

Available in Digital and Paperback

www.elizagreenbooks.com/genesis-code

Genesis (Book 0) Get this teaser story for free only when you sign up to my mailing list. Check out **www.elizagreenbooks.com** for more information.

Ω

DUALITY
(adult standalone, adult language, moderate violence)

A delusional man caught between two realities. Two agencies fighting to access his mind. Could one false move trap him in the wrong existence?

Get *Duality*

Available in Digital and Paperback

Kate Gellar Books

Eliza also writes paranormal romance under the pen name, Kate Gellar.

THE IRISH ROGUE SERIES
(adult series, adult language, steamy romance)

A mysterious family bloodline. A novice witch without a clue. Can she get on the right side of magic before the underworld claims her?

After a mysterious illness kills Abby Brennan's mother, she believes things can't get any worse. It's then a powerful magic awakens inside her, turning her ordinary life chaotic.

Her sudden ability to sense magical energy attracts the attention of four mysterious Irish men. When she receives an invite to spend the summer in their Irish castle, Abby jumps at the change of scenery. But the second she sets foot on the ancient grounds, a negative energy makes itself known.

If that wasn't bad enough, the sexy-as-hell men are acting weird around her. She doesn't need magic to know when she's being lied to. What she can't explain is why she hungers for them—and not in a good way.

If Abby can't figure out fast what her mother was—
who she is—she might be adding murder to her list of
summer activities.

The Irish Rogue Series begins with *Magic Destiny.*

**Available in both digital and paperback from
Amazon.**

Get *Rogue Magic* (a free prequel to *Magic Destiny*
when you sign up to my mailing list) Check out
www.kategellarbooks.com for more information

Word from the Author

The final book is here! Quintus has been stopped and it looks like the gang will get back to living life instead of fighting for it. But I'm not ready to say goodbye to this series yet. There will be another book, set in the time before the Region.

This cover is super cool. As usual, the team at Deranged Doctor Design have nailed the idea I gave them. My editor, Sara, is brilliant to work with and a champion for this series. Love to the launch gang for reviewing the book for me. Special mention to Jessica for beta reading the book.

It's been a strange year for everyone, but for me writing has kept me sane and busy. I hope my books gave you that escapism we really needed this year. No negative thoughts. Vaccines are coming. We will be returning to normality soon—whatever that looks like for you. And I hope we'll appreciate the little things more, like making connections that matter and discarding anything that no longer works.

As always, drop me a line, even if it's only to say hi.

Oh, and reviews: hate writing em, love getting em. If you decide to leave one, thank you.

Reviews

Word of mouth is crucial for authors. If you enjoyed this book, please consider leaving a review where you purchased it; make it as long or as short as you like. I know review writing can be a hassle, but it's the most effective way to let others know what you thought. Plus, it helps me reach new readers instantly!

You can also find me on:

www.twitter.com/elizagreenbooks
www.facebook.com/elizagreenbooks
www.instagram.com/elizagreenbooks
www.wattpad.com/elizagreenbooks
Goodreads – search for Eliza Green

Printed in Great Britain
by Amazon

71769703R00218